SOUL BLADE

BOOK III OF THE SWORD OF LIGHT TRILOGY

AARON HODGES

Written by Aaron Hodges
Edited by M.M Chabot
Proofread by Sara Pinnell
Cover Art by Christian Bentulan
Map by Michael Hodges

The Sword of Light Trilogy
Book 1: Stormwielder
Book 2: Firestorm
Book 3: Soul Blade

The Praegressus Project
Book 1: Rebirth
Book 2: Renegades
Book 3: Retaliation
Book 4: Rebellion
Book 5: Retribution

Copyright © November 2016 Aaron Hodges.
First Edition
All rights reserved.
The National Library of New Zealand
ISBN-13: 978-0473375188

Aaron Hodges was born in 1989 in the small town of Whakatane, New Zealand. He studied for five years at the University of Auckland, completing a Bachelor's of Science in Biology and Geography, and a Masters of Environmental Engineering. After working as an environmental consultant for two years, he grew tired of office work and decided to quit his job and explore the world. During his travels he picked up an old draft of a novel he once wrote in High School – titled The Sword of Light – and began to rewrite the story. Six months later he published his first novel, Stormwielder. And the rest, as they say, is history.

Wow, I can hardly believe I've come to this point. It's done – the story I conceived in my first year of High School has reached its epic conclusion. I have to admit, it did take a few unexpected turns along the way, evolving as I grew and learned more about the world. I'm sure my closest friends and family will be able to pick up a few of those influences.
But anyway, don't let me keep you – enjoy the story!

For Dad, with love.

THE THREE NATIONS

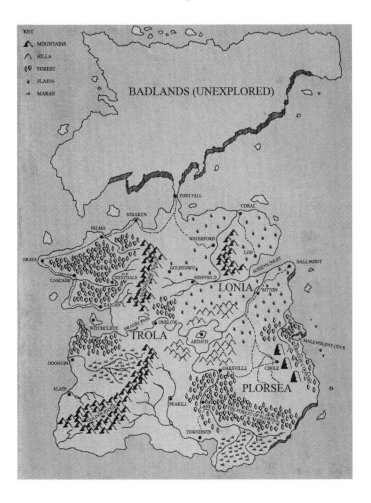

PROLOGUE

May strode along the silent battlements, her sharp eyes sweeping out to search the night. Stars sprinkled the sky overhead and torches lit the frozen stones beneath her feet. Darkness gripped the world around her, concealing the wasteland to the north.

Her short sword slapped against her leg as she walked and her breath misted in the winter air. The cold enveloped her, eating its way through the thick woollen coat she wore. Ice crunched beneath her boots as she made her rounds.

Shivering, May picked up the pace.

Ahead, a guard looked up at her approach. A thin frost sprinkled his white beard, but the smile he flashed her was genuine. Lowering the giant war hammer he carried, he stood to attention and offered a short salute.

"Commander May, what brings you to the outer wall at this time of night?" He spoke in a gruff voice, but the tone was soft.

May smiled back. "At ease, Alan," the man was a familiar face in the fortress, and a legend amongst the Lonians. Tales of his exploits as a youth had been circulating for weeks, and if even half of them were true, May was glad to have him. "If anything, I should be saluting you."

She moved to stand beside him, looking out into the darkness. After a moment's silence, she addressed his question. "I couldn't sleep."

"The reinforcements will come," the old soldier offered.

May glanced at him, raising an eyebrow.

Alan laughed. "It doesn't take much to guess what would keep the commander of Fort Fall up at night," his smile faded as he looked out to the north.

May followed his gaze, unable to find a response. Men and women had been trickling in for weeks now, answering Jurrien's call to arms. Alan had been amongst the first to appear – an old man with his hammer. Yet his arrival had been greeted with a hushed silence. Even at sixty years of age, Alan dwarfed most of the garrison, and he was a legend amongst the Lonians. In his youth he had strode these very walls, and ridden out to quash the small rebellions amongst the banished. Tales of his exploits were still told around the campfires of the young.

"What if they're not enough?"

"They will be," Alan replied.

Listening to his confidence, May could almost believe him. Silence fell then, and together they stared out into the empty darkness. Except they both knew it was not truly empty. Somewhere out in that wasteland, the banished waited. Centuries' worth of criminals and exiled, those deemed unworthy of living amongst the citizens of the Three Nations. Yet left on their own, those banished had formed a civilisation of their own, of sorts. Towns had grown from the rocky hills, the inhabitants surviving on what little water and food they could find.

That was all well and good. As far as May was concerned, they could have their lawless civilisation. So long as they kept to the north. Far from the Three Nations, they could do whatever they wished.

Unfortunately, she knew things would never be that simple. North of Fort Fall the land was a wasteland, barren of life. The people there craved something better, to escape the deathly plains of their existence. They wanted the land of the Three Nations for themselves.

And it was her duty to stop them.

At least with the massive walls of Fort Fall, that task had never been particularly difficult. Three walls stood between the towering citadel and the northern wasteland, each higher than the last. With the standing guard of five hundred men, few enemies had ever come close to mounting a successful attack. It would take an army ten times their number to breach those walls.

Only once had the unthinkable happened – the last time Archon marched south.

And now the whispers spoke of Archon's return.

May shuddered, struggling to find the courage that drove men like Alan to join such a war. She glanced at the big man, and found herself caught in his grey eyes.

He smiled. "Is that the sword?"

May's eyes widened, her thoughts thrown off by the question. "What?"

"The sword, missy. The one the king gave you. Is that it?"

May looked down at the short sword sheathed at her side and nodded. "Yes, it's the one King Fraser gave me when I was awarded this appointment," she sighed. "The sword of the Commander. It seems so long ago now."

"Good," she looked up at the tone in his voice. "A magic sword might be useful right about now."

May stared as he reached down and pulled the horn from his belt. Before she could speak he had lifted it to his lips.

Three long, pealing blasts rang out through the night. Lowering it, he flashed her a grin.

"Just doing my duty," tossing aside the horn, he picked up his war hammer. "They're coming, Commander. Best prepare yourself."

Even as Alan's horn had sounded, May had caught the glint of metal below, reflecting from the light of the defenders' torches. She nodded back at Alan, the hackles on her neck rising. Reaching down, she drew her blade as the first men below appeared in the light of their torches.

Torchlight flickered on the grizzled faces of the enemy, revealing their matted beards and unkempt hair. Hard eyes stared up at them, alerted by the horn, their lips drawn back in scowls. Scar-crossed hands gripped hard around the hilts of swords and axes.

The final ring of the horn faded away, returning the night to silence.

Then, almost as one, the men below charged.

Staring down at the enemy, May struggled to guess at their numbers. But in the darkness the task was impossible, the enemy beyond count. May sent a quick prayer for the Gods to grant her soldiers speed. Half the garrison slept below them at the foot of the wall. In her mind's eye she pictured them leaping from their beds and sliding into their chainmail; sweeping up swords and helmets as they rushed for the door. With luck they would reach the battlements in minutes.

In the meantime, it was up to the night guard of fifty to see off the first attack.

Returning her attention to the invaders, May clenched her sword tight in her fist. She glanced at Alan, surprised to find his presence comforting.

She smiled. "Are you ready, soldier?"

Alan hefted his hammer. "Always."

Light burst across the plains below as the guards tossed bales of hay into their flaming barrels. The glow caught the shadows of the men below, revealing the stark truth of the challenge they faced. May forced herself to stand still as she heard whispers from the men around her.

"Stand strong!" she called out over the thumping of the enemy's boots.

Turning her eyes back to the force below, May swallowed hard. This was no raiding party, that much was clear. They were too numerous and too well-equipped for that.

Where did they get chainmail and steel weapons?

Sharing a glance with the aging warrior beside her, she gave him a nod. She could trust him to hold the men together here. Her presence would be needed elsewhere though; to add steel to the backbone of the defenders. Turning, she strode along the battlements, shouting encouragement to her men as she went.

Sixty feet down the line May found a space and stepped back up to the crenulations. Mouth dry, she cast a glance to her left and right. The fifty men of the guard lined up either side of her, their faces grim but determined. She felt a rush of pride when she saw their fear had retreated behind masks of courage. Whatever challenge they faced, these men and women would stand to the last against the enemy.

Below, the enemy roared and rushed across the last patch of ground before the wall. Swords and axes crashed against shields and a wave of sound swept up over the defenders.

May stepped up as a grappling hook clunked onto the stone battlements. Sword in hand, she waited until the rope went taut before slicing down. A shout rose up from below as the rope split on the second swing, sending the climber toppling back into his companions. All along the wall, the other guards did the same.

Moments later, the first scream of a defender split the

night. She looked up in time to watch two axemen dispatching the guard to her right. They had clambered up one rope while he sliced at another, taking him unawares before he could defend himself. Another foe had appeared at the top of the rope and more would no doubt be following behind him. If they were not stopped now, the wall would be lost long before the reinforcements arrived.

Screaming a battle cry, May leapt at the nearest axeman. Grinning, he watched her come, the axe held loosely in his thick hands. May allowed herself a smile of her own, glad to be underestimated. But you did not become commander of Fort Fall without earning the position.

As the man hefted his axe May moved to the side, ducking his first clumsy swing. Then she slid forward beneath the man's guard and stabbed out with her short sword. The blade crunched through the gap in the chainmail beneath the man's arm.

The man swore and swung his gauntleted fist, but swift as a cat she moved back out of range. He tried to follow, but only managed two steps before he collapsed to the ground, blood bubbling from his lips.

May sprang past the man, eyes already studying the second axeman. The man on the rope joined him and they eyed her warily, apparently realising now the threat she posed.

Smiling, May beckoned them forward. Blood pounded in her head, adrenaline feeding strength to her limbs. In her three years as commander, she'd had little practice in real combat. She had almost forgotten the thrill that came with it.

As the axeman stepped towards her, May danced sideways out of range, eager to engage the smaller swordsman first. The axeman made to follow her, but suddenly found himself tangling with his comrade. The swordsman stumbled, pushing back as he turned to swear at the larger man.

May's blade slammed into his exposed back and the words never left his mouth. He toppled without a sound.

The remaining fighter roared and swung his double-headed axe, forcing May back a step. But the man was a novice and the force of the blow carried the blade past, burying it in the body of his fallen comrade. Another curse echoed through the cool night air, but he tore the blade free before May could close on him.

The thug eyed her closely now, edging back to give himself room to swing. May laughed, hoping to ignite the rage she glimpsed behind the man's eyes. She was not disappointed.

In silent fury he stepped forward, axe raised in a two-handed grip. May almost laughed again, pleased by the man's lack of skill. While someone had clearly taken great effort to arm these men, their preparations had obviously not extended to training. Stepping sideways to avoid the blow, she thrust out with her blade. The tip slipped beneath the man's guard and sliced through his exposed throat.

As she leapt past, the man gave a gurgling cry and staggered backwards. He managed a single step before his feet gave way beneath him and he collapsed to the bloody ramparts.

Looking up, May grinned as she saw another guard had reached the rope. Steel rang on steel as he fended off the next man attempting to reach the battlements. She moved towards him, eager to offer her aid, but the man suddenly reared backwards. He staggered, the sword slipping from his fingers as something pushed him back from the ramparts.

May swore as he twisted, revealing the dagger buried in his throat. She reached out to catch him, but she was still too far away and he pitched to the ground before she could reach him. He gave one last gurgling cry, and lay still.

Turning back to the rope, May felt an icy hand wrap about her heart. A figure clambered into view, pausing to straighten and survey the battlements. Black robes flapped in the wind, revealing the pale flesh of the creature beneath. Black eyes stared out from a deathly face and a host of shadows clung to the figure, rippling against the light of the torches.

Demon, the word sent a tremor through May's soul, but there was no denying the truth. The creature standing atop the wall wore the body of a human, but there was no humanity left in those eyes. Her mind reeled at the implications.

The demon turned, its black eyes finding hers, and grinned. Its head tilted to the side in detached curiosity.

"Commander," its gravelly voice carried through the night. "What brings you here on a night like this?"

May shuddered, and gripped the sword her king had given her tighter.

The creature laughed, the sound sending dread down to the pit of her stomach. Her knees shook, but she stood her ground, determined to do her duty to the last.

The thing cackled again and stepped towards her.

With a roar of defiance, May shook herself free of her fear, and attacked. Silently she prayed whatever spells had been cast over her blade would be enough to combat the creature's power.

A blade slid into the demon's hand and shot out to parry May's attack. Steel screeched on steel and she felt a reverberation go through her arms, but the sword held firm. Surprise flashed in the demon's eyes and it drew back, suddenly hesitant.

Drawing courage from its surprise, May pressed the

attack, unleashing a string of blows that drove the creature backwards across the wall. But its hesitation was short-lived, and with supernatural speed its blade moved to fend off her attacks. Then it spun, black cloak sweeping out around it, and its blade flashed for her stomach.

Twisting, May threw herself sideways, but even her speed was not enough to avoid the blow. A sharp pain lanced from her side and then she was clear, dancing backward out of range. Instinctively, her hand dropped to her hip. It came away streaked with blood, but she was relieved to find the wound was not serious.

Keeping her eyes on the dark creature, May began to circle. It smiled and mimicked her, wary too of the skill she had shown. Her eyes narrowed as she studied it, seeking a chink in its defence. She was confident now this was not one of Archon's more powerful demons – she would be long dead if that were the case. Nevertheless, its skill with the sword was phenomenal, and who knew what other magic it might possess. She needed to finish it now, before it could work any further mischief.

Sliding into a fighting stance, May beckoned the creature forward. It growled and leapt for her. She sprang to meet it and their blades rang as they came together, flashing in the firelight. Stepping to the side, she made to stab for the dark thing's head.

As the black sword swept up to parry her blow, May pulled back, then hurled herself at the demon's legs. Her shoulder struck first, driving straight into the creature's knee. She heard a satisfying crack as the joint shattered beneath her weight. Then her momentum carried her forward, sending the two of them toppling to the ground, limbs and weapons flailing.

Gritting her teeth, May fought to free herself from the entanglement. A hand clawed at her neck and the demon's iron fingers grasped at her wrist, but she refused to give in. The thing had not made a sound as its leg broke. The demon within was well beyond the realm of mortal pain, but the damage had still done its job, crippling the demon's movement.

Swinging her sword, the blade finally found flesh. Roaring, the demon released her and she broke free, rolling away and scrambling to her feet. She fumbled to bring her sword to bear as the demon writhed on the ground. It struggled to regain its feet, but the shattered knee would no longer take its weight and it collapsed back to the stone.

Springing forward, May drove her blade down through its back. She felt a satisfying crunch as the tip slid home. Then a hideous cry shattered the night, ringing from the towers of the citadel behind them. May clapped her hands over her ears as pain sheared through her head, the high-pitch scream cutting to her very soul. Strength fled from her legs and she sank to her knees.

When the noise finally ceased, a fragile silence fell over the ramparts. Across from her the demon had rolled onto its back, driving the blade through its chest. The black eyes found hers, its face twisted with hate. Its chest still rose and fell, but she could see it was finished, its energy spent.

May edged closer, drawing the dagger at her side. It watched her come, breath still coming in ragged gasps.

When she reached its side she raised the blade, ready to plunge it through the black skull. Before she could strike, a pale arm shot out to catch her by the shirt. She gasped at the icy touch, struggling to free herself, but even dying its grip was like iron. It pulled her closer, a deathly grin on its pale lips.

Sucking in a breath, May ceased to resist the demon's pull. She still had the dagger and she raised it to strike.

The demon laughed and released her.

May hesitated, the dagger hovering over the creature's head.

Their eyes locked and a shudder went through her soul. There was no fear in the depths of its black stare. Instead, she saw triumph.

"Archon has come," the words rose from its lips like death itself.

Almost without thought, May plunged the blade into the demon's skull. But she felt no joy at the victory now, no pleasure. Despair crept through her heart, the demon's words hovering like a ghost in the air around her. She did not hear its last gurgling gasp. Her mind was already far away, lost on a tide of dread.

The demon's words meant the end of peace, the end of the Three Nations, the end of life as they knew it.

The cries of the reinforcements as they finally reached the wall came from around her as the defenders swept the last of the enemy from the battlements. May hardly noticed, her mind consumed, lost in the grip of the demon's final words.

Archon has come.

CHAPTER 1

Eric staggered as a stray root caught his boot. Before he could right himself he found himself falling, toppling to the muddy ground. The breath whooshed from his lungs and he choked, thrashing in the puddle he'd landed in. When he finally managed to suck in a breath of air he swore, pulling himself to his knees.

Climbing back to his feet, he tried to wipe the brown muck from his clothes. It coated him from head to toe now, the result of days spent trekking through the untamed wilderness. Looking around, he took stock of his progress up the steep hill.

Thick forest rose all around him, making it difficult to determine how far he'd come. Lichen clung to the branches overhead, thriving in the cool damp climate of Witchcliffe Island. Dense ferns dominated the undergrowth and low-lying vines threaded their way through the mossy carpet, making movement anywhere within the forest a constant battle.

If he'd had a choice, Eric would have been a long way from the cursed island by now. Yet over a week had passed since he'd slain the demon, the cool days giving way to freezing nights, and still he remained. His clothes were torn and filthy and he'd hardly eaten for days, but he refused to quit. He would not leave his friend, would not abandon Enala to the forces that had taken her.

Of course, she was more than a friend now – though he doubted he would ever adjust to their true relationship.

"*Sister*," he whispered the word to himself. "Where are you?"

Even now the revelation still shocked him, though there were more pressing concerns to distract him from that now.

Despair clutched his heart. It had grown with each passing day, weighing on his soul as he marched through the dense forest, clambering up the muddy hills and searching the empty forest. In the week that had passed, he had not glimpsed a single sign of his sister, not a footprint or stray thread of clothing.

Nothing.

He saw again the burning temple, his last glimpse of the girl as she disappeared into the trees. Earth magic had radiated out around her, surging from the *Soul Blade* clutched in her hand. Its power had taken her, and Eric had been powerless to stop it.

Shuddering, he prayed for the thousandth time that he would find her in time. The longer the magic held her in its thrall, the less chance there was Enala could be saved.

For all he knew, it might already be too late.

Pushing down the thought, Eric sucked in a breath and started off again. The pommel of the sword strapped to his back struck him in the neck with his first step, forcing him to reach back and readjust it. As his fingers brushed across the leather grip he felt a crackling of power race down his arm.

He flinched back, his chest constricting with fear. He'd almost forgotten it was the Sword of Light he carried, not some ordinary blade. The weapon possessed power far beyond his understanding, and was not to be taken lightly. Only members of the royal bloodline of Trola could touch the blade – though their direct line had now come to an end.

Thankfully, Eric and Enala were distant relatives.

Even so, he had hesitated to touch the blade since his battle with Archon's demon. Its power was overwhelming and only his desperation had given him the strength to wield it. Now though, fear made him pause. He had no wish to suffer the same fate as his sister.

Worse yet, the demon's second *Soul Blade* slapped at his side. *That* he had absolutely no desire to touch. It contained the Storm God, Jurrien, and if Enala's transformation was anything to go by, to touch it meant a fate worse than death. Enala had awakened the Earth magic of the other *Soul Blade* in time to heal them, but before she could release it, the God magic within the blade had overwhelmed her.

Willingly or not, she had sacrificed herself to save him.

Eric could not let that stand.

Reaching out, he tore aside another fern frond, anger fuelling his limbs. For days he had eaten nothing but berries and beetles; in his desperate flight from Kalgan, he had not thought to pack supplies. At least the two years he'd spent in self-imposed banishment had taught him how to survive in the wilderness.

Pressing on, he reached out with his senses – sight, sound, *magic*. He was desperate to catch any whiff of Enala or the magic controlling her. Even inexperienced as he was, he had sensed the magic of others before and knew its taste. Yet he had felt little of the God magic within the *Soul Blade* – only flashes of power now and then. It gave little hint of his sister's location.

Eric smashed his way through the trees, unconcerned by the noise he made. As far as he could tell, Witchcliffe Island was deserted. That was probably why the traitorous King Jonathan had hidden the Sword of Light here in the first place.

A breeze rustled the branches overhead, catching in his hair, and he was again tempted to fling himself skyward. His own magic gave him power over the weather, and with a little effort the wind could carry him high above the island. Unfortunately the island's dense vegetation made searching from the air an all but impossible task.

Eric stumbled again as the ferns ahead of him gave way to an open field. He breathed a sigh of relief, pleased for a moment's break from the fight with the dense undergrowth. He strode forward, eyes searching the open grass.

He paused as the hairs on his neck rose in sudden warning. Closing his eyes he reached for his magic, felt its power rising at his touch.

"*Don't,*" a voice challenged from the treeline opposite him.

Goosebumps pricked Eric's skin. He hesitated, searching the trees. "Why? Who are you? *Show yourself!*"

Movement came from across the clearing as men stepped from the trees. Eric's eyes raced over the men, counting ten in all. Each held a bow with arrows nocked, their tips pointing in Eric's direction.

Except for one, he realised, his eyes returning to the man at their centre.

His white robes had been stained by the muck of the forest, but there was still no mistaking the markings of a priest of the Light. His face was lined with the beginnings of age and his fiery red eyes were locked on Eric. He wore a sword at his side and Eric guessed from his stance he knew how to use it.

"Who are you?" he asked again. Despite the presence of

the priest, he was not about to trust the strangers. He had been betrayed too many times for that.

"Who are you?" the man in the white robe replied. His voice was gruff, but Eric recognised it as that of the original speaker. "You are trespassing on royal land."

Eric hesitated, uncertain of his next move. The priest was clearly a Magicker – and he had already sensed Eric reaching for his magic. There was no way to know what powers he might possess, but from prior experience he knew it was best not to guess.

Then, of course, there were the archers.

Still, despite his fear of the weapon, he had the Sword of Light. Its magic was more than enough to deal with a Magicker, and its power would incinerate any arrow before it came close. His fingers twitched as he weighed up his options.

"I warn you, trespasser, our patience is short. We have other matters to attend to. Tell us your name, now."

Eric grimaced, making his decision. For all he knew these were Archon's men, or King Jonathan's. Quick as lightning, he reached up and drew the Sword of Light clear. The blade ignited at his touch, bathing the clearing in its brilliant light. Heat washed across his face as he pulled it down and held it in front of him.

He swallowed as the first wave of magic washed through him. White fire swept up his arm, spreading to fill his body, to flood his mind. It burned within him, lighting up the darkest confines of his mind, illuminating his every secret regret. Eric shrunk before its strength, withering beneath its glare.

Then his own magic flared, its stormy blue glow erupting outward to mingle with the white. The sight gave him strength. He had mastered that dark force – now he would use it as a weapon against this new power. Reaching out with his mind, he gripped his magic and pulled it to him, twisting it into ropes of power.

Staring at the white flame, Eric gathered his courage and unleashed the threads of his magic. They raced from him, wrapping about the power of the Sword. Flashes of white erupted through his mind as it fought for freedom, blinding his inner eye, but he held strong. Slowly, the strands of blue wrapped around the white, binding it to his will.

At last Eric opened his eyes. Though only a second had passed, the clearing had changed, bathed now by the white fire of the Sword.

"I am Eric," he announced.

As one, the men who faced him dropped to their knees, heads bowed.

Eric blinked, turning to look behind him to ensure it was not a ploy. But the clearing remained empty but for himself and the kneeling men.

He turned back to the leader, the Sword gripped tight in his hand. He could feel its power writhing within, fighting at its bonds.

"Who are you?" he growled through gritted teeth. "I will not ask again."

The priest looked up from the ground. "I am Christopher, priest of the Temple of the Light. I am here representing the Trolan council," he waved at the other men. "We are here to find King Jonathan and the girl known as Enala. The Magicker, Eric, too – though I guess we have found him," he trailed off. "But how? How is this possible?"

Shaking his head, Eric allowed himself a smile. He could hardly think with the power wrapping about his insides. Without another thought, he extinguished the Sword's flames and sheathed it.

"That is a long story – but the short of it is Enala and I are twins, separated at birth by our parents to protect Aria's line. When Jonathan betrayed us and injured Enala, I was forced to take up the Sword."

The man stood as the light of the Sword died away, his head still bent. "I am sorry; we did not know. Please, allow us to start over. I am one of the few remaining councillors left in Kalgan. We were sent to rein in our wayward king. But we had no idea how far he had sank."

"I would say he was far more than wayward," Eric growled.

Christopher raised his hands. "I would have to agree. From the signs I saw at the temple, it appears he tried to steal your... sister's magic. We found his body and guessed one of you had put an end to him," a hint of uncertainty hung in his voice.

Eric almost smiled. If they had been to the temple, they had also seen the forest created by Enala as she fled. It had taken him an hour to cut himself free; even healed he'd been too exhausted to use his magic. More than enough time for her to vanish.

"I killed him," he answered Christopher's unspoken question. "He didn't leave me much choice. He stabbed Enala in the chest and would have done the same to me if he'd had the chance."

Whispers spread amongst the men and Christopher bowed his head again. "I am sorry for your loss."

"My loss?" Eric shook his head. "Enala is not dead. She saved us both. She was able to use the Earth magic trapped within the *Soul Blade* carried by Archon's demon to heal us."

Christopher frowned. "So that's where the trees in the temple came from, why there was such evil in the air. I could not begin to decipher what had happened there. Where is she then?"

Eric clenched a fist. "Lost. She has not even learnt to use her own magic. The God magic in the *Soul Blade* overwhelmed her and she fled before I could stop her. I have been searching for her, but…" he trailed off, his voice trembling.

Christopher glanced at his men. "I might be able to help you. I have felt the power shaking through the island. From its strength, I thought it was the Sword at first. But it moved too quickly and did not feel like Light magic. Together, I'm sure we could track it though."

"I've tried," Eric ran a hand through his hair. "I have only sensed flashes. And there's been no trace of her anywhere."

"Like I said, together we may have more luck," Eric looked up as the priest stepped closer. "A magic like that cannot hide, not while it possesses your sister. We will find her."

Eric felt a surge of hope, but crushed it down. "Why should I trust you?"

King Jonathan had warned them about the council, and though obviously his word meant little now, Eric was still wary.

Christopher's face darkened at Eric's implication. "I don't know what our dear king told you of the council, but they have done their best to fill the void left by his melancholia. While he vanished with the Sword, we have provided Trola with what leadership and guidance we could. And when Jurrien came to us, desperate for aid, we mustered our armies and sent them north. Did you not notice Kalgan is all but abandoned?"

Eric nodded, remembering the empty corridors of the citadel.

"I was one of the only Magickers left in the city. Without me, the Kalgan is all but defenceless to magic, but I came all the same."

Eric took a breath and nodded, shamed by the fire in Christopher's eyes. He could read the truth there, his sense of betrayal that Eric and Enala had fled their custody. Jonathan had tricked them all with his lies. Thinking back, he remembered the kindness the guards had shown him, the comfortable room he'd been left in. They had not even taken his sword.

Shaking his head at his own stupidity, Eric met Christopher's gaze. "I'm sorry. I should have guessed the truth."

Christopher gave a sad smile. "He fooled us all, had us believing he was a broken man when all along he was scheming," he waved a hand. "But we must put that in the past. Come, tell me all you know of Enala and this *Soul Blade*. If she remains on Witchcliffe Island, we will find her. You have my word."

Nodding, Eric began to tell him their tale.

CHAPTER 2

Elton stifled a yawn and then swore as the horse shifted beneath him. The creature was eager to return to its stable and it took a firm tug of the reins to put the animal back on track. In truth, he could not blame the gelding's nerves. They were close now, and even his own heart had begun to thump hard in his chest.

Raising a hand, he squinted up the hill, seeking for a glimpse of their quarry. The first rays of the morning sun peaked over the horizon behind them, casting shadows across the rolling hills. Below, their ship still bobbed at anchor, awaiting their return. The ride across the lake had been rough, the winter winds tearing at their clothes and flinging freezing water over the sides. It was a relief to escape, though it did not seem to have helped King Fraser's mood.

He stared at the king's broad back, wondering again at the change in the man. His temper on the journey across the lake had set the men on edge. Glancing around, Elton glimpsed nervous fingers lingering close to swords and swore silently to himself. This was not the disposition one would expect of a welcoming party.

Especially not when treating with creatures as sensitive as gold dragons.

Swallowing, Elton resolved to ignore the tingle of warning raising the hairs on his neck. Memory of the dragons' arrival was still fresh in his mind. Their appearance over the waters of Lake Ardath had sent panic through the ranks of men manning the city walls. Unsure of their intentions, the city defenders had come within seconds of firing on the dragons. Only his friend Caelin had prevented the disaster.

If only he had done it without bloodshed. Elton closed his eyes, seeing again the body of Katya, the blood pooling around her. The king's rage at the woman's death had been terrifying to behold. In his anger he had locked away Caelin and his companions, at least until their true allegiance could be determined.

Shaking his head, he returned his thoughts to the present. Before the dragons had departed they'd invited the king to join them and plan for the war to come. Elton had expected King Fraser to meet with them within a day, but it had now been over a week since their arrival. He hoped the dragons did not consider the delay an insult.

Ahead the winding trail was finally approaching the top of the hills surrounding the lake. Long grass grew up on either side of them and the mud-streaked trail had made the trek difficult for the horses. It had clearly not been used for some time. Even so, the trip had taken less than an hour and the scouts reported the dragons were nesting at the top of these hills.

A low growl came from overhead and Elton felt a tremor run through his horse. Craning his neck, he looked up at the ridge and saw a massive head rise into view. Sunlight glittered off golden scales as the blue globes of its eyes shifted to stare at them. Another rumble carried down to them as the jaws opened, revealing rows of sword-like teeth. It shifted again, dragging one giant claw into view, then another. Bit by bit the lumbering body appeared as it pulled itself onto the ridge.

Stretching out its wings, the dragon watched their approach, intelligence glistening in its eyes.

Elton's horse shied as they drew level with the ridge. He tugged at the reins, struggling to keep the horse in line, and cursed as it jostled against his control. Around him the other guards were experiencing similar problems. Glancing at the dragon, he swore he caught a glint of amusement in the curl of its jaw.

The king's horse had no such problems. It trotted between the scattered guards and drew up beneath the dragon. The king glanced back from the saddle, anger in his eyes as he surveyed them.

"When you're ready, men," he growled.

Elton ignored the king's barb and kicked his horse forward. The others followed, white fists now wrapped tight around their sword hilts. Elton resisted the urge to copy them, his nerve wilting beneath the shadow of the dragon.

"Dragon!" Fraser boomed. "I am King Fraser. I have travelled here to meet with your leader. He is called Enduran, I am told."

Elton winced at the king's lack of courtesy. A rumbling came from the dragon's throat as it lowered its head to their level.

We do not have leaders, King of Men, the dragon's voice vibrated through their minds. *But Enduran seems to have developed a patience for your kind.* At that, the dragon turned away and moved down the other side of the ridge. *A patience I do not share,* its voice carried back to them.

The king dismounted from his horse, muttering under his breath as the others moved to join him. Elton hoped the man would keep his temper – it would not do to alienate their allies any further than they already had. They needed all the help they could muster against Archon's forces, and the dragons were more powerful than most.

Climbing down from his own horse, Elton handed the reins to another of the guards and walked to the edge of the ridge. His mouth dropped as he looked down the other side. Dragons lay strewn across the open field below, basking in the warm rays of the morning sun. Gold glittered wherever he looked, all but blinding him, but he thought he counted around forty of the beasts.

The dragon who had greeted them had already disappeared amongst the crowd, but another now climbed towards them. Though there was little to differentiate between the creatures, Elton felt a tingle of recognition. This could only be Enduran, the dragon that had spoken to them on the wall.

"He's coming," he turned back to the king.

Fraser nodded and waved for him to join the other guards. Elton hesitated a moment, wondering if he should offer his assistance, but a scowl from Fraser sent him on his way.

King of Man, Enduran's voice echoed in their minds as the dragon reached the ridge. *You are late.*

"My apologies, dragon," the king replied. "I had pressing matters to deal with. We have a war to fight, after all."

Elton winced at the abrupt tone to Fraser's voice. There were courtesies to be observed when speaking with the gold dragon tribe, and the king had all but ignored them.

Enduran gave a slight nod. *Very well*, he turned, surveying their company. Elton shrank as the eyes found him. *You, I know you. You were on the wall. Where are the others, the ones I spoke with in Dragon Country?*

"They could not be here," the king answered for Elton. "They send their regards."

Smoke puffed from the dragon's nose. *You are a busy*

people, it seems, Enduran paused, staring down at the king. *So how can my people assist in the war to come?*

Fraser waved a hand. "A good question. You are mighty creatures, but it seems your numbers are few. How many of you remain?"

Forty-five joined me in this journey. There are others, old or with child, who remained behind. But we are a great deal more steadfast than you brittle creatures.

"I have no doubt," Fraser nodded. "Even so, I must consider how best to employ your people. Our armies have gathered, but we have not yet decided on the best course of action."

A rumble came from Enduran's chest. *It was our understanding that Jurrien wished the armies of the Three Nations to march north, and defend Fort Fall against Archon's forces.*

"Yes," Fraser snapped. "But that was before the Storm God went and got himself killed and left us without the protection of the Gods."

A dim growl escaped Enduran's jaws, and there was no missing the flash of anger in the dragon's eyes. The king's tone clearly did not agree with it. The great head lifted back, the globes of its eyes studying the king.

The passing of the Gods only means the rest of us must stand together, Enduran rumbled. *You cannot hope to defeat Archon alone?*

The king smiled. "As I said, dragon, we have not yet decided. But our plans are our concern, not yours."

An awful silence stretched out at the king's words. Elton exchanged a quick glance with his fellow guards and saw his own confusion reflected there. The king's anger was clear, his tone brisk. But whatever the reason, the stakes were too great for him to address Plorsea's ally in such a fashion.

And then there was the matter of his plan. Did he truly mean to hold their army back?

Elton shook his head. He knew this man, had served under him for years. He would not abandon the other nations in their time of need.

A wave of heat swept over them as the dragon let out a long breath. Its eyes glittered and Elton saw the anger there, bubbling beneath the surface. The great claws shifted, slicing massive grooves through the soft ground.

Very well, Enduran's words came at last. *When you decide your course, we would be pleased to know your plans. But do not delay long, king. We will not wait forever.*

"Very well, dragon," Fraser nodded his head. "Until next time."

Without another word, Fraser turned his horse and rode back down the hill. Elton stared as the king passed through the men, searching for sign of… what? He kept waiting for the man he knew to appear, the kind soul edged with strength, the man who had ruled Plorsea for more than a decade.

Can this truly be the same man?

Their eyes met as he rode past and for an instant Elton thought he glimpsed a smile on the king's lips. His stomach clenched with anger, and he felt a desperate need to speak his mind, but he held back. Fraser would not welcome open criticism, and it would not do to alienate himself now. He had already seen what became of those who crossed the man.

Yet doubt clung to the back of his mind. Questions whirred through his thoughts, feeding his uncertainty.

He shook his head, trying to ignore them. Yet as he mounted and turned his horse down the hill, a single thought clung to him, persistent and undisputable.

This cannot be the same man.

❧

INKEN WRAPPED her arms around her knees and rocked herself in the darkness. It stretched out all around, endless in the tiny space of the cell, wrapping them in its doom. Beneath her the damp stone seeped through her thin pants, sending a shiver through her body. Despair hung around her like a blanket, dragging her down.

A steady stream of tears ran down her cheeks, but she did not make a sound, determined to keep her sorrow to herself. Somewhere in the empty darkness sat her companions: Caelin and Gabriel, and the other one. The one who had sucked the last droplets of hope from her soul.

Sucking in a breath, Inken fought down another bout of sickness. She had hardly eaten in… she could not say how long had passed since the events in the throne room. The darkness offered no hint; only her steady pangs of hunger suggested the passage of time. Food had come once, a tray sliding through a slot in the bottom of the door, but that seemed a long time ago now.

Panic gripped at the edges of her mind as she scrunched her eyes closed. It made no difference, but at least it stemmed the tears. She could feel herself teetering on the brink of some abyss, one from which she would never return. Around her the silence stretched out, thick with its own presence, filled with a dark promise.

This will be your tomb, it whispered to her.

A long, drawn out groan came from her left. Gabriel, she guessed. He had been the first to break, to lose his mind to the lure of the darkness. His whispers woke her sometimes as she slept, though it grew harder each day to distinguish between reality and dream. He spoke to some creature in the darkness, one only he could see.

Inken released her legs, drawing another lungful of air from the suffocating dark, as if that alone could sustain her.

The nausea came again and she retched, though there was nothing in her stomach. Her chest ached and her throat burned as she spat bile onto the grimy stones.

She struggled to stay strong, to keep herself from the madness which had claimed her friend. But knowledge of the man in the cells with them drove away all thought of hope. A scream rose up within her, but she fought it down.

In the darkness the world seemed to spin, drawing her further from reality. She grasped at the ground, her fingernails scraping through the muck coating the bricks. She felt a stab of pain as a fingernail caught and broke, but the ache at least drew her back from the edge.

Gasping, she looked around again, desperately seeking some break in the darkness. But there was only the unrelenting nothingness.

She swallowed and felt the action catch in her parched throat. Her chest heaved and she began to cough, the sound coming out like a bark in the tiny cell. Shuddering, she swallowed again, desperate to stop the fit.

When it finally subsided, Inken leaned her head against the wall. The cold bricks collected what little moisture was present, providing a small supply of water. It was all that sustained them now. She licked at a droplet, biting the inside of her cheek to keep herself from choking at the taste.

Her stomach growled and she wondered if they would ever be fed again. Their new companion said food came occasionally, but they had no way of knowing how long had passed since the last delivery. It would not be enough to sustain them anyway. She could feel her strength fading away.

Inken struggled to think, to keep her mind occupied. How many days now since Eric and Enala fled? Since they had lost Michael? How many days had the Three Nations survived without their Gods? How many more would they last?

Frustration grew in her chest, rising up to fight down the fear. They could not remain locked up in this wasting darkness; she would not allow it. The world outside hung in the balance, the threat of Archon pressing in from all around. His servants were everywhere, could get to anyone. The presence of their new cellmate proved that.

She needed to get out.

Rising, Inken felt her way to the door and slammed a fist into the wood. The dull thud echoed in the darkness, but the panels did not move an inch. She was not surprised – this was not the first time she'd tried. Even so, anger flashed within her and she lashed out with her boot. Then, with a screech of rage, she threw herself at the heavy door.

When her rage finally subsided, Inken leaned against the door and slid to the floor. She panted heavily, exhausted from even that brief exertion. A shudder went through her as the despair returned. No one had come; no one had even acknowledged her screams. They did not post guards in this dungeon; there was no need.

Caelin had already told them where they were. This was not the citadel's regular dungeon and this was no ordinary cell. This place had been created a century ago for a single purpose – to hold the dark creatures Archon had unleashed upon their world. The darkness still stank with their evil.

"Are you finished then?" a voice came from the darkness.

Inken closed her eyes and forced her breathing to slow. She clenched her fists, feeling the sticky wet of blood on her palms. She had done far more than break a nail in her mad fit. Turning, her eyes searched the dark, drifting to the empty space where the voice had come from. She knew where he sat, where he had sat for untold weeks and months before their arrival. He was a broken man, of that she was sure. The fight had gone from him, stolen away by the black cell.

"No, Fraser," Inken hissed. "I will never be finished. I will not allow the darkness to win. Never!"

"So be it," replied the king.

CHAPTER 3

Eric stared across the sunlit clearing. His heart thumped hard against his ribcage and he struggled to swallow the lump crawling its way up his throat. His eyes flickered sideways as Christopher and the others stepped up beside him, but they quickly returned to the vision in the centre of the field. Silence hung in the air, thick and heavy.

Enala stood opposite them, her face bathed in the sickly green glow of the *Soul Blade*. Long strands of grass rose up around her, twining their way around her legs and knitting through her blond hair. She held her arms open, the *Soul Blade* clutched in one, the other clenched tight in a fist. Her eyes were closed, her face lined with concentration.

Sucking in another breath, Eric fought down his panic. He could hardly believe they had found her. With Christopher's help they had sought out the tendrils of God magic seeping across the island, finally tracing them back to this clearing high on the mountainside.

Except now they had finally found her, Eric had no idea what to do next. Unclenching his fists, he wiped the cloying sweat from his fingers and glanced at Christopher. A chill fog hung on the morning air, hovering just above the treeline. His chest heaved and he could feel the blood thumping in his head, but he knew they could not afford to hesitate. If Enala fled, they might never find her again.

Looking back to Enala, Eric stepped towards his sister.

As his feet touched the damp grass, Enala's eyes snapped open. Eric froze as their unnatural green glow found him. Not a trace remained of Enala's usual sapphire blue, and with a wrench in his stomach Eric felt another trickle of hope leave him.

When she did not speak, he gathered his courage and took another step.

"*Stop*," his sister's voice screeched like steel on stone.

Ice spread through Eric's stomach, doing nothing to slow his racing heart.

Even so, he locked eyes with Enala, willing the girl within to break free. "Why?"

"I told you not to follow me," the forces holding Enala ignored his question. "I told you –"

"I will not abandon you, Enala," Eric interrupted.

Watching her closely, Eric thought he glimpsed a trace of recognition sweep across his sister's face. Then the iron glare returned and her teeth flashed, her lips drawing back into a scowl.

"Leave, *now*," the rasping voice growled.

"No," Eric took another step forward, alone in the clearing. He stared at the thing possessing his sister, refusing to back down. "I will never leave you, Enala."

"Then you will *die!*" the voice roared.

The hairs on Eric's arms stood up as he felt the crackling of magic. Then the clearing erupted into chaos. Screams came from behind him as tree branches swung down to smash the Trolan soldiers from their feet. He heard Christopher cry out, and then he had no more time to worry about their fate. Grass erupted beneath his feet, twisting up to bind his legs in place.

Eric acted without thought, his hand already reaching up to draw the Sword of Light. He knew from bitter experience only God magic could match God magic. Steel hissed on leather as the Sword slid free of its makeshift scabbard, white flames igniting at his desperate touch. Heat washed across his face, and then the flames were all around him, burning the green tendrils to ash.

Turning quickly, Eric risked a glance at the Trolans. The men huddled in a circle with Christopher at their centre. Flames leapt from his hands, incinerating any branch that came near. Together they retreated backwards from the clearing and their mad princess.

Glad they at least were safe, Eric turned back to Enala. Thoughts twisted in his head as he searched for a plan to free her. Looking at her expressionless face, the haunting green eyes, Eric felt pain twist in his heart.

Are you still in there, sister?

Enala strode towards him, the long grass billowing out in waves around her. Green light flooded from the *Soul Blade*, contorting the features of her face, revealing the wild magic within. Purple veins stood out stark against her pale skin, her muscles tensed with the power of the *Soul Blade*.

With a roar, Eric pushed back his emotion and slashed through the grass, stepping up to stand before her. He stared into the emerald green eyes, seeing the power swirling within but seeking out the girl he knew so well. But there was only the madness of power there. The same power he felt each time he touched his own magic, but magnified a thousand times by the ancient might of the Gods.

She is gone, the thought hissed in his ear, trickling into his soul.

Yet Eric would not give up. He could not abandon her to this fate. Somehow, he would find a way through.

"Enala!" he yelled through the chaos of the clearing.

This time his cries seemed to give the wild magic strength. A twisted grin spread across Enala's face and a dark laughter followed.

"There is no Enala here," she raised the *Soul Blade* and swung at Eric.

It was a clumsy swing but Eric leapt back all the same, terror in his heart. The God magic was gaining strength, driving Enala deeper inside, away from the light of life. If that light went out, there would be no coming back for the girl within.

She would become a demon.

They had already witnessed the destructive powers of one such creature. In his old age their ancestor Thomas had been overwhelmed by his magic, losing his soul to the dark depths of the power within him. The demon that took his place had wreaked havoc across the Three Nations, slaying the Gods of Earth and Sky before Eric finally destroyed him using the Sword of Light.

Eric had no intention of watching the same fate take Enala. In his heart, he knew he did not have the strength to do the same to her as he had to Thomas.

"Enala, you have to listen. This is not you, you do not need this power. *Fight it!*"

The laughter came again. This time when she raised the *Soul Blade* it was not the grass that came for Eric. The ground shook, and with a roar it tore apart beneath his feet. He leapt, reaching now for his own magic and its power over the Sky.

Winds raced around him, his magic leaping at his desperate need to propel him into the sky. Looking down, Eric watched the crevice tear its way through the forest. Trees groaned as the fissure widened, sending them tumbling into the depths below.

Wiping sweat from his brow, Eric turned and searched for Enala. His eyes swept the shattered clearing and found her hanging over the crevice, suspended there by a host of vegetation springing from the earth below. Her murky green eyes watched him, the breeze toying with the copper lock hanging across her face.

Tears stung Eric's eyes as he watched her. "Enala, please, please, you have to break free!"

This time he caught a flicker of doubt in his sister's eyes. A surge of hope washed through him – he had not imagined that! It could only have been Enala. Somewhere in the dark depths of her mind, her soul still fought for freedom. He just had to find a way to help her break free

But the wild magic had other plans.

"*Die!*" the voice screeched, and green light flashed across the clearing.

Eric gripped the winds in threads of magic and drove himself higher as vines flashed towards him. He ducked as a tree branch swung for his head, then he was clear of the trees, racing upwards as the vines chased after him.

Then, growling, he spun in the air and raised the Sword of Light. White fire swept down, incinerating the vegetation below. He coughed as smoke wafted up to catch in his nose. Rising higher, he searched again for his sister, eyes watering.

She rose through the smoke, the vines lifting her above the treetops. Gripping the Sword hard in his hand, Eric drew more power from the blade. The white of its magic blazed within him, but his magic wrapped it tight. A grin tugged at his lips as he revelled in its power.

The grin faded as he stared at his sister. He could not allow the magic to corrupt him, not if he wanted to keep his sanity. His joy faded as he realised raw power could not free

Enala. He could not fight the power possessing her, not without risking her in the process.

The Sword could draw on any aspect of the Light element, but he had yet to master even the simplest aspects of its power. Without that mastery, it offered little more than protection against the power possessing Enala. The rest was up to him.

Taking hold of the winds, he dropped towards Enala. The emerald eyes watched him come, the power behind them studying his descent. The corner of her lips rose in a deathly smile.

Eric shuddered as he saw the demon within, its confidence growing with every clash. If it was allowed to escape, the God magic it possessed would wreak untold havoc.

Lightning flickered as Eric drew on the power of a distant storm. A bolt raced across the sky, striking his outstretched hand with a crash of thunder. It flickered in his palm and danced up his arm, a faint numbness lingering with its touch. He watched it with detached curiosity and then turned his gaze to Enala. Silently he prayed the lightning and the Sword would be enough to protect him.

The earth below them groaned and snapped shut with a dull boom. The vines holding Enala began to contract, lowering her back to the ground. Letting out a breath, Eric followed her down until they both stood again in the clearing. The silence stretched out as they stared across the broken clearing.

"I will not allow you to be born, demon," he addressed the magic for the first time. "Fight it, Enala!"

"*Oh, Eric,*" the thing within his sister cackled, mimicking Enala's true voice. "You are already too late."

Eric stared into the depths of his sister's eyes as she raised the *Soul Blade*, searching for a hint of recognition. His stomach twisted in a knot as the truth of her words crept through the cracks in his mind. The magic was too powerful. For more than a week it had burned its way through Enala's body, tearing at her soul, driving her deep into the depths of her conscious.

"Not yet," he breathed as he recalled his battle within the otherworld known as The Way.

There, Eric's magic had come close to possessing him. Only Enala's desperate, dying cries for help had given him the strength to beat it back.

Closing his eyes, Eric lowered his head.

The risk is too great, the thought whispered in his mind. If things went wrong, both of them would be lost. They were the only ones left who could wield the Sword of Light. Without them, the Three Nations would fall to Archon.

Yet he could not turn his back now, not if there was still a chance to save her.

Eric's hand trembled, his thumb running along the diamond embedded in the hilt of the Sword. He could sense the power throbbing within Enala, preparing for another attack. He had only seconds to react now, mere moments to change his mind. But even as dread spread through his chest, he knew he would take the risk.

Enala would come through for him. He knew the girl's strength, the courage she possessed.

She would not let him die.

Closing his eyes, Eric felt the weight lift from his soul. Right or wrong, the die had been cast. A smile tugged at his lips as he unclenched his hand and released the Sword.

The snake-like tendrils were on him before the blade had even touched the ground. They whipped from all around, rippling out from Enala in a wave of earthly power. The strands twisted around him, binding him tight.

The lightning died in Eric's palm as the pressure grew, stealing the breath from his lungs. He stared through the writhing mass of green, seeking out Enala, seeking out those haunted eyes. Blood throbbed in his arms, trapped by his bindings.

As the last vines wrapped about him the air cleared, revealing Enala's approach. She stared across at him, hate twisting the features of her face, a smirk on her lips. Arms folded, she held the *Soul Blade* in a casual grip, and watched as her creatures squeezed the life from her brother.

Summoning the last of his strength, Eric sucked in one last breath.

"Enala," he gasped. "*Help me!*"

A shadow crossed Enala's face, her eyes widening. For a second he thought he saw a flicker of blue in her eyes, and to his surprise the vines around him loosened. He sucked in another gulp of air and screamed. "You can do it, Enala. Don't let it kill me!"

A tremor swept through his sister and her irises swelled, reducing the whites of her eyes to thin circles. Blue swirled amidst the green and she stumbled back a step. The *Soul Blade* trembled in her hand.

"Come on, sis. You can do it," he mouthed.

His bindings loosened further, almost freeing him. He did not move, knowing Enala was locked in a desperate struggle with the force within her. Any change might shift the balance, destroy the desperate strength with which she fought.

Slowly the colour in his sister's eyes shifted, the green retreating before the sapphire blue. Her lips quivered and her breath came in great, gulping gasps. Yet still her fist remained clenched around the hilt of the *Soul Blade*. So long as she held it, the flow of Earth magic would not cease.

Swallowing caution, Eric spoke again. "You're almost there, Enala! You can do it, just let it go. Cast out the God magic!"

Enala's eyes drifted back to Eric and for the first time he saw again the girl he knew in their crystal depths. Fear lined her face, matched by a great, all-consuming fatigue. But the steely determination he knew all too well was there too. It just had to hold out a few more seconds, for one final push.

Their eyes caught and Eric gave a short nod.

Enala's eyes closed as she summoned whatever strength remained to her. Her shoulders heaved and she raised the *Soul Blade* above her head. Then, with a final scream, she hurled it from her. The weapon spun in the air, sunlight glinting from the suddenly dark metal. It slammed point first into the ground and quivered there.

The vines around Eric collapsed to the ground as one, freeing him from their grasp.

He looked up in time to see Enala's eyes roll back in her skull. He stepped forward and caught her as she fell. Holding her close, he pulled her tight against him.

"You did it, Enala. You're safe."

ENALA GROANED as sensation returned to her, agony lancing through every muscle of her body. Light burned into her skull as she opened her eyes, struggling to take in the world around her. A thumping pain came from the back of her head and a sharp jolt came from her neck as she tried to move. She fell back to the ground with a whimper, surrendering to the waves of agony.

"Enala?" she heard Eric's voice from nearby. "Are you okay?"

She cracked open an eye, squinting against the fiery light. Her brother's face hovered nearby and branches clawed across the sky behind him. Concern touched his lightning blue eyes and his auburn hair was slick with oil. Dirt streaked his face and his tunic was stretched and torn. Even so, the sight of him warmed her heart.

"Where are we?" she croaked.

Eric smiled. "Someplace on Witchcliffe Island. How do you feel?"

Memory was slowly returning to her as she lay there. She shivered, recalling the helpless horror she'd felt in the clutches of the traitorous King Jonathan. Images flashed in her mind: Eric falling from the sky, the Sword of Light spinning towards her, the agony as it tore through her chest.

Enala shuddered. "I don't know," she whispered, still caught in the tide of memories.

She recalled with horror Eric's battle with the king, then the arrival of the demon, Thomas, and a final surge of elation as the Sword burnt the creature to ash. She watched with growing dread her desperate crawl across the temple floor, her helpless cry as she reached for the *Soul Blade*.

She remembered the healing light that had shone from the weapon, and then the wave of power that surged from the blade. It burned through her veins, flooding her mind and washing her soul away in its current.

Enala shot upright, a deep, rattling gasp rising from her lungs. She felt Eric's touch on her arm and flinched away, a scream on her lips. She could still *feel* the shadow of the power within her, the God magic burning at her soul, her helpless fear as it tore away control.

If not for Eric, she would never have found the strength to overcome it.

Sanity returning, Enala opened her eyes and reached for her brother, desperate to feel his touch, to reassure herself the nightmare was truly over. Pulling him close, she held him for dear life, drawing comfort in the solidness of his skin, his body.

"It's okay, Enala. You're safe."

Another tremor took her. "I've never felt anything like it, Eric. It was like a wave, sweeping me away, taking everything that was me and leaving only the magic. I thought I would drown in it."

"I know," Eric drew back from her. Enala looked into his eyes and saw her own fear reflected there. "It is the same with all magic. It has a life of its own, a longing for freedom. When you touch it consciously with your mind, even your own magic will try to overwhelm you. I can only imagine the strength it would take to fend off God magic."

Enala took a deep breath and forced herself to look around. Her eyes took in the clearing around them. She remembered it from before, though the memories were distant, as though she had dreamt them. Several people stood nearby, doing their best to ignore them.

"Who are they?" she murmured.

"Trolans," Eric answered. "They helped me find you. The council sent them. Turns out Jonathan misled us all along. It was the king who abandoned Trola, forcing the council to step in and govern the nation."

Enala nodded, the last pieces of the puzzle falling into place. "I'm glad he's dead."

Leaning on Eric's shoulder, she pulled herself to her feet.

"Thank you for your help," she looked around at the Trolans. "I am sorry we fled the city. We should not have run."

A man wearing the white robes of a priest smiled as he walked up to them. "Do not worry, we place the blame squarely on Jonathan's shoulders. The man did not deserve the title of king."

Enala smiled. "I can agree on that."

Something in the corner of her eye drew Enala's attention. Turning, she stumbled back a step as her eyes fell on the *Soul Blade*. It still lay on the grass where it had fallen, a faint green seeping like water from the black blade. An icy hand gripped her heart and a cold sweat dampened her forehead. She gripped Eric's shoulder tight, her hands like claws.

Eric followed her gaze and squeezed her hand. "It's okay, it's gone, you're free. You don't have to worry about ever touching that foul thing again."

Relief swept through Enala, but before she could reply the priest spoke. "I'm not so sure, Eric," Christopher paused as she turned on him. He raised his hands, and went on. "We have no way of knowing how to free either Jurrien or Antonia from those blades, and the Three Nations are desperately short of God powers just now. If we cannot find a way to free them, someone will need to confront the power of those blades."

"I will never touch that thing again," Enala hissed.

Christopher stared back, his face grim. "I pray you won't have to."

CHAPTER 4

Elton strode down the dimly lit corridors of the citadel, his thoughts lost in a whirlwind of questions. Two days had passed since the king's meeting with the dragons, and nothing he'd seen or heard since had lessoned his suspicions. There was no longer any doubt in his mind – something was very wrong with the king.

He had done his best to find Caelin and the others, but they had not been seen since the king ordered them imprisoned. They were not in the dungeons or locked away in any of the towers reserved for noble 'guests', and the king had yet to set a date for their trial. To make matters worse, as far as the councillors knew, no one had come forward yet to corroborate their tale.

Yet Elton knew that could not be true. Yesterday he had spoken with the guards on the stairwell up from the lake and heard from them that a Lonian priest had arrived several days ago. The priest's presence could only mean the Sky temple in Lon had sent someone to verify his old friend's story. But still there was nothing.

The more Elton searched, the less he could deny the

truth of Caelin's suspicions. Something was wrong in Ardath, and it seemed the king sat at the middle of it all.

What has happened to him?

Still, Elton could not bring himself to believe Fraser could be at the centre of such a conspiracy. No, he had to be under some spell, some corruption cast by one of Archon's agents. Caelin had already slain two of the creatures; there had to be more.

He had considered going to the king himself, but so far had held back. He was no Magicker and had no way of breaking the king free of such a spell. And what if he was wrong?

No, he could not risk it. Not if somehow, impossibly, the king had truly been turned.

Thankfully, as a soldier, Elton had plenty of friends amongst the guards and soldiers of the Plorsean army. The councillor's might not know a priest had arrived in the capital, but all news in the city eventually made it to ears of the guards. It had not taken long for him to discover a small pool of men had been assigned to guard a room deep within the citadel.

It only took a few pints of ale to convince one of the guards to exchange shifts.

Picking up the pace, Elton took the next right and turned into a poorly lit corridor. It had taken longer than expected to navigate the maze of hallways in this section of the citadel, and he was running late. Ahead he glimpsed the shadow of a man in the light of a single lantern and smiled. He had arrived.

The guard turned and flashed a grin as he saw Elton approaching. "Ah, Elton, good to see you. I heard you changed shifts with Alexandar. I think you pulled the short straw on that one; nothing to do but stare at this here wall."

Elton laughed. "Sorry I'm late, I haven't been back here

often," he shrugged. "Truth to tell, after a few run-ins with those dragons, I could use a little quiet."

Chuckling, the guard shook his head. "True, true. I'll not forget the sight of that beast landing on the walls till my dying day," he clicked his neck and groaned. "But that's me for the night. Best of luck. Hope you find something to keep yourself entertained."

With that he turned and wandered away down the corridor. Elton waited a few minutes after he'd turned the corner before facing the door. Reaching up, he thumped on the heavy wood. He wondered how the priest had taken the reception here in Ardath – it was not exactly customary to post guards outside a guest's door.

He didn't have to wait long for his answer.

"*What?*" a woman's voice growled from inside the room.

There came a scrambling from the door and then the creak of hinges as it opened. A woman stood in the doorway, her blue robes scrunched with lines as though she'd just pulled them on. Angry eyes glared up at him, blinking in the lantern light, her long white hair muddled with sleep.

"What do you want?" she growled. "Has the king finally given up this nonsense?"

"Nonsense?"

"About whether he believes the news I brought?" the priest snapped. "I am tired of this room. It was not my intention to spend my days in Plorsea locked in the citadel. Do you treat all your guests like prisoners, or is this treatment reserved just for priests?"

Elton held his hands up in surrender. "My apologies, ma'am. I am just a simple soldier – I am afraid I do not know the king's mind. But I am interested in your story. I believe you may know my friend, Caelin?"

The old woman nodded. "I do, though we did not speak much with the bunch of them. We were busy preparing the soldiers and equipment for their expedition," she eyed him closely. "What did you say your name was?"

"I didn't," Elton nodded to the room. "But perhaps this is a conversation better had in privacy, away from any prying ears."

The priest studied him for a long moment before finally stepping from the doorway and beckoning him inside. "Very well. I take it you are *not* here at the request of the king then."

"No," Elton moved into the room, his eyes sweeping the interior. An unmade bed had been pushed into the far corner, while a table took up the opposite side of the room. Otherwise the room was unadorned.

"I'm afraid I can't offer you anything to drink…" the priest spoke in a wry voice.

"My apologies…" Elton shook his head, realising he did not know the woman's name. He held out his hand. "My name is Elton."

"Lynda," she took his hand in hers.

Elton lowered himself into a chair at the table. "Nice to meet you, Lynda," he sighed. "I am afraid I don't know why you're here. I don't know what is happening in this city, what is happening to the king."

Lynda sat opposite him. "Perhaps you could start from the beginning."

"You're right," Elton shook his head. "I'm afraid there is something very, very wrong happening here in Ardath."

Bit by bit, he explained how the king's demeanour had changed over the past weeks and months. It had started with the occasional outburst and rages, but with the arrival of Caelin and his companions, things had quickly descended into madness. The tale of his friend's reception by the king rushed out, followed by the arrival of the dragons and the insanity that had almost shattered the ancient alliance between the beasts and man. As he spoke he could feel a burden lifting from his shoulders, the weight of his suspicions fading away in the warmth of the woman's gaze.

When he finished he fell silent, looking up at Lynda for a response.

She took a long time to reply, her old eyes studying him closely. At last she gave a short nod.

"I am afraid my part to this story will only confirm your suspicions. I spoke to the king two days ago in his private chambers. Everything Caelin and his friends said was true – I confirmed as much to the king. He told me he would consider my words and sent me away. I have been locked in this room ever since."

"How can this be?" Elton lowered his head into his hands. "He has always been a good king. Could he be under the control of one of Archon's servants?"

Lynda shrugged. "I do not know. I did not sense anything from him myself. But there are many ways for the dark to turn the light. For now though, we must get to the bottom of this rabbit hole," her voice was firm, resolute.

"How? I cannot accuse the king of treachery. Even with your word to support me, the council is clearly with him. His power is indisputable. What can I do?"

"You could free Caelin and his companions. That would be a start. We will need allies if we are to wrestle control of Plorsea back from whatever influence Archon has over the throne."

"I do not even know where they are being kept," Elton groaned.

"I believe I do," Lynda offered. "When I met with the king, he mentioned they were being held in the dungeons."

"No, I already checked. There's only the usual thieves and riff-raff down there."

"Are you sure?" she frowned. "The king mentioned it

several times. He was angry, refused to take my news as fact. He insisted they could not be trusted after murdering his councillor, that they were exactly where they deserved to be."

"Strange," Elton stood and started to pace.

He had checked most of the citadel in his search, but there had been no sign of the company. And he could not have missed their presence in the dungeons.

Pausing mid-stride, Elton turned to face the door.

They are not the only dungeons, the thought whispered in his mind. There were others, ones far older than those used today. As far as he knew, the black cells had not been used in decades. They were from another time, a darker time. They had been used to hold the prisoners of Archon's war – beasts and humans alike.

Elton shuddered, thinking of the cursed cells far below the keep. Untold horrors had transpired in those cells and darkness clung to the air itself. He had walked down the stairs once, but had never made it to the bottom. The darkness had driven him back, and not even the warmth of the torch in his hands could convince him to return. There was a presence about the place, a creeping evil that chilled the soul.

They are exactly where they deserve to be…

With sudden clarity, Elton knew his suspicion was right. If the king had truly been turned to Archon's cause, then those dungeons made a chilling sort of sense, offering a perverse revenge for the dark things that had once taken place down there.

"I know where they are," Elton breathed.

Lynda nodded. "Good. Then let us go find them."

"Us?" Elton questioned. "You can't come with me, you're a priest…"

"Ay, I am," there was steel in Lynda's voice now. "A priest entasked by the Gods to defend this world from darkness. I will not stand here, trapped in this room, and wait for that darkness to triumph. This is my fight as much as yours, young Elton. Besides, you may need my help," as she spoke a wind whirled through the room.

The hairs stood up on Elton's arms as he felt the bitter kiss of winter on the air. "You are a Magicker?"

"I am," Lynda smiled. "I have a gift with the wind. Perhaps it will help in the fight to come."

Elton stared at the priest, trying to guess her age. Beneath the blue robes her body looked frail, the skin of her hands thin and wrinkled. She must be well past sixty. But there was no denying the strength of resolve in the woman's grey eyes. And he did not know if he could continue this fight alone, not against the men and women he had served beside for the better part of a decade.

She was right, he would need her help.

"You're right," he nodded and moved to the door. "Let's go find our friends."

GIVE IN, the demon's voice hissed in the darkness.

A groan crackled up from Gabriel's parched throat as he tried to block his ears to the whispers. But the voice came from all around him, reverberating through the deepest confines of his mind.

Give in, and I will free you from this place, it persisted, tempting, irresistible.

Gritting his teeth, he fought the call. Dried blood congealed beneath his fingertips from where he had dragged them down the stone walls, desperate for distraction. The pain cut through the haze, offering a brief respite from the lure of the demon's call. But as the pain faded the voice would return, unceasing.

"*No!*" he screamed again, no longer caring what his

companions thought. In truth, he hardly remembered their presence. There was only the darkness now, only death.

And the voice.

"No, no, no," he sobbed.

He swung his fist and jumped when it connected with flesh. "Gabriel, stop," Caelin's voice echoed off the stone walls. Strong hands grabbed his wrists. "Stop this, get a hold of yourself!"

"Leave me!" Gabriel screamed, wrenching himself free, hardly aware it was Caelin who grabbed him and not the phantom stalking the darkness. "Just leave me alone," he sobbed.

"Gabriel," sadness tinged Caelin's voice, but the word was followed by scuffling as the sergeant retreated further into the cell.

Gabriel slumped back against the wall, closing his eyes, trying to close his ears.

They do not understand, the voice came again. *These mortals, they do not understand your greatness. Surrender, and I will free you from their presence.*

Tears welled in Gabriel's eyes. Why had it returned? Why would it not leave him be? Its presence radiated through the cell, its perverse evil sending chills down to his very soul. He reached inside for some defence, for some weapon with which to fight it, but there was nothing. Its thoughts crept through his mind, whispering dark secrets, washing away his sanity.

It's too late, Gabriel. You will never be one of them. It is not your destiny. There is blood on your hands, innocent blood. Join me…

Gabriel bit his tongue to keep from crying out again. Guilt swept through him. The voice was right; he had made a terrible mistake. Katya had not been the traitor. The truth had been before them all along. Some foul impersonator sat on the throne in place of the king. Katya had been no more than a pawn.

And he had killed her. The blood of an innocent woman was on his hands.

Fool, fool, fool, the words rang in his head, digging deeper until only pity and hate remained. *I swore, I swore to do good. And I failed.*

It is only your nature, the demon's voice twisted through his thoughts. *You cannot deny what you are, the darkness in your heart. Surrender, and I will give you the world.*

"Who are you?" Gabriel cried. "Leave me!"

"Gabriel, it is only us, your friends," Inken spoke now, her voice soft but weak. "We are here, only us, only ever us. Whatever speaks to you, leave it be."

"Inken?" Gabriel groaned. "What have I done? I killed her… She was innocent, and I killed her!"

"It was not your fault," her voice was sad. "We all thought it was her. The way she acted, the spell that was cast over us. You could not have known."

"Ay," it was King Fraser who spoke now, his words thick with despair. "It is a treacherous creature, well-versed in deception. It spent weeks in our court, garbed in the body of one of my councillors. I suspected something was amiss, but it whispered in my ear, sending me after the wrong suspect. I did not realize my mistake until it was too late. The man it had impersonated was waiting in here for me. It killed him once it had me."

"It doesn't matter," Gabriel replied. "Her blood is on my hands, mine alone. I deserve to be here."

For a while there was silence.

Then the whispers of the demon returned.

CHAPTER 5

Enala rolled onto her back, sighing as her head sank into the soft pillow. The bed beneath her was more comfortable than anything she could remember, but sleep would not come. Closing her eyes, she tried to lose herself in the crackling of the fireplace, in the gentle snoring coming from the other bed. Struggling to relax, she allowed her thoughts to drift over the events of the past few days. The revelations rose one after another – though her mind kept returning to the one, inconceivable fact.

I have a brother.

The word still felt strange on her tongue, the notion beyond belief. A twist of pain swept through her as she remembered her parents and the fierce love they had given her. Even amidst the poverty-stricken streets of Chole, she had never wanted for much.

More than anything, she cherished the time they had spent together amongst the Gold dragon tribes to the east, the summers spent in the wilderness of Dragon Country.

She could only imagine the pain they must have felt to

give up their child, to pass Eric into the arms of another family.

Where did you find the strength, Mum, Dad?

A tear ran down her cheek. She would never get to ask them. Eric would never get to meet the ones who had brought him into this world, who had given everything they had to protect him. He would never share in the joy her parents had given her.

Enala rolled in her blankets again, desperate for sleep but knowing now it would not come. Her restless mind ate away at the long hours, the passage of time marked by the dying light of the fireplace. Exhaustion clung to her mind, but her fear kept her awake.

"What if I have to use it, Mum, Dad?" she breathed to herself.

"Then you will pick it up and conquer it," Eric's voice came from across the room.

She turned to see him watching her, the firelight reflecting in his blue eyes. Eyes that matched her own.

"How long have you been awake?"

"I've been drifting in and out of sleep," he glanced at the window, and Enala noticed a hint of light had appeared on the horizon. "Did you sleep?"

Enala shook her head. She sat up in the bed, staring down at the covers. "What if it happens again, Eric? What happens if I can't come back this time?"

"It won't," Eric's voice was strong. "Next time, you'll be ready," he shook his head then. "Anyway, it won't come to that. Christopher will find a way to free them."

Enala should have taken heart from Eric's confidence, but the dread in her chest whispered a different song. In a flash of intuition, she knew the priest would not succeed. Even so, she smiled and nodded at her brother.

"Come on," Eric said, pulling himself from the bed.

"We're awake; we may as well get ready. We're meant to meet the council at dawn."

With a groan, Enala followed Eric's lead, rolling from the bed. She cursed her whirling mind for keeping her from sleep. She needed it desperately, and the soft bed was difficult to leave behind.

An hour later, they moved slowly up the red carpet of the throne room. Enala's feet dragged as she walked, an entirely new sense of dread wrapping around her throat. She had betrayed the Trolan council's trust when she fled with Jonathan, spitting on their hospitality. Now she had to face that same council, and beg for their aid.

Without the help of the Trolan Magickers, Eric would never master the true power of the Sword.

Eric stood beside her, his lips pursed tight. He carried the *Soul Blades* wrapped in a bundle – neither of them had any desire to touch the cursed things – and the Sword of Light strapped to his back.

A raised stone ceiling stretched high overhead, carrying echoes of the councillor's whispers across the hall. Sunlight streamed through the wide windows to their left. Enala attempted a smile as the warmth caught in her hair, her eyes drifting to the table at the end of the room. A dozen seats ringed the wooden slab, though only four were occupied. Enala guessed those who had marched north with the army usually filled the empty chairs. She felt another twist of guilt in her stomach but shook it off. Crossing the last strip of red carpet, they drew to a stop and stared at the collection of men and women facing them.

She recognised Christopher in his white robes immediately, and felt a surge of relief to see the smile on his face. The relief faded as her gaze swept across the others: another man and two women. Each wore neutral expressions, though the thin line of their lips suggested they were not impressed by their presence.

Biting her lip, Enala held her hands behind her back and gave a short bow of her head. Eric followed, and then there was nothing left to do but talk.

Enala opened her mouth to introduce herself, but broke off as one of the woman stood and walked around the table towards her. Her hair was grey and her face aged, but her eyes were sharp. They caught Enala's gaze and held her. The words in Enala's throat shrivelled and died as the woman drew to a stop in front of her.

"Welcome," the older woman spoke in a soft voice. Even so, it carried to the furthest corners of the room. She raised an eyebrow. "Again."

Enala winced, looking away from the iron in the woman's eyes. Then a surge of anger gripped her and she looked up into the woman's amber gaze.

"We have already apologised to Christopher, and the soldiers you sent. Must we bow and grovel for your forgiveness too?" her eyes flashed. "Or will you apologise for the actions of your king, for allowing such a man to wander your citadel unsupervised?"

To her surprise, the woman chuckled. Warmth spread to her face as she smiled. "I see my fellow councillor did not exaggerate when he spoke of you," she gestured them towards the table. "Come, let us leave the past in the past. My name is Angela. Christopher you already know, and this is Heather and David. Please, join us."

Enala hesitated as Eric moved past her, then nodded. Striding across to the table, she lowered herself into the chair beside Eric.

"These are dark days indeed," Angela looked around the table, as though expecting someone to disagree. "With the Gods gone, the world is descending into chaos. In truth, I see little hope for our nation's survival without divine intervention. It is a welcome sight to see the Sword of Light back in the hands of one who can wield it."

Beside her Eric nodded, and Enala tried to relax. She managed a short smile. "We were lucky things turned out in the end," she paused. "I am sorry that we ran. It was a costly mistake."

Angela smiled. "As I said, it's in the past."

"So, are you all Magickers?" Enala decided to change the subject. "The king... he told me his people no longer respected him as a ruler when he lost his magic. Or was that another lie of his?"

"A half-truth, at best," the woman named Heather answered. "Jonathan was the one who abdicated his duties and left the council with the burden of governance. Although myself and Christopher are Magickers, it is by no means a requirement."

"No," Angela added. "For myself, I am glad not to carry that burden. Most of our Magickers marched north with the army, along with half the council. We have been left rather short-staffed, as you may have noticed."

"That was why the citadel was empty when we... left," Eric's cheeks reddened as he stumbled on the last word. "Is the guard... the one outside my room, is he okay?"

Christopher chuckled. "Ay, although a little embarrassed about letting someone half his size get the better of him."

Eric smiled. "I had help, from a Magicker by the name of Laurel," his smile faded. "She was a Light Magicker."

Christopher's eyes widened. "Laurel, you say?" when Eric nodded he turned to Heather. "Could it be the same Laurel?"

"What?" Enala asked. "You knew her?"

"I believe so," Christopher nodded. "I knew a Laurel once, when I was a senior apprentice to the Temple of Light. She vanished several years ago, not long before I graduated.

We have always wondered what happened. How did you come to know her?"

An image of the feisty Baronian woman drifted through Enala's thoughts, and the smile faded from her lips. Eric had told her of the woman's sacrifice, that she had held the demon long enough for Eric to escape.

Making a decision, she interrupted Eric's reply. "We would never have made it here alive without her," she nodded at Eric. "And she sacrificed her life to save Eric from the foul demon Archon sent to hunt us."

Eric's eyes widened at her omission of Laurel's unsavoury past, but said nothing.

Christopher's eyes wrinkled in sadness. "A brave woman. Would that she had lived, we could have used her skills now. Despite lacking the Light's more aggressive powers, she was rather adept in its subtleties," he nodded at Eric. "You will need such skills if you are to wield the Sword against Archon."

Enala shivered at the name. Even now she could not bring herself to think of the confrontation to come, though it seemed all but inevitable now. Without the Gods to aid them, there would be no spell to banish the dark Magicker from their lands. No, it would be up to the men and women of the Three Nations to confront Archon.

"Is there anyone left here who *does* wield the Light?" Eric asked.

Christopher chuckled. "Well, as you might have guessed from my robes, my magic comes from the Light. It allows me to manipulate fire."

"I think I've got that one fairly well under control," Eric grinned.

"Yes, I noticed," Christopher sighed. "I do still remember most of the theory from my years as an apprentice. That may have to be enough."

"What about you, Heather?" Enala jumped in, turning to the older woman.

Her face wrinkled as she smiled back. "I am just a simple healer, I am afraid. I was one of the ones who worked on you when you first arrived."

Enala felt a sudden welling of tears. "Thank you," she murmured, blinking rapidly to clear her eyes.

After a moment of silence, Eric spoke again. "At least you'll be able to help with Enala's magic too, Christopher."

Enala's brow knitted at the thought of her power. In truth, she wanted nothing more to do with the force within her – not after everything that had happened on the island.

But Christopher was already nodding. "Yes, a budding fire Magicker I can help."

"What about the *Soul Blade*?" Enala cut in a little too sharply. Taking a deep breath, she continued. "Are you going to look at them, to see if you can free Jurrien and Antonia?"

The eyes of everyone at the table slid across to the bundle Eric had placed on the table in front of him.

"We will," Heather answered. "If you allow it, Christopher and myself will take them and do what we can to inspect them. I suspect it will take stronger powers than our own to break such a curse though."

Enala bit her lip, finding the kind eyes of the healer. "Do you think the same as Christopher? Do you think I will need to wield it?"

Heather stared back. "It may very well come to that, Enala."

Shuddering, Enala turned away. "What if I'm not strong enough?"

"You will be," Christopher spoke into the silence following her question. "I will make sure of it."

"How?" Enala hissed, still unable to meet his eyes.

Christopher stood and walked around the table until he

stood beside Eric. Reaching down, he flicked the cover off the *Soul Blades*. Enala suppressed a shudder as the faint blue and green lights bathed their faces.

"It is my theory that these blades can only be used by anyone with magic strong enough to control them," he looked across at Enala. "From what I saw on the island, I believe the magic of the *Soul Blade* overwhelmed you because you could not summon your own magic to protect yourself. From what Eric has told me, you have never consciously tapped into your power. Without that preparation, you never stood a chance against the God magic trapped in the *Soul Blade*."

"So what are you suggesting?"

"That before you even go *near* this sword again, I will train you to use your own magic."

Enala bit her lower lip, her thoughts turning to the fire magic that had appeared within her such a short time ago. It terrified her still, though it was nothing compared to the force waiting in the *Soul Blade*. At least this power was a part of her, had aided her when she had been threatened. But could it truly protect her against the God magic?

Only time will tell.

Taking a breath, she met Christopher's eyes. "When do we start?"

"WHAT DO YOU THINK?" Eric sat up as Christopher walked into the snowy courtyard.

He stretched as Christopher approached, then rubbed his arms to fight off the chill. Even in the woollen clothing they'd given him, the Trolan winter was bitterly cold. He would rather have waited near the large fireplace in his room, but the old Magicker had asked to meet him here.

Shivering, Eric wiped the sprinkles of snow from his shoulders.

"She is a fast learner," Christopher replied. "But she's not ready yet. It can take months before a Magicker is able to make the final leap with their powers."

"We don't have months. We don't even have weeks."

"I know," Christopher raised his hands. "But I will not push her before she is ready. I can sense her fear; it holds her back. And who could blame her, after what happened…"

They both fell silent then, remembering the scene in the clearing, the demonic distortion of Enala's face.

Shuddering, Eric nodded. "Okay, you're the teacher."

Christopher chuckled, shaking his head. "There's a first time for everything. I was never much of a student; I guess I'm going to learn how my teachers felt. Are you ready?"

Eric glanced down at the Sword of Light. He held it by the scabbard, the soft leather separating him from its power. Even so, light seeped from the diamond in the blade's pommel, dancing across the snowflakes falling around them.

"Well?"

Glancing up, Eric caught Christopher's eye and smiled by way of reply. Then he reached down, wrapped his frozen fingers around the pommel, and drew the blade from its sheath.

The familiar power raced up his arm, burning away the tingles of ice in his fingers. The warmth spread through his chest, pulsing with the beat of his heart. He could feel its light touching every part of him, seeping into every shadow of his mind. A shiver of fear touched him and he reached for his magic, eager to bind it to his will.

Eric breathed a sigh of relief as the blue lines of his power wrapped about the white, pulling it back from his mind. He felt the warmth of the Sword's flame and opened his eyes with a satisfied smile.

Looking up, he saw Christopher staring. "I don't think I'll ever get used to that," the Magicker offered. "I can feel the power radiating from it. Like a second sun. Unbelievable."

"I'm just glad it's under control," Eric gave a sad smile. "I have wreaked enough havoc with my own magic. I can only imagine what this would do."

"The destruction would be beyond anyone's imagination," shaking his head, Christopher clapped his hands. "But enough of such thoughts. There is much you must learn about the Light. As you may know, the Light is the most powerful of the three elements. It controls the raw energies of nature – the heat of fire being just one of them."

Eric nodded. "I saw Laurel become invisible several times – so it also controls the light itself?"

"That's correct. Although invisibility is just the beginning. A true master can also project illusions, make others see whatever the Magicker *wants* them to see."

"And Alastair's power?"

"Yes. While I only met him a few times, Alastair's power to move objects also came from the Light. With the Sword, you can do the same," Christopher took a breath. "Even more than that, the Light has dominion over magic itself. True mastery of the Sword would allow you to suppress the magic of others."

Eric gave a sad smile. "Laurel was rather adept at that particular skill," he frowned then, thoughts turning to the confrontation to come. "Could I do the same as she did – use the power of the Sword to steal the magic from Archon?"

Christopher took a while to answer. "It could be possible, but I don't think it would work. I believe it would take knowledge beyond mortal comprehension to bind dark magic as great as Archon's. Darius himself could possibly do so, but with just his raw power?" he shook his head. "If it was

SOUL BLADE

possible, I would have thought Thomas or one of his ancestors would have done so."

Eric bit his lip, struggling to hide his disappointment. Even so, he would keep the idea in mind. "When I was fighting the demon, I could feel the sword giving me energy, giving me the strength to keep going."

"That's not surprising," Christopher replied. "As you know, the Sword is God magic. Unlike our own power, it can create energy from nothing. It does not need to draw heat from the air or manipulate what is already there. In theory, you could draw unlimited energy from the Sword, though I would not recommend it."

"Why not?"

Christopher looked down at him, a hint of fear in his eyes. "We are not immortal creatures. Our souls are fragile, unlike the spirits of the entities we know as Jurrien, Antonia and Darius. We are not meant to wield such power. If you draw on the Sword's magic too much, there is no way of telling what the side effects might be."

Eric's stomach clenched in a knot, but he asked his next question anyway. "So in theory, I could use the energy of the Sword to recharge my own stores of magic?"

"It should be possible," Christopher sighed, then shook his head and grinned. "But enough with the questions. Let's see what you can do."

Eric hefted the Sword and grinned. "Let's begin."

CHAPTER 6

Elton paused at the top of the stairs, glancing back at Lynda. A few steps below, the light of the torch came to an end, engulfing the world in shadow. Staring at that darkness, he was suddenly glad he'd brought the old priest with him. He did not know whether he had the courage to continue down those steps alone.

"We had better move quickly," Lynda hissed. "Before someone comes."

Drawing in a deep breath, Elton nodded and took his first step down into the darkness. He shivered as the icy air touched him, the warmth of the torch in his hand providing scant comfort. Together they moved downwards, the darkness swallowing them up, reducing their world to the globe of light cast by the torch.

Beside him Lynda's footsteps were soft on the stone, a stark contrast to the rhythmic thud of his own boots. He glanced at her, taking strength from the courage on her stern face. Whatever the consequences, the woman intended to see this out to the end. Swallowing the lump in his chest, Elton continued their downward march.

Minutes dragged by, punctuated only by the scuffling of their feet on stone and the rhythmic thump of his heart. As they reached each landing he found himself praying they were finally at the bottom, finally within reach of his friend. But with each turn they would find another empty wall, and see another set of stairs continuing down. Down into the never-ending darkness.

"How far do they go?" Lynda whispered.

"I don't know. This dungeon was built to hold the worst of Archon's followers; those creatures and Magickers captured after his defeat in the last war. There were many who escaped the net cast by the Gods' spell, and our people were all too eager to extract their revenge."

He heard the priest swallow. "No wonder you can almost taste the evil on the air. The actions of our own people, let alone the stink of those creatures, it will never come out."

Feeling the swirling shadows around him, Elton couldn't help but agree. But there was no time to reply now – ahead, the torch had finally illuminated the bottom of the staircase. The stone steps came to an abrupt halt, replaced by a smooth, unlit corridor disappearing into the darkness. Their light reached the first of the cells, but there was no telling how far they stretched.

"This is it," Lynda murmured.

Elton looked around as a breath of wind stirred his clothing. Glancing at the priest, he stepped back in shock to see her robes flapping around her, caught in the grip of a great gale. But other than the briefest of whispers, the air in the dungeons was still, dead.

Lynda smiled. "I thought I'd call the wind now, in case we are cut off from the surface. You never know what we might find down here."

Forcing his mouth shut, Elton nodded. Lynda must be more powerful than he'd thought, to summon wind from so far above them, into a place as dark as this. Then he shook his head, returning his thoughts to the task at hand.

Somewhere down here, Caelin and his companions waited.

Stepping into the corridor, Elton made his way to the door of the first cell. Reaching up, he pounded the wood with his fist, then stepped back, waiting anxiously for a hint of life within.

After a few moments of silence, he moved to the next door, heart clutched tight in his chest. Down in this darkness with no source of light or heat, Caelin and the others could easily have succumbed already. It had been almost two weeks since the incident on the wall; he could only imagine the horror they had suffered in this place.

They made their way quietly down the corridor, Elton's hopes fading with every silent door. Lynda walked beside him, lips pursed, silent but for the gentle flapping of her robes. But he could see the determination in her eyes. If they did not find anything, he had no doubt she would blow every door from its hinges before she gave up.

Finally, they reached the door at the end of the corridor, the only one left unchecked. Elton's head throbbed with the cold, the beginnings of a migraine starting in the back of his skull. Icy despair touched his heart, but he pushed it back and held the torch aloft to cast its light over the door. From the outside it looked the same as the others. There was no sign of recent use.

Holding his breath, he reached up and banged his fist on the wood.

They waited together, breath held, the only sound in the darkness the gentle whirring of Lynda's wind. Elton closed his eyes, fighting the racing of his heart, and tried to push his panic down. The seconds stretched out, slipping away like sand from an hour-glass. And still no sound came from within.

At last Elton released his breath, the weight of defeat heavy on his shoulders.

"They're not here," he hissed.

As he spoke, the faintest of taps came from beyond the door.

Elton almost jumped, reaching for his sword before reason could take hold. In this dark place, the faintest of noises was as loud as a drum. He glanced at Lynda, eyes wide in question.

She nodded, and raised her hand.

The wind roared in the narrow corridor, rushing outwards to slam against the door. Wood groaned as the bottled up fury of the Sky crashed against it, followed by the scraping of hinges on stone. Elton stumbled back a step, sparing a glance at the priest. A vein throbbed on her forehead and her teeth were bared with exertion.

Then with a heavy crunch, the door buckled inwards, the wood splintering before the fury of the Sky. A second later it vanished into the black depths of the cell.

Elton stared, eyes searching the darkness within for a hint of movement. For a moment there was nothing, then he glimpsed a shadow in the light of the torch. He stared, waiting with anxious breath to see who would emerge.

The shadows shifted again, a figure taking shape within. It stepped closer, stumbling as it moved towards the light. Elton glimpsed an upraised arm, warding off the brilliance of the torch, and cursed his own stupidity. After so long in the darkness, the flame would be blinding. Shuttering the torch to just a slit, he waited for the figure to emerge.

The figure took the final step from the cell, and the slit of light fell across his face.

The air went from Elton's mouth in a sudden hiss. He stared, mouth agape and eyes wide, unable to comprehend this vision in the darkness.

Matted hair covered the man's face and his grey hair hung in a tangled mess. Dark brown eyes squinted out from beneath bushy eyebrows, struggling with the light. Lines marked his forehead and his limbs were shrunken and thin, starved of the power they had once wielded. The long weeks had reduced his clothes to little more than rags.

Yet even filthy and unkempt, there could be no mistaking the King of Plorsea.

"Elton," the king's words were barely a whisper. "So glad you came. You're a little late."

DEEP IN HIS THOUGHTS, Caelin did not notice the first knock on the door. The sound echoed in the tiny room, trickling slowly into his conscious. It found him there, locked away where the darkness outside could not find him.

He studied the noise, curious as to what could have disturbed him. Certainly it could be nothing within the cell: he had long since filtered out Gabriel's mad rambling and the quiet sobs from Inken's corner.

What could it be?

The question continued to bother him. Had the guards finally returned with food? Or were they here to take them up again, to go before the imposter on the throne and plead their innocence?

Yet he had long since given up that hope. There was no reason for the creature to return them to the light, not now that they knew the truth.

No, they were meant to wither and die here in the darkness.

But there had been a sound, an echo of the outside world. The knowledge seeped through him, growing and spreading out to light the candles of his mind.

What could it be?

His mind was waking now, searching out the answer. It would not be the guards – they did not knock. The only time they had come, a tray had slid through the slit beneath the door.

Someone else then.

The thought finally gave him the strength to open his eyes and move. The darkness greeted him once more, but then, even his dreams were of the darkness now. The light seemed but a distant memory, a lifetime ago. Only the Gods could guess how long they had been here.

But then, they were dead too.

Drawing on the last dredges of his will, Caelin pulled himself back to his feet. In a daze he stumbled to where he knew the door stood. Reaching out, he tapped at the hard wood.

The noise seemed unbelievably loud in the narrow confines of their cell. Or perhaps that was because it had been so long since there had been noise.

Staring into space, Caelin found his energy withering, trickling back down to the depths of his soul.

It was nothing – a rat or nothing.

Then the darkness roared, and before he could think he was throwing himself to the side as the shattered remains of the door bounced past where he'd stood.

Light split the darkness, burning his eyes with the intensity of the sun. Tears spilt down Caelin's face but he could not look away from the light. The wonderful, unbelievable light. Around him the shadows peeled away, lifting from his soul. Strength flowed back to his muscles, lifting him from the ground. Light could mean only one thing.

Freedom.

Looking around the room, he saw the others blinking back. Inken wore a sort of wonder on her pale face, her hazel eyes glistening with tears and her fiery red hair shining in the light. Grease marked her face but he could see the strength there, flooding back to wash away the despair.

Gabriel sat beside her, but where Caelin had welcomed the golden glow, Gabriel flinched away, curling up and turning away from the doorway. His black hair was thick with oil and his forehead wet with sweat. But Caelin could not spare the young man his help yet. His thoughts were returning now, the memories rising up to meet the light. And with them, questions.

To his surprise, the king was already standing and staggering towards the doorway. The ravages of Fraser's captivity were clear in the light, his body shrunken almost beyond recognition. But despite it, there was a light in the man's eyes now, one Caelin had not expected after the man's earlier despair.

Perhaps the king was not broken yet.

Fraser was the first to reach the light, stumbling through the doorway to the corridor beyond. Gasps came from outside and Caelin's suspicions were confirmed; whoever was out there had not been sent by the false king.

Listening to the voices, Caelin drew on his last reserves of energy and stumbled out after his king. He heard Inken behind him, offering Gabriel her hand, and hoped the young man would find the strength to bring himself back from the grip of madness. It would take all they had to overthrow the demon on the throne.

Pain stabbed at his eyes as he emerged, though he saw the lantern held by their rescuers had been reduced to a slit. He stared at the man with the light, struggling to make out his features. A priest stood beside him, that much was clear from the blue robes. The woman's face appeared as a blur, but he guessed she was from the temple back in Lon. Probably the one they'd sent to verify their story.

Hope rose in his chest as the man's face came into focus.

"Elton, you found us," he croaked, his throat rough from thirst.

"Caelin," his old friend's voice shook. "How... how is this possible?"

Caelin gave a weak shake of his head. "I do not know," sorrow clung to his voice. "Archon's reach has stretched further than any of us could have imagined."

"Ay," the priest spoke now. "Without the Gods to protect us, there is little to stop the dark tendrils of his power spreading south. Us mere mortals are easy pickings for the likes of him. And it seems this time, he does not intend to be slowed by the armies of the Three Nations."

"What can we do?" Inken emerged with Gabriel on her shoulder. Her face was a sickly white, but she stood straight. "What will *you* do, Fraser?"

Elton winced at the casual way Inken addressed the king, but he had not been locked in that cell with them. Whatever happened now, they were bound by the shared horrors of the darkness.

Fraser stared back, his eyes pits in the shadow of his brow. He had lost so much to the darkness. Anyone who saw him now would call him imposter to the demon upstairs. There appeared to be little left of the man Caelin knew.

But he prayed the darkness had not taken everything, that a spark of the man still remained.

Staring at the king, Caelin held his breath and waited.

Fraser looked back, his breath misting in the icy dungeon air. The flames of the lantern reflected in his eyes, reminding Caelin of the man that had sent him to find Alastair so long ago. He was in there somewhere; they just needed to find him.

"Fraser," he whispered. "We need you."

The king drew in a great breath and looked around, his eyes lingering on each of them.

He took another breath. "I guess… I guess we go to war."

CHAPTER 7

L ight, light everywhere. Emptiness, a vast open void, stretching out to eternity. And it burned, burned wherever it touched, consuming him, devouring him.

Eric opened his mouth to scream, and woke.

He snapped upright, struggling to bite off his cry before he woke Enala. His chest heaved and a cold sweat ran down his brow. He turned his head, his desperate eyes searching the room. But there was no one, nothing but the gentle snores of his sister from across the room.

Slowly his panic began to subside. He took another breath, trying to still his racing heart.

The memory of the Sword's magic lingered in his mind. His eyes drifted across the room until they found the blade leaning against the foot of his bed. He shivered. It had just been a dream; the vision had not been real. The blade remained out of reach, its magic locked within.

Yet the memory of its touch lingered in his mind. They had been training for days now, and Christopher's warning about the Sword's magic was becoming all too real. Its magic was never far from his thoughts.

Each time Eric touched it he felt its hunger, its harsh light burning away the shadows of his mind, searching for a weakness. And each time he touched it, he feared it would find it.

Shivering, Eric pulled back the covers and stood. His legs trembled and his mouth stretched in a yawn, but the dream still clung to him. He would not sleep now.

"Eric?" he heard the sleep in his sister's voice. "Are you okay?"

He saw her sitting up in bed and sighed. Sinking back onto his bed, he looked across at her.

"Sorry, I didn't mean to wake you."

"It's okay. I was hardly asleep," she shrugged, hesitating. "The magic, it scares me. Every time I close my eyes I can feel it, waiting. It may not be the same as the power in the *Soul Blade*, but it still terrifies me. I am afraid to close my eyes."

Eric rubbed his hands together and glanced at the fire. It had burned down to embers, and without its heat the room was beginning to cool. Without speaking he moved across the room and tossed one of the smaller pieces of firewood onto the ashes. Flames licked at the wood as he crouched down in front of it, hands out to the heat.

"I know how you feel," he spoke without turning, his voice soft. "Before we reached Chole, Alastair began to teach me how to use my magic. I began to meditate, to look within the shadows of my inner mind. Before Alastair could prepare me, I found my magic. Not knowing the risks, I reached out and touched it. When I did, my magic took me. If not for Alastair…" Eric shook his head. "Afterwards, I was gripped with the same terror you feel now. But you cannot let it rule you, Enala. If you let it fester the fear will only grow, until it becomes a beast you can never face."

He turned and saw tears in Enala's eyes. "Why is this happening to us, Eric?" she whispered. "How can we possibly hope to defeat Archon, when even the Gods have failed?"

Standing, Eric moved across to his sister and drew her to her feet. "We take one step at a time," drawing her across to the fire, they sat on the fur rug. "You need to face the beast within you, Enala. You need to prove to yourself you have the strength to face it. Remember, your fear is the only weapon it has against you."

He watched Enala take a shuddering breath, and then her sapphire eyes met his. Eric added another log to the fire, closing his eyes as the flames licked up the fresh morsel and the heat washed over him.

"Are you ready?" he asked in a whisper.

"Are you ready?" Eric asked.

Enala smiled back at her brother, glad for his support. "I'm ready."

Without another word, she closed her eyes and turned her thoughts inward. She had spent the last few days practicing meditation with Christopher, but it still took time to concentrate. Thoughts rose to distract her, the bitter tang of fear at the forefront. Swallowing, she pushed them down, focusing on the rise and fall of her chest.

In, out. In, out, she breathed.

Slowly, her thoughts faded away, the simple words rising up to swallow them. Sensation fell with them, until all that remained was the gentle in and out of her breath. She found herself drifting in a world of shadows, alone, free from the trappings of her earthly worries.

Then, in the distance, she glimpsed the faint flicker of light. Curious, she turned towards it. The darkness slipped past her, as though she were soaring through a night sky, and the light grew. Within seconds it had turned from a dim speck to a vast pool of flame. It flickered beneath her, tongues of fire leaping up from its depths. And she knew she had found what she needed.

My magic, the words echoed all around her, as though spoken aloud.

Drawing on her strength, Enala cast aside her hesitation and reached for the light. A flame licked up in response, a finger of power reaching out to meet her. A tingle swept through her as it touched, curling up to wrap around her.

She gasped as the power drew suddenly tight, trapping her in its heat. Red flashed before her eyes and then it was burning, its touch searing through her spirit form. In the empty darkness, she screamed.

The pool of flame beneath her twisted, turning in upon itself. It rose in a column before her, shifting, changing from benign light to a creature of fire. Great jaws took form within the darkness and fangs of fire reached for her. The sleek body of a lioness grew out from the jaws, its sharp ears flat to its head, the wicked tale flicking out behind it.

Enala's fear came rushing back and she shuddered in the bonds of flame. The lioness swelled, drawing strength from her fear. It stepped towards her, fangs and claws poised to strike.

You can do it, Enala, from someplace far away, she heard her brother's words. *Face it; defeat it.*

Enala stared at the beast, the fear within her alive, swelling to engulf her. She clung to Eric's words, her lifeline in the darkness. The fear swelled, seeking to consume her, but as she stared at the lioness she found her courage returning.

Clenching her fists, Enala looked into the eyes of the beast.

You are nothing, she hissed.

To her shock, she felt the bonds of fire loosen. The lioness growled and took another step towards her. Enala ignored it. Summoning her own strength, she stepped towards it. The flames around her roared as she stepped into their midst, their hungry tongues licking at her spirit. But Enala pulled her courage around her like a cloak and took another step forward.

As she emerged from the flame she saw the lioness shrinking, withering before the power of her courage. A house cat now stood before her, hissing as she approached it. Its paws swiped out in rage and its hair stood on end, but she felt no fear now. Reaching down, she grasped it in her hands.

And the flames went out.

With a rush of warmth, she felt the magic surging within her, flowing through her veins. It swept through her soul, carrying with it images of smoke and flame. But it was hers to command now, and she would not release it.

Smiling, Enala opened her eyes.

"Welcome back, Enala. You did well," Eric grinned back at her.

Reaching up, Enala wiped the sweat from her brow. Her body felt hot, far hotter than the fire burning in the grate.

"Thank you, Eric," she shook her head. "Thank you for your belief in me. I could not have defeated the lion without it."

"I have every confidence you could have. You are the bravest person I know, Enala. If anyone could conquer their fear, it's you. And without fear the magic has no hold on you," he paused. "Although personally, my magic takes the form of a wolf. Much scarier," he winked.

Enala sucked in a breath. "Maybe, but I think I still have a lot to learn. Whatever you think, it almost had me. It will take time to master it," she paused. "And the *Soul Blade...*"

"One step at a time, remember."

"I know," even so, Enala could not stop her thoughts turning forwards. "Do you think we'll be able to free them? Antonia and Jurrien?" It seemed that was the only way she could avoid touching the cursed blade.

Eric shook his head. "Not here. I don't think the Magickers remaining in the capital have the power. In Fort Fall, maybe…" his voice trailed off.

Enala found herself biting back tears, the worry in her heart rising up to overwhelm her. It seemed that with every challenge they overcame, a greater one waited to take its place. She may have conquered her magic this one time, but she could not even enjoy that triumph, knowing the *Soul Blade* lurked in her future.

She felt Eric's hand on her shoulder and looked up. "It's not fair, I know."

A great, shuddering sob tore through Enala and she buried herself in his shoulder. "I can't do it, Eric. I can't face that *thing*, whatever it is in that sword."

Eric said nothing, just held her there in the light of the fire, offering his silent comfort. There was nothing he could say, nothing either of them could do to escape the destinies waiting for them. It was as Eric had said – unfair.

At last her sobs started to subside and she pulled back from her brother. She attempted to smile through her tears. "You know, I bet we find Inken and the others at Fort Fall," she said the words to give Eric cheer, but felt a warmth swell in her own chest at the thought of a reunion with Gabriel.

Eric smiled back. "I hope so. The Gods know we could use their help."

"There will be a lot of catching up to do," Enala nodded at the Sword of Light. "How do you think Inken will react to *that*?"

Laughing, Eric shook his head. "She'll probably ask what took us so long."

"When will we go?"

Eric frowned, watching as an ember rose from the fire to settle on his sleeve. "I don't know. Soon, I guess. We cannot afford to wait. Archon won't. Without the Gods holding him back, there is nothing left to stop him from marching south."

Enala nodded, her mind distant, thinking of the men and women manning that lonely fortress far in the north. "No," she whispered. "You're right; we can't linger here for long. As much as we need the rest, Fort Fall needs every soul they can get."

"We had better talk to Christopher and the others in the morning. Perhaps we can take a ship up the coast to the Gap."

A shadow wrapped around Enala's heart at the words, but she nodded all the same.

Silence fell between them then, as their thoughts turned inwards. Enala stared into the fire, her mind a thousand miles away, consumed by a fortress she had never seen.

Fort Fall.

She prayed the place would not live up to its name.

ERIC FROWNED as the muffled *whoosh* of flames erupting against stone echoed through the courtyard. Wiping the sweat from his forehead, he looked up at the two combatants as they fought their way through the heavy snow. The clash of steel followed as they closed on each other, the blades little more than blurs in their hands.

Sighing, Eric shook his head. It was good to see Enala making progress; he only wished he could say the same for himself. He sat on a stone bench at the other end of the courtyard, the Sword of Light lying across his lap. So far he had achieved little more than the first time he'd felt the rush of its power. It was galling to think unlimited power lay in his lap, yet he could do little more than create fire.

He watched Enala dive sideways into the snow to avoid a column of flame. It had been three days now since their midnight lesson, but they had made little progress with their plans to travel north. A blizzard had moved in over the city that night, burying the citadel in white and freezing the harbour solid. Things had only begun to thaw today, though Eric could still taste the ice on the air.

At least they had made the most of the extra time. He could see Enala's confidence growing each day, the fear lurking behind her eyes retreating before it. Christopher was proving to be a good teacher, although he'd had less luck with Eric. The Magicker had explained the basic techniques to wielding the different parts of the Light element, but so far Eric had failed to grasp even the most basic of them.

Across the courtyard, Enala rolled and regained her feet. Flames flickered along her arms, the snow coating her clothes turning to steam. She glared across at Christopher and with a scream, swept out her arm.

The flames roared and rushed towards her opponent, the snow sizzling at its touch. Across from her, Christopher raised both arms and a wall of orange fire leapt up in front of him. A dull boom rang across the courtyard as the two forces came together.

But Enala was already moving, sprinting across the burning stone with sword in one hand, fire in the other. Christopher waved a hand and the tangling flames went out with a rush, then Enala was there, flaming hand swinging for his face. Before the blow could land Christopher leaned backwards and her fist swept past, finding only empty air.

Then a burst of orange roared from Christopher's open

hand, taking Enala full in the stomach, and suddenly she was airborne.

Eric suppressed a chuckle as his sister tumbled backwards, disappearing into a mound of snow.

A groan came from somewhere within, followed by a string of curses. Her head reappeared, flushed with anger.

"You couldn't have pulled your blow?"

Christopher laughed. "I *did* pull my blow."

Enala swore again and shook her head. Eric could see the attack had rattled her. She still struggled to focus on both her magic and physical combat, a skill he himself had yet to even attempt. He did not envy her the challenge.

"I think I'm getting the hang of it," Enala offered as she climbed to her feet and brushed snow from her jacket. "It's a difficult balance."

"It takes practice," Christopher agreed. "But it is also an excellent way to help you get a grip on your power quickly. And I imagine it could prove useful in the north."

"I know. It's just *hard*."

Smiling, Eric shook his head. Turning back to the Sword of Light, he let out a deep breath and began again. Sinking into the confines of his mind, he reached out for the magic of the blade. The white flames leapt at his touch, their heat searing at his thoughts, but his own magic quickly rose to combat it. The blue lines of his power wrapped about the white, binding it tight.

Taking another breath, Eric opened his spirit eyes and allowed his soul to take flight. Rising from his body, he drew the white fire with him, holding it firm in his grasp. Looking now at Enala and Christopher, he saw the burning red within them, bright as torches in the darkness.

Eric had already attempted to suppress their magic as Laurel had done to his, but without success. Now as he reached out he decided on another course. It seemed an age

81

ago now, but he had watched Alastair work his magic a hundred times. His mentor's strength had been prodigious, but Eric only needed the gentlest of touches for what he intended.

Drawing the Sword's power with him, Eric drifted across to where Christopher stood watching Enala's approach. Lines of power wrapped around the Magicker, some flashing red with the power burning at his core, while others seemed to appear from the air itself. Praying he knew what he was doing, Eric reached out and pressed the white fire of the Sword to the lines of power.

Light flared as the two forces met, then pale fire raced down the line towards Christopher. Eric's spirit shivered as the power reached the priest. The air popped as they met, but nothing changed, and Christopher stepped forward to knock aside Enala's next attack.

Frowning, Eric repeated the process sure he must be onto something. The lines had to be connected to some part of the Light – otherwise the Sword's magic would not be able to interact with them. Some intuition told Eric they must be related to how Alastair's power had worked.

This time as the white swept along the line, Eric reached out and gripped it with his mind. To his surprise, the surging white froze, its energy tingling beneath the soft touch of his conscious. Then, almost by instinct, Eric drove the energy into Christopher and gave one final, gentle push.

Christopher gave a shout of surprise as his legs whipped out from beneath him, tripped by some invisible force. The flames in this hand died away as his concentration snapped, and Enala leapt in to tap his chest with her practice blade.

Chuckling to himself, Eric retreated into his body and stretched his arms. His chest swelled with pride, that he had managed to replicate the magic of his mentor. Smiling, he stood and sheathed the Sword of Light, then walked across to join the others.

He laughed out loud as he caught Christopher's glare.

"Made some progress at last I see," the priest raised an eyebrow.

Eric grinned back. "Slowly but surely."

"A bit of warning would have been nice," Christopher shook his head. "But well done. You will need every skill you can muster to face Archon."

"I thought the scales could use a bit of balancing. Enala looked a little outmatched."

His sister scowled. "I didn't need you to cheat for me, Eric."

Eric raised his hands in surrender, but could not keep the smile from his face. "I just hope I'll have time to learn the rest. I want to at least *try* and use the Sword to suppress Archon's power."

Christopher sighed. "Would that it could be so easy. Only time will tell I guess."

"How goes the training?" they all looked up at Angela's voice.

"Progressing better than I had hoped," Christopher answered with a thin smile.

Angela nodded. "I have news. Heather and the other Magickers have finished inspecting the *Soul Blade*. It is as you suspected, Christopher. They are not powerful enough to break the enchantments. Unless we find someone stronger, the Gods will remain trapped in the weapons."

Eric's heart sank. He shot a glance at Enala and caught the despair sweep across her face. She masked it quickly, but not before their eyes caught. She looked away before he could say anything.

"There's still hope, Enala," Christopher spoke from between them. "By the time you reach Fort Fall, the greatest

Magickers of the Three Nations will be there. If anyone can free the Gods, it will be them."

"That is my other news," Angela interrupted.

Eric looked up, catching the hint of warning in her voice. "What is it?"

He saw then the weariness in Angela's eyes, the rings of exhaustion lining her face. She held her shoulders tensed and her fists were clenched tightly around a scrap of paper.

"This just arrived by pigeon," Angela paused for a breath. "It's from Fort Fall…" her voiced faded off.

A wave of weariness swept through Eric's legs. He stumbled a step, struggling to find the strength to keep his feet. "What's happened?"

"The invasion has begun," the old councillor's voice trembled. "Fort Fall is under siege, and the majority of our armies have yet to reach them. With the standing guard and the advance parties from Plorsea and Trola, they only have a thousand men."

"How far off are the rest of our forces?" Christopher's forehead creased with worry.

"The last word we had from our army put them a week out from the fortress. The Lonians are likely closer. But with only a thousand men, Fort Fall will be hard-pressed to hold on long enough for reinforcements to arrive."

"We will leave today," Eric growled, a desperate idea taking form in his mind.

Angela shook her head. "Even if you leave now, it will take weeks for the ship to traverse the Trolan coastline. It could be all over by then…"

Beside him Enala cursed, but Eric was already shaking his head. "You're right; there's no time for that now. We will not go by ship," he tapped the pommel of the Sword of Light. "We will fly. The Sword can give me the energy I need to make the journey. We could be there in days."

Christopher shook his head. "Remember what I said, Eric? Using the Sword for such a long period of time… there is no telling what the consequences would be."

Eric drew in a breath of the icy air. "It doesn't matter; we have to take the risk. If we don't we'll be too late to make a difference anyway."

"What about the Plorsean army?" Enala interrupted. "Could they be closer?"

"We have heard nothing from King Fraser," Angela answered. "But even if they marched as soon as Jurrien sent out word, the Lonians would still be closer."

Eric swallowed. "Then we have no choice."

"Are you sure?" Angela stared at him. "There will be no second chances here. You know what waits for you up there."

Eric nodded. "I know. But I doubt I could ever be ready for what is to come – not if I had a decade to prepare. Either way, it doesn't matter now. Our time is up."

"He's right," Enala added. "Ready or not, we have to do this. Archon will not wait for us."

Tears in her eyes, Angela stepped forward and drew them both into her arms. "Then good luck, my king, my queen. How I wish you had come to us sooner."

"May the Gods bless your journey," Christopher murmured from beside them.

CHAPTER 8

Inken staggered down the corridor, Gabriel and the priest Lynda at her side. Gabriel had regained some of his colour and now walked unsupported, but the haunted look remained and she still feared for his sanity.

Ahead Caelin, Elton and Fraser strode through the door of the barracks. Swallowing her doubts, Inken moved after them. They were taking a terrible risk, but there was no arguing with Caelin's logic. Circumstances left them little choice – they needed reinforcements. She just prayed Caelin and Fraser could convince the guards to follow them.

Stepping through the doorway, she reached unconsciously for her sabre and then swore at its absence. Elton had not been able to arm them, and he held their only sword. Not that it mattered; if they were forced to draw their blades now, they had already lost.

Even so, the sight of a dozen men stepping towards them with blades drawn did not give her much confidence in their plan.

Caelin and the others raised their hands and the guards

paused, exchanging uncertain looks between themselves. That was all the time they needed.

"Men, you know me," Fraser spoke now, his voice soft but with a quiet confidence Inken had not expected. "You know my face, beneath the filth. I have fought beside many of you, spilt my blood to defend you. I am Fraser, your king."

Swords wavered in indecisive hands as the men stared hard at the filthy beggars who had invaded their barracks.

Finally one of the guards stepped forward. "What is going on here?" he growled. "You *look* like our king, but it cannot be. I was in the throne room not an hour ago. The king was as strong and *clean* as I have ever seen him. You, you look as though you have not eaten in weeks, *imposter*."

Fraser bowed his head, and for a second it looked as though their cause was lost. Then he looked up, and saw the fire in his eyes. "*Ay*, I have not eaten in weeks, Robin. No, I have been locked in the old dungeons, shut away from the world, starved and kept alive for the Gods only know why. And in my place has sat a demon, or some other cursed creature of Archon."

The man reeled back before the king's fury, but others were not so easily cowed. Another man stepped forward and waved a hand. "Yet another traitor named by Caelin?" he shook his head. "No, I will not believe the words from this man's mouth, not with this murderer standing beside him," his voice broke. "I will not believe Katya was a traitor."

Inken sensed the sorrow behind the man's words and guessed the councillor had meant more to him than most.

"I am sorry, truly, Antony. I know you two were close," Caelin drew in a breath. "And I fear you are right, we were tricked. I now believe Katya truly was innocent, that the creature sitting on the throne manipulated us into believing she was the one wielding the dark magic against us."

"But the truth stands before you now. This man is your king, filthy and withered from starvation as he may be. If you wish for me to suffer, let it come later. For now, believe the truth of your own eyes, the whispers of your conscious. You know the king has not been himself, and he has not. A traitor sits on our throne, one who means to see our nation fall before the might of Archon. We cannot let that happen."

Antony's eyes swept the room, lingering on each of them in turn. He settled on the priest standing beside her and raised an eyebrow.

"What's your place in all this, priest?"

Lynda bowed her head. "I was sent from Lon to verify their story," she waved at Caelin. "Everything he has said is true. The thing on the throne had me locked up before I could confirm their story to the council. Elton freed me, and together we found where they had been imprisoned. We were as surprised as you to find the true king locked away with them."

As her words spread around the room, Antony's shoulders slumped. Inken held her breath, hand twitching with anticipation. If Antony denied Lynda's words, it would come to bloodshed. She could see the anger in his eyes, his desire to revenge the fallen councillor.

Air hissed between Antony's lips and he bowed his head. "Okay," when he looked back up, the rage had faded. "But this is not the end of this discussion, Caelin," he turned to Fraser then. "Your majesty, please, forgive us. We should have seen through the creature's deception long ago. Things have been… wrong… for weeks."

The others in the room nodded, and Inken breathed a sigh of relief as swords were returned to their sheaths.

Fraser waved a hand, dismissing the soldiers' guilt. "The fault is not yours, but Archon's."

"Well that's a relief," Lynda smiled beside Inken as the soldiers gathered around Fraser and began to discuss their next move.

Inken nodded, the tension fleeing her shoulders. "That's half the battle won."

"The easy half, I imagine," Gabriel's voice was thick with self-loathing.

Inken glared at him. He turned away, unable to meet her eyes. "If we can convince the guards in the throne room the same way, there won't be a battle at all."

Gabriel nodded, his eyes to the floor. Inken reached out and grasped his chin, forcing him to look at her.

"We will make this right, Gabriel," she stared into his eyes, refusing to flinch at the darkness she saw there. "You understand?"

"How?" he croaked.

"By banishing this evil, by sending that creature screaming into the void," she paused, taking a breath. "But it will take everything we have to do it, Gabriel. We cannot afford to hesitate. We need you, Gabriel, all of you. So, are you with us?"

Inken glimpsed a spark of light in the young man's eyes and smiled as Gabriel nodded.

Before she could respond a roar went through the room, and then the soldiers were sweeping past her, Fraser in the lead. Caelin tossed her a sheathed sword and she reached up to catch it, nodding her thanks. She glanced at Lynda and raised an eyebrow in question.

The priest shook her head. "I have my magic. It will be enough. Shall we join them?"

Inken smiled. "Let's go to war."

GABRIEL SQUEEZED HIS EYES SHUT, swallowing his fear as he followed the others from the barracks. The whispers came in a constant stream now, the shadow of the demon hovering always just out of sight. He pushed them down. He needed to concentrate, to find the strength to fight. His friends needed him.

At least day had finally broken, the light of dawn streaming in through the windows of the corridors. The sun's warmth offered him comfort, banishing the icy chill clenched around his soul.

Ahead, Caelin, Fraser and Elton led the group of guards. They had been armed from the stockpile of weapons in the barracks, though the sword Gabriel now carried felt heavy in his hand. His stomach rumbled and he wished they'd eaten more than the scraps they'd pilfered from the kitchens earlier. Even with the food he felt exhausted, his muscles starved of energy.

Hopefully we won't need to fight, he thought to himself. Twelve guards had joined them in the barracks, yet he wondered whether they would have the courage for such a fight. If they could not sway those protecting the false king, they would be forced to kill their own comrades. Such a decision was not to be taken lightly.

They encountered few people on the short march to the throne room. Those who spotted them were easily fooled though – after all, it was clear the guards were escorting a group of prisoners to the king for judgement. Fortunately, no one bothered to give them a closer inspection. If they had, they would have noticed Gabriel and the other prisoners were armed.

Gabriel kept his sword low and tucked out of sight beneath his old coat. The muck from the dungeons still clung to him, leaving his skin itchy and raw. Still, at least they had left the darkness behind. Though the light hurt his eyes, it also gave him hope, and the strength to push back the voice.

The guards in front reached the great double doors of the throne room and thrust them open. The gold-embossed doors swung open without so much as a creak, the hinges obviously well-oiled by whichever servant was in charge of maintaining the throne room. Gabriel held his breath as the company raced inside, and waited for the shouts to start.

It was not a long wait. As he strode after his friends the first cry of rage came from the dais. The false king stood on the dais, towering over the room from his position at the head of the council table. His eyes swept the room, anger burning in their depths – though it quickly turned to shock as he found Fraser in their midst.

"What is the meaning of this?" the false king shouted. "Guards, why have you bought these beggars before me?"

Fraser stepped forward and pointed at the false king. "I am no beggar, foul creature. I am Fraser, the true king of Plorsea. You are naught but some foul beast of Archon, sent here to betray our land."

Shouts raced around the room as councillors leapt to their feet. The guards surrounding the dais wavered, looking from the false king to Fraser and his circle of men. He saw the indecision on their faces. But it seemed clear to Gabriel which king they would pick. Fraser still wore the ruined clothes of his imprisonment, while the false king stood atop the dais in all his finery, the picture of royalty.

If they chose the false king, it did not bode well for their chances. The guards in the throne room outnumbered them two to one.

Fraser turned to the ring of guards, his eyes filled with fire. "You know me; you know who I am. Do you truly believe that thing on my throne is your king? You know the truth; you've seen it each day with your own eyes. That is not the king; that is not *me*."

The words swept through the ranks of men and Gabriel saw the doubt in their eyes. Then a slow clap carried through the hall, echoing down from the false king. As the eyes of every man and woman turned to him, he reached down and drew his sword.

"You know your true king, men. And it is not this traitorous beast. Let us put an end to the lies of this foul imposter."

With a roar the false king leapt from the dais. Gabriel's heart sank as the guards fanned out around him. They had lost the war of words; it would come to blades now. Outnumbered and drained by starvation, Gabriel feared he and his companions would not fare well.

"*Stop!*" Lynda's voice cracked through the room. She moved through the soldiers until she stood beside Fraser. "Stop," she repeated. "And listen."

"No," the false king growled. "We will hear no more of your lies," with a roar, he leapt towards them.

Lynda smiled and raised a hand. A howling whistle filled the room as wind rushed through the open windows. With a nod from the priest, the wind struck the false king and his men, forcing them backwards.

"You will listen," Lynda snapped. She waved at Caelin and the others. "Caelin and Fraser speak the truth. It is here for all of you to see. Why would a creature of Archon come before you as a beggar? Why would your fellow soldiers join him, if not for the truth of his claim?"

"Who are you?" Gabriel looked up to see a councillor still standing atop the dais.

"I am Lynda, the Lonian priest you sent for to verify the story of Caelin and his companions."

"Where have you been?" the councillor moved closer to the edge of the dais.

"That *thing* had me locked away," Lynda nodded to the false king.

The councillor stood silent, staring down at them with a strange look on his face. Gabriel held his breath, praying this might be the turning point they needed. The councillor's red robes rustled in the breeze still whipping about the room. Then the man crossed his arms and smiled.

"I do not believe you," before any of them could react he threw out a hand.

A beam of light lanced across the room and caught Lynda in its brilliance. The old priestess raised a hand as the light reached her and the wind roared once more. It billowed up over the heads of the soldiers, up to the councillor atop the dais. There came a muffled thud as it caught him, followed by a sickening crack as he spun head-first into the wall.

Then the light spiralled around Lynda, and she threw back her head and screamed. Gabriel stumbled back, staring in horror as her body began to convulse. Lines of purple spread across her face, and the sound of her screams drove splinters into his head. But he could not look away. The woman stood frozen, her eyes filled with pain and fear.

Then the screaming stopped and an awful silence fell over the throne room. As one Caelin and Elton stepped towards the woman, but before they could take two steps she crumpled to the ground and lay still.

Gabriel looked away as Caelin reached her and searched for sign of life. In his heart he already knew the truth – Lynda had given her life to protect them from the other Magicker. Turning to face the false king, he resolved to make her sacrifice count. To his relief, the others in their party did the same. Not a man wavered; each had made their decision, and now they were determined to see it through.

The same could not be said of those opposing them. Already some of the false king's guards were stepping back, retreating to the far wall and taking themselves out of the fight. None of them made a move to join Fraser, but it was clear they had no wish to fight their comrades for a cause they did not quite believe in.

Even so, there were still some twenty guards left supporting the false king. Even counting their weakened fighters, they remained outnumbered and outmatched.

Gabriel's eyes found the false king and locked on the greatsword he carried one-handed. If he fell, would his true identity be revealed? Even if it did not, surely his death would rob his remaining supporters of motivation, and stop the slaughter of innocent men.

That has to be our best chance, Gabriel resolved, and began to inch his way around the ring of guards, searching for an opening.

As the first clash of steel rang through the throne room, Gabriel leapt at the nearest guard. His sword swept for the man's helmet, but found only empty space as the man leaned backwards. Then Gabriel was jumping back as the man's sword stabbed out for his stomach. He heard the tearing of cloth as the blade sliced through his cloak and swore at his feeble movements.

The man smiled as Gabriel retreated out of range, but stayed in formation with his fellow guards.

Swallowing, Gabriel edged forward with more caution now. These men were accomplished fighters and even at full strength he would have trouble besting one of them. His heart sank as he realised there was only one way through the guards. This was a fight to the end, and each would give their lives to protect the false king.

Not that the false king appeared to need protecting. He had stepped into his ring of guards and now swung his greatsword as though it weighed no more than a feather. Already one of their side had fallen to his blows, the heavy blade shearing through chainmail and flesh alike. If he was not stopped soon, their resistance would be over before it began.

The guard facing him sneered as Gabriel closed on him, the contempt plain on his face. His sword flicked out and Gabriel struggled to deflect the blow from his throat. His arm already felt heavy and his chest burned with the exertion. He was no expert in the best of conditions, but he usually relied on the strength he'd built from years in the forge to defeat his opponents.

Now that strength was failing him. He felt a tingle of fear in his spine as the man came for him again.

I can give you back your strength, the demon's whispers came again, but there was no time to consider the words.

His opponent hacked at him with his short sword, driving Gabriel backwards. As he retreated his foot caught on the edge of the carpet and he stumbled. The guard could have killed him then and there if he had not hesitated to leave the circle of men.

Gritting his teeth, Gabriel straightened and threw himself back into the battle. A dozen men were already down between the two sides, their blood staining the royal floor, but so far Caelin and Fraser still held their own. Gabriel knew it could not last. A few more losses, and their remaining fighters would be overwhelmed by sheer numbers.

They had to end this, now.

Tightening his grip on his blade, Gabriel charged at his opponent, determined to smash his way through to the demon beyond. There at least was a guilty soul, the one truly responsible for the chaos hovering over the capital.

The guard grinned as Gabriel came at him, blade at the ready. Drawing on every ounce of his strength, Gabriel swung for the man's helmet again. The guard raised his sword to deflect the blow but stumbled as one of his comrades staggered into him. Knocked off balance, the guard's sword went wide and Gabriel's blow crunched home.

The guard's eyes widened. A trickle of blood ran down his forehead as a low groan hissed from his mouth. Then he dropped without another sound.

Gabriel released the hilt of his sword, its blade still embedded in the iron helmet. He stared at the dead man, the familiar guilt rising up within him. Looking down, he looked at the blood speckling his hands.

You have to move, a voice hissed in his mind, returning him to reality. *Slay the king!*

Sweeping up the fallen guard's sword, Gabriel leapt through the gap left by the man's absence. The guards to either side were caught up in battle and he passed unnoticed. Ahead the false king stepped back from the line and wiped sweat from his forehead, grinning as his men slayed another of Gabriel's comrades. He froze as he turned and saw Gabriel approaching.

His hesitation did not last long. His eyes studied Gabriel and he began to laugh, clearly unimpressed.

Swallowing, Gabriel closed the gap between them. He held his sword straight, ready for anything the massive man might throw at him. Even so, the greatsword wielded by the imposter made Gabriel's blade look like a toothpick by comparison.

"Come on then, boy, try your luck. Let's see the kind of man you would have been," before Gabriel could reply, the imposter charged at him, swinging his blade like an axe.

Fear ran down Gabriel's spine as he ducked the blow. Then he leapt to the attack, his sword snaking out in search of flesh. The imposter grinned and batted his blows away with a gauntleted fist. Bringing his sword around, he swung again, attempting to split Gabriel in two.

Gabriel stepped to the side, feeling the breath of the blade's passage as it sliced past. His hackles rose on the back of his neck but he pressed on. All that mattered now was destroying this creature, before it led Plorsea into the abyss. Fist clenched around his sword, Gabriel attacked again.

The false king stood waiting for him, sword held in a casual grip. As Gabriel attacked, the greatsword came sweeping down to block the blow. Pain shot through Gabriel's hands at the impact and the blade slipped from his numb fingers. Gabriel retreated backwards as his sword clattered to the ground.

The imposter strode after him, the greatsword raised for the final blow. Gabriel scrambled for the dagger he'd slid into his belt back in the barracks. The air hissed as the greatsword sought his flesh. Without looking, Gabriel hurled himself to the side.

He struck the edge of the dais as the greatsword smashed into the ground where he had stood. Chips of tile scattered across the room and a jagged piece sliced across Gabriel's face. Then his dagger finally came loose. He raised it before him like a talisman, looking up to see the false king preparing to swing again. Before the blow could descend, he hurled the dagger at the traitor.

The imposter screamed as the blade caught him in the shoulder and sent him staggering backwards. His greatsword clattered to the ground as he reached up and grasped the hilt of Gabriel's blade. With another cry he tore it loose. Blood splattered across the tiles as he turned and glared at Gabriel.

"You will pay for that," he raised his empty hand.

Gabriel's stomach twisted as darkness began to gather in the man's palm. It swirled between his fingers, gathering force.

"What?" he whispered, scrambling to find his feet. He glimpsed the fallen greatsword nearby and swept it up, turning to face the king. His body ached, battered from his fall. He was utterly exhausted, but he strained to keep the massive blade pointed at the imposter.

"Die," the false king growled, and Gabriel saw his eyes had darkened to pure black. He pointed his fist and a ray of darkness shot towards Gabriel.

There was no time to move or think, only react. Gabriel drove himself forward, the greatsword raised to strike down the imposter.

The wave of darkness rushed towards him and caught him in the chest. At its touch sickness swept through him, sucking the strength from his failing body. Gabriel's advance slowed, yet even as the sickness spread he could feel the dark force weakening.

With a cry of defiance, Gabriel forced his way forward and to his surprise, the darkness fell away.

Gabriel glimpsed panic on the imposter's face a second before his blow struck. The greatsword swept out, sliding beneath the king's outstretched fist to take him in the chest. Without armour or chainmail there was little resistance, and he drove the blade in to the hilt. Then he stepped back, watching the rage turn to fear in the traitor's eyes.

The false king tried to take a step towards him, but his legs suddenly gave way. He collapsed to the ground, a thick blackness spreading out around him. Then, as every soul present turned to stare, a sickly black fog rose to cover the creature's body. A foul smell filled the room, sending grown men staggering backwards in disgust.

As quickly as it had appeared, the fog vanished.

Gabriel stared at the spot where the false king had fallen. There was nothing left of the creature but a dark scorch staining the white tiles.

Taking a breath, Gabriel turned to Fraser and sank to his knees.

One by one, the guards and councillors did the same.

"All hail the king," the cry rose up from around the room.

Head bowed, Gabriel stared at where the imposter had fallen, and smiled.

CHAPTER 9

"We must march north," Caelin sat at the council table and looked around at the assembled faces.

Only a day had passed since the events in the throne room, but all signs of the battle had already been removed. The blood had been cleansed from the tiles and the ruined carpet removed. If he looked closely he could spot where the tiles had been cracked by stray blows, but otherwise the room was clean. Even the black stain left after the traitor's death had been scrubbed spotless.

Yet despite their best efforts, a darkness still hung over the capital. Their victory may have given them a chance, but the damage caused by the traitorous creature might yet prove irreparable. Men and women ringed the council table, many of whom had sat in judgement of them only two weeks ago. These were the same people that had left them to rot in the darkness, who had supported the false king to his dying breath. It was difficult to ignore that fact.

"Of course," Fraser replied, his tired eyes scanning the table. "There is no other option. Alone, we cannot hope to match the forces Archon will muster; we found that out last time when Fort Fall was lost," he turned to Caelin. "But even with the army mustered, it could take a week or more to be ready to march. And with winter setting in, the journey itself will take weeks."

Caelin swallowed. The demonic king had done its job well, delaying their forces to the point where their arrival at Fort Fall would likely come too late to make a difference. A letter had just arrived from the north – Archon's forces had arrived and were now preparing to make siege on the fortress.

"Even so, we cannot abandon our allies at Fort Fall."

"Of course," Fraser eyed the room again. "And anyone who thinks otherwise can join the traitor who replaced me," he growled. Several men winced and dropped their gazes, unable to meet Fraser's eyes.

Beside him Inken chuckled. He glanced at her, glad to see the colour back in her face. Cleaned and fed, they were all looking better after a good night's sleep. Though in truth he had slept with a lantern lit near his bedside. It would be a long time before he was ready to face the darkness again.

Despite the rest, Fraser still looked weary. Caelin saw through the man's facade, seeing the darkness he hid from his councillors. That he could sit here and give orders at all was a minor miracle. The man had spent weeks locked alone in the pitch black of that cell. The mind of a lesser man would have been shattered into pieces.

Even a man such as Fraser had come close.

But there was no time for weakness now. Archon would not wait and they had no time to spare. They needed the king Caelin remembered, the one the people knew and respected. Only that man could get them through the coming days.

"Okay, what do we do then?" Fraser questioned the table. "How do we reinforce Fort Fall in time for it to matter?"

"The dragons," Inken surprised Caelin. She blushed as the table turned to look at her. "Unless the imposter managed to insult them beyond repair, the dragons could reach Fort Fall within a few days. If we are lucky, they might be able to carry a hundred men between them. It may not be much, but it's better than nothing. And the dragons themselves would also be a formidable boost to Fort Fall's defences."

As whispers spread around the table, one of the councillors came to his feet. Caelin recognised him as one of those who had supported their imprisonment. "But can we trust them? They are beasts; what is to stop them from turning on us?"

Caelin's anger stirred in his chest and he struggled to keep his voice even. "Sir… despite what you might think, the gold dragons are for all intents far more civil than our own species. Certainly more polite than some humans I have met."

The man's face coloured and he made to respond, but Fraser spoke over him. "Oh get out, Councillor Richard. And do not come back, or I will have my guards introduce you to my accommodation from the last few months."

The councillor paled. He stared at the king, his chest heaving as he fought to keep his rage in check. Then with a final exhalation of breath he spun on his heel and stamped from the room.

Fraser waited until the doors at the end of the hall swung shut before he continued. "I like your idea, Inken. You and I shall visit the dragons today and offer my apologies for the insults my… predecessor gave them. I just pray the damage he caused was not permanent."

Inken smiled. "They are a prickly bunch, but they are also reasonable creatures. I am sure we can convince them to forgive us."

"What about the rest of the army? Can we send an advance party now?" Caelin asked. "A thousand men a week earlier may mean the difference between finding Fort Fall in our ally's possession, or Archon's when the rest of our forces arrive."

"But what if they're still too late?" another councillor spoke. She looked around the room, her face apologetic. "If Archon's forces have already broken through they would come on our men in the open. A thousand men would be slaughtered for nothing."

Fraser passed a hand across his face, his exhaustion palpable. "You're right, of course... both of you. But there are no good choices here. We have been robbed of the time we needed to do this right. But even so, I have to agree with Caelin. It's a gamble, but if we lose Fort Fall, we are doomed whether our army is separated or not. We will send a thousand men as an advance party. They will leave first thing in the morning."

He turned to Elton, who had sat quietly through the meeting, clearly uncomfortable with his sudden elevation to the council. "Elton, there are few I trust now more than you. I want you to lead the advance force."

Elton blinked. "But your majesty, I have never led men in open battle! I am only a guard captain; how can I lead a thousand men? There must be others... better suited."

The king nodded. "Ay, there might be. But none I trust, not now. I have other plans for Caelin, so it must be you. Can you do it?"

Elton swallowed, eyes wide, and nodded.

"Good. Go and prepare your men. I award you now with the rank of Commander. I will leave you to choose which men to take with you. I suggest you talk to the sergeants of each unit and go from there."

Elton rose and saluted. "Thank you, my king. I will."

Fraser nodded back. "Good luck, Elton. Do not let us down."

As Elton left the room, Fraser turned his attention back to the council. "Well, we have a plan. Let's get to it. Caelin, you are to select a hundred of our best fighters and have them ready to depart at a moment's notice. If Inken and I are successful, you and the men you select will be flying north by the day's end," his gaze swept the table. "The rest of you know your roles. I want the army ready to march within the week. Get to it."

Caelin took a breath as he watched the others stand and file out of the room. Gabriel, Inken and himself remained at the table, sitting in silent thought.

He watched Gabriel closely as the last of the councillors disappeared. Gabriel had hardly spoken since slaying the false king, and Caelin still wondered how the youngster had managed it. The thing had been a demon or worse, a dark creature that no doubt possessed an equally dark magic.

So how had Gabriel, an unskilled youth weak with starvation, managed to best it? Starved of his strength, Caelin himself had hardly been able to hold his own against the royal guard, let alone go up against the false king.

But that was a mystery for another day. For now, they had work to do. All going well, they would be a-dragon-back come nightfall.

He glanced at Inken. "Do you want one of us to go with you?"

She flashed him a wry smile. "I think I'll be fine, Caelin. And don't worry, I'll look after Fraser," she winked at the king.

Fraser scowled back. "Watch yourself, Inken."

Inken only laughed and stood. "Don't worry, I will. Come on, let's go see the dragons."

Caelin smiled as the two left trading barbs. Inken had a

knack for getting the best out of people, for bringing them back from the darkness. Her strength had helped him keep fighting after his friend Michael had been killed in Sitton, and he had not missed the talk she had given Gabriel. If anyone could keep the king on his feet, it was her.

Standing, he nodded to Gabriel and followed them out. They were already disappearing down the corridor as Caelin pushed through the great double doors, a host of guards at their back. Caelin made to follow them, already thinking ahead to what he would say when he reached the barracks. He would need to find men with a particular breed of courage if they were to ride the gold dragons to Fort Fall.

"Caelin," a voice came from the shadows to his left.

Caelin turned, his heart sinking as Antony stepped forward to block his path. He knew the man from his days as a recruit. They had never been more than friendly rivals, but he could see the hate on the man's face now.

"Katya wasn't a traitor," he croaked, and Caelin saw there were tears in the guard's eyes. "I knew her. She never changed, not like the king. It was *her*."

Caelin bowed his head. He'd been dreading this confrontation, but knew there was no avoiding it. Raising his chin, he looked Antony in the eye. "As I said yesterday. I was wrong. You're right. She was not a traitor."

"Then why did she have to die? *Why?*"

"I don't know," Caelin shook his head, guilt eating him from within. Since the battle he had heard more from the other guards about the relationship between Antony and the councillor. "I know you loved her, Antony."

"Do you?" he took a step towards Caelin. "How could you? How could you know what it's like to see someone you love killed by her own people?"

"I have seen my fair share of treachery, Antony. But this

was an accident, and the only one to blame was that creature."

"And that boy, Gabriel," Antony growled, taking another step. "He was the one who killed her. I cannot let him get away with it."

"No," Caelin stopped Antony with a word. "It was not his fault; he did what he thought was right. And he did the same thing when he killed that treacherous creature. If anything, you should thank him for avenging Katya's death."

Antony stared at Caelin, his arms trembling with anger. Caelin met his eyes, refusing to waver. He would not let this man anywhere near his friend. Slowly, the rage in Antony's eyes cooled and they started to water. The man took a great, shuddering inhalation and bowed his head.

"Fine," he breathed, then looked back up. "Then take me with you, Caelin. I heard the others talking as they went past; I know what you're doing. Take me with you to Fort Fall. Let me avenge Katya's death with the blood of Archon's people."

Caelin looked into the man's eyes and saw the desperation behind his rage. In that instant, he knew the truth. Antony wanted to die. He sighed, wanting to refuse the man's demand but knowing he could not. Antony was one of the best fighters they had. His skill would be needed in the north.

"Very well, Antony. You can join us."

With that he pushed past Antony and moved away down the corridor. Guilt hung in his throat, the weight of the man's life heavy on his shoulders.

INKEN DROPPED to her knees on the damp grass, struggling to keep the measly remains of her breakfast down. The rough ride across the lake had not been kind, and it was a relief to have solid ground beneath her again. She had already thrown up once as they neared the shore, but she was determined not to repeat the event.

"You okay?" Fraser asked from nearby.

Inken forced a smile. "Fine," they were alone now on the shore. The small sailboat rocked on the beach, the sailor who manned it leaning back against the mast with his eyes closed. Fraser had ordered him to remain in the boat while they went ashore. He had left his usual guards in the city, already growing weary of their constant presence. That, and he claimed it would be difficult enough to apologise to the dragons without marching up to their camp with a small army at his back.

"Okay, whenever you're ready then," Fraser grinned, no doubt drawing some satisfaction from her discomfort after her joke earlier in the throne room.

Her stomach swirled again, but Inken pushed it down and stood. Nodding, she strode past Fraser and began the short trek up the hill. Despite the seasickness, it was a relief to be in the fresh air again. Overhead the sky seemed huge after her time in the cell, filled with the untold vastness of nature. A bird flew past and she smiled, setting aside the unpleasant feeling in her stomach and deciding to do her best to enjoy herself.

Yet she knew it would take more than the open sky and sun to lift the darkness from her soul. It clung to each of them still, waiting in the backs of their minds to strike. Not for the first time that day she found herself missing Eric's quiet confidence. She prayed he had survived whatever trials had come his way since they separated.

"There doesn't seem to have been any word of them," Fraser appeared to read her thoughts. "Eric or Enala. Although we cannot be sure the creature did not hide news of them."

Inken nodded. "Eric is used to travelling in the wild, and Enala's parents trained her for this – whether she knew it or not. They would know how to go unnoticed."

"Good. As we've seen, Archon's people are everywhere now."

They fell silent as the top of the hill loomed. Elton had given them an account of the false king's encounter with the dragons and they did not expect a friendly welcome. Inken was surprised the creatures had stayed at all.

The breath caught in her throat as a golden head lifted into view. Her heart thudded hard against her ribs and the nausea in her stomach was suddenly forgotten.

It's okay, but despite her own reassurance, she could feel the fear sweeping through her. Faced with the giant creature, it was all she could do to force herself to stand still.

Fraser, however, seemed to suffer no such fear. He continued on a few more steps before noticing her hesitation. He glanced back and grinned. "After all we've been through, don't tell me you're afraid of a little dragon?"

Inken scowled. Biting her tongue, she forced down her instinctive fear and continued up the slope. The dragon watched them come in silence.

As they mounted the rise, Inken could not suppress a gasp. Even Fraser seemed taken aback, though he hid it well. The dragon camp lay spread out below them, stretching away for miles across the green fields. The hulking forms of the gold dragons sprinkled the grass, the light reflecting from their scales almost blinding. Each dragon appeared to have a range of its own; an area the size of a small village which the others avoided. A few lay in pairs, but the majority appeared to prefer their own space.

Welcome, humans, the dragon on watch growled, moving to block their view of the camp.

Inken turned to look at the creature and found its eyes

looking back. She could almost imagine the hunger there, the desire of a wild beast to consume such lesser creatures.

Shaking her head, she dismissed the thought. This was no beast. As far as she was concerned, the dragons seemed to be far more intelligent than any man she'd ever met. Woman, however…

Before she could finish the thought, Fraser bowed low to the dragon. Inken quickly followed suit, cursing the king for beating her to the act. The dragon watched them with an amused tilt to its head.

You have suddenly found your manners, oh king of man?

Fraser straightened, a sad frown on his lips. "Would that it had truly been me to greet you last time, dragon. Alas, it was an imposter who came to your camp and offered you insult. I was imprisoned beneath the keep, and have only just managed to find my freedom once more."

The dragon leaned closer, the great slits of its nostrils opening to sniff them. *Ay, there is a different smell about you,* the dragon straightened. *I am Enduran. It was I who spoke with your imposter,* there was a threatening edge to the dragon's tone.

Fraser bowed again and Inken followed suit. "My deepest apologies, Enduran. My people were tricked and I was imprisoned while the creature took my form and stole control of the kingdom."

A growl rumbled up from Enduran's chest and sent tremors down to Inken's stomach. The dragon took a step closer, its claws digging grooves in the untouched earth.

Another? there was open anger in the dragon's tone now. *What creatures are you, to allow such things into your midst?*

Fraser met the dragon's gaze, unflinching. "We are weak, all of us. But do not forget, mighty Enduran, the creature tricked you as well. No one was immune to its guile."

Silence fell, and then another rumble came from

Enduran's chest. Inken smiled as she recognised the sound as laughter. *You speak the truth, king of man.*

Fraser smiled back and continued. "The creature has done us great damage, but it is not irreparable, not yet. I am sorry for the way you and your kind were treated, Enduran, but from this day forth I promise to treat your people with respect. We need you."

Enduran's head twisted down until it hovered eye level with the king. *And what do you need of us, king of man?*

Inken struggled to hide her grin as Fraser gaped, taken off-guard by the question. *Definitely smarter than men*, she chuckled softly to herself.

Enduran's eyes turned her way. *Do not think I have forgotten you, little one*, there was humour in the dragon's voice. *It is good to see you again. You have progressed.*

Inken blinked, staring at the dragon in confusion. "Progressed?"

Your child, the dragon answered. *I could not be sure when last we spoke, but I smell the change in you now.*

Gaping, Inken looked from the dragon to the king. "Wh... *What?*" she all but shrieked.

The dragon looked to Fraser. *She did not know?*

Open mirth sparkled in Fraser's eyes as he turned to her. "The dragon is telling you you're pregnant, Inken," he grinned. "It seems congratulations are in order."

Inken would have beaten the smile from Fraser's face if she could have found the will to move. She stood frozen on the hilltop, staring at the king and the dragon, unable to form the thoughts to speak. Her heart hammered in her chest like a runaway wagon and she struggled to catch her breath.

Sinking to her knees, she was surprised to find Fraser suddenly beside her, his hand firm on her shoulder.

"Are you okay, Inken?" he murmured, concern in his eyes.

She nodded, and found herself smiling up at the king. A warm fluttering spread through her stomach, washing away the illness that curdled there. Her eyes watered.

Oh, Eric, where are you? She whispered to the void.

When she finally caught her breath, she looked up at the dragon. "Are you sure, Enduran?"

Yes, child. We are not wrong about such things, she could almost imagine a grin on the dragon's giant jaws.

"Then can you take me to Fort Fall?" she asked, desperate now to reach the fortress. "If Eric is alive, he will be there."

The dragon's head dropped down to stare at the two of them. *Is that what you wish as well, king of man?*

Fraser nodded. "It is, Enduran. Archon's forces have reached the fortress. They desperately need reinforcements. My man, Caelin, is gathering our best fighters as we speak. If you agree, I would have you carry them north to bolster the defences at Fort Fall. Together, you could make all the difference..."

Fraser's words trailed away as Enduran stood and spread his wings. At full height he towered over them, casting the hilltop in shadow. Stretching back his head, the dragon opened its jaws and roared. The sound echoed across the hills, rebounding and growing louder with each second. Flames licked from Enduran's lips as he turned to look down at them.

Then let us fly, little one.

CHAPTER 10

Eric stared down at the fortress far below, a creeping awe spreading through his chest. Fort Fall stretched out beneath them; a behemoth of sprawling walls and towers nestled on the narrow straight of land known as The Gap. Its three massive walls carved across the barren land, standing in silent defiance to the forces of the north. The outmost wall stood fifty feet high, and each grew larger than the last. To the east and west they came to an abrupt halt atop the ocean cliffs, impassable by even the most skilled of climbers.

The rumble of the waves smashing into the cliffs of The Gap carried up to them, covering the fortress in a fine mist. From so far above the men and women manning the ramparts appeared as ants, scurrying about their business with an insect-like determination. Yet even from their vantage point, there did not appear to be enough soldiers manning the walls.

The towers of the citadel stood behind the third wall, the stone spires reaching up towards them. This was the fortress' final defence, though in truth, the battle was already lost if the third wall fell.

Beside him, Enala hung in silent contemplation, the wind ruffling her golden hair and sending her single scarlet lock fluttering across her face.

"There's a lot of them," she said as she noticed his gaze.

Eric nodded, his eyes drifting to the north. There the forces of the enemy waited, the light of their fires stretching out to the horizon. Bathed in the crimson red of sunset, it appeared as though the land itself were bleeding.

Swallowing, Eric pushed the dark thoughts from his mind. His strength was flagging, his body aching with the power he'd spent in the three days of flight. They had stopped only to eat and sleep, with Eric drawing on the power of the Sword to replenish his own store of magic.

Yet despite its support, Eric felt weary to his very soul. Each time he used the Sword's magic the white fire would sweep through him, burning at his spirit, eating at him in a way he could not quite explain. And even with the Sword's heat, he would find himself shivering, clinging to the warmth of Enala's hand. But he had little choice; they could not afford to wait for his magic to recover on its own.

Eric took another breath, preparing to descend, but the winds lurched suddenly in his grasp. The air stilled and then they were falling, plummeting towards the ground far below. Heart hammering in his chest, Eric sent his magic racing outwards, regathering the winds and catching them mid-air.

"Eric!" Enala shrieked, her face white with fear. "What was that?"

Eric shook his head, his thoughts turning inwards, gripping the swirling ropes of blue tighter. He could sense a change in the air, the presence of another magic. With a curse he wrapped his fingers around the hilt of the Sword, prepared to summon its power if necessary.

"Who approaches?" the voice boomed from all around them.

Enala glanced at him, her question clear. *Is it our side, or theirs?*

Taking a risk, Eric shouted over the cracking of the wind, unwilling to test his fading strength against the might of whoever faced them. "We are Eric and Enala of Plorsea. We have come to aid Fort Fall," he did not mention the Sword of Light.

There was a long pause before the voice answered. *"If you speak the truth, you are welcome. You may land to the south of the fortress, not within. Approach the gates and we will speak more."*

The voice cut off and Eric guessed they would hear no more from the Magicker – unless they disobeyed the command.

With a sigh of relief, Eric directed them down towards the small southward wall. The gates stood closed, but he could see a group standing on the ramparts in the shadows of the gate-house. As they closed he began to make out individuals, and saw a mixture of concern and relief on their faces. Only a woman in the centre of the group kept her expression neutral, her arms folded across her chest as her dark eyes followed their approach. She stood a foot taller than her companions and wore a red cape and tunic of the Plorsean army. Her fingers hovered close to the hilt of the gold-embossed sword she wore at her side.

From the way the others glanced at her, Eric guessed her to be Commander May. Christopher and Angela had spoken of her before they left, and had nothing but praise for the woman.

Keeping a tight grip on the wind, Eric settled them gently to the ground. Even in the dim light of sunset, he could see that the northern wasteland had extended south of the fortress. The ground beneath their feet was hard and dry and there was no sign of vegetation.

"You're getting better at that," Enala commented.

Eric grinned, remembering their first crash landing after they had fled Sitton. It was a cheering thought, to think he had improved in such a short span of time.

"At least we'll have beds to sleep in tonight," he pointed out as they started the short walk to the gates.

Enala rubbed her back. "Thank the Gods, my back couldn't take another night on the cold ground."

Eric laughed. "And no more frostbite," that morning they had woken in their blankets to a world of white. A thin ice had settled around them over night, coating their hair in a white frosting. The cold had seeped into Eric's very bones and his teeth had chattered halfway to the fortress. For the hundredth time in three days, he wished he'd had the strength to carry a tent with them.

But at least they'd made it.

Ahead the southern wall loomed with its waiting company of men and women. Eric and Enala walked with their swords sheathed and the *Soul Blades* hidden in their bundle of blankets. They had eaten the last remnants of their food for lunch and Eric was looking forward to a hot meal.

They came to a halt before the wooden gates and looked up at their welcome party. The group stood at the edge of the ramparts, looking down at the strangers below. Eric glimpsed curiosity in the eyes of some, wariness in others. This was a fortress under siege and it was clear they would not allow them through the gates unchallenged.

"Who are you?" the woman he'd guessed to be Commander May shouted down. "Who sent you?"

Eric stepped forward. "My name is Eric, and this is Enala. Your letter about the attack reached us in Kalgan. We came as fast as we could."

"Well, Eric and Enala, welcome. You must excuse my suspicion, but how, pray, did you come here so quickly? Kalgan is a long way from here," she paused, then shook her head. "And I am rather confused as to why our Trolan brothers would send us two children as reinforcements."

Eric grimaced, his patience wearing thin. Obviously talk was not going to get them far here – these people would never believe their tale. And May was right, there was no way any ordinary Magicker could have come so far so fast. His magic would have run out long ago without the Sword.

No, he would have to show them. Drawing on the last of his strength, Eric reached up and pulled the Sword of Light from its scabbard. Above, the guards nocked arrows to their bows and he sensed the power of the Magickers beginning to gather, but he was not overly concerned.

Light swept across the wall as the blade slid free and ignited in the crisp winter air. The warmth of its flame flickered across Eric's face as he looked up at those gathered above.

"Commander May," he boomed. "We have come a long way and I am tired. This is the Sword of Light and I am its wielder. By blood and by magic, we claim the Trolan throne. Open the gates, if you please."

The colour had fled May's face and her mouth hung open. He gave her a second for his words to sink in, then smiled as she finally came back to life. Looking around, she shouted an order and a moment later the gates gave a groan and began to open.

Below, Eric glanced at Enala and grinned.

Together they walked through the gates, and into greatest fortress in the Three Nations.

~

ENALA GROANED as she sank into the chair nearest the fire, her joints aching from the icy cold. Even with the thick woollen clothes Angela and Christopher had given them, the winds holding them aloft had still sucked the warmth from her. The nights had been worse still, the ice creeping across the clearing each evening to freeze their sleeping bodies solid. Or so it seemed when they woke in the mornings.

It was more than a relief to be indoors again.

Eric's knees cracked as he took a seat across from her and stretched his hands out towards the flames. A shiver racked his body and his face was pale, but he was looking far better than the first time she'd flown with him. He'd hardly been able to move that day. The memory seemed an age ago now.

Commander May stood between them, shifting nervously from one foot to the other. She had dismissed the rest of her people and brought them here – her private meeting room deep within the citadel.

Her discretion came as a welcome relief. Enala did not have the energy to be interrogated by half the fortress. Although the eager look on May's face suggested she had more than enough questions of her own.

"Please sit down," Enala sighed, to weary for manners.

May straightened. "If you are who you say you are, I should stand, ma'am."

Enala would have laughed if not for her utter exhaustion. "Oh Gods, please, Commander, just take a seat. We're too tired for pleasantries. As you said, it's a long journey from Kalgan to here."

Eric nodded and May finally gave in. As she sank into her chair Enala could not help but smile. They had been told of the woman's fierceness in battle – apparently she had even defeated a demon in the first attack on the wall – but now she seemed almost a child, eager to please her guests, if only to get the answers to her questions.

Her eyes slid to where Eric had discarded the Sword of Light beside his chair. "It's true then, the Sword is back? What happened to the old king, Jonathan?"

"He's dead," Enala growled. "He was a traitor, tried to kill me and steal my magic. Eric killed him."

May swallowed and sat back in her chair. "It seems treachery is everywhere now. What has happened to our land?"

"Archon," Eric answered. "Without the Gods to protect us, we have little to defend us against his subversions. Only the strength of our own courage can protect the Three Nations now."

"And the Sword?" May raised an eyebrow. "Is it as powerful as they say?"

"It is, and it isn't," Eric answered, then continued at the confused look on May's face. "I am yet to master most of its power."

"It's better than we had this morning," May shrugged.

Enala looked from Eric to May and then swallowed her hesitation. "We may have more than that," reaching down, she unwrapped the bundle at her feet. The green and blue glow of the *Soul Blades* rose up from the blankets. "These... these are the *Soul Blades* that killed Antonia and Jurrien. They contain their magic, the God powers of the Earth and Sky. We are hoping that the Magickers here might be able to free them."

May stared at her, eyes wide, and gave a slow nod. "You're saying we can bring them back?"

"Maybe," Eric corrected. "The Magickers in Kalgan could not, but their strongest had already marched north. Perhaps those here can."

May swallowed, her eyes shining in the light of the fire. "That's all we needed last time – the Sword and the two Gods," her eyes shone with hope. "Thank you for coming."

Enala gave a soft laugh. "Do not get ahead of yourself, May. The Magicker, Christopher, did not think it would be possible. Not without knowledge of the spell first used to summon their spirits."

The Commander waved a hand. "Even so…" her eyes were drawn to the creeping glow of the *Soul Blades*. "Could we use their power still, if we cannot free them?"

Pain twisted in Enala's stomach and she dropped her eyes. May had a sharp mind; she had seen their problem and was already looking for an alternative plan. Enala just wished that plan did not inevitably include her.

"Enala already has," Eric murmured over the crackling of the fire. "She was able to draw on Antonia's magic and heal us. But it was too powerful, and she was overwhelmed. We almost lost her."

"But it is possible," May mused.

"It is a terrible risk," Enala said grimly. "To the Magicker and everyone around them."

"I take it you do not wish to try again?"

Enala's heart sank as she looked into the Commander's eyes, but she refused to look away. "I will do anything I can to help my brother," she looked down at the *Soul Blades,* her blood curdling at the sight. "I am stronger now. I can control my power. I will try, if it comes to it."

May nodded. "You are a brave girl."

"No. The thought terrifies me. But I will do what I must."

"Let's hope it won't come to that," Eric put an end to the discussion.

"Of course," May leaned back in her chair. "I shall have our Magickers begin examining them in the morning. But I will also make enquiries for the other blade, in case it *does* come to that."

"What about your forces here?" Enala changed the course of the discussion. "How many defenders do you have?"

"Just over a thousand," May answered. "The standing guard, plus the advance force Lonia sent, and volunteers that have been arriving for the last few weeks."

"Not enough," Eric said grimly. "I cannot even guess how many men are waiting to the north."

"No, but the rest of the Lonian army is close. And word from the Trolans put their army less than a week away."

"Will it be enough?" Enala asked.

"By ourselves, I do not think the combined might of every man, woman and child in the Three Nations would be enough. But with the Sword, and these *Soul Blades*... maybe," she let out a long sigh and seemed to shrink in her chair. "In truth, I was beginning to lose hope. We have suffered terrible losses these last few days. We did not even have the men to hold the outer gates; we were forced to seal them with rubble to prevent the enemy from smashing their way through."

Standing, the Commander moved to a cupboard and reached inside. Enala smiled when she saw her hand emerge with a wine jar. She stood and retrieved some glasses as May unstopped the jar.

"It's a Lonian red," May offered as she poured. "I've been saving it for a special occasion. We might not have won the war yet, but I think your arrival is worthy of the vintage. Cheers," she offered when their glasses were full.

"Cheers," they echoed her, joining their glasses to May's.

Enala took a sip, enjoying its dry touch and fruity richness. "We heard you were on the wall during the first attack?"

May nodded with a shudder. "Our cause was almost lost before it began. Despite our best preparations, the enemy still took us by surprise. If the outer wall had fallen..."

"But you held," Eric interrupted her. "You're still here.

Fort Fall still stands because of you. The Three Nations owes you a great debt for that."

Enala frowned as she took another sip of wine. "Why do they call it Fort Fall? I've always wondered."

"From the last war," there was sadness in May's eyes. "Archon's final attack, when he rained fire from the sky, became known as 'The Fall'. Somehow the name stuck when the fortress was rebuilt."

Enala stared into the fire, imagining the fear and horror of the defenders as the sky turned to flame. She shuddered. "How can we stop magic like that?"

"I don't know," Eric replied. His eyes were fixed on his glass of wine, but she saw them flicker as he glanced at the Sword.

"You will find a way," May replied, her voice firm.

"What about his army?" Enala asked. "Who are these people, how did he gather so many to him?"

"They live in the wasteland, surviving off what little food and water exists up there," May swirled her glass of wine, deep in thought. "For centuries we have banished the worst of our criminals to the north. It always seemed a good solution – remove them from our society, wash our hands of their evil," she paused. "We did not expect them to thrive. They have built a society of sorts, and their numbers have grown. But locked in that wasteland, we have given them no hope of redemption, no reason to change. And so they and their children have grown to hate us. In truth, I cannot truly blame them."

"There are children up there?" Enala asked, surprised.

"There are entire *cities*," May replied. "Though we only know of a few, I am sure there are more hidden in those lands. Many of the families there have survived for generations, scavenging a meagre living from the harsh land," her eyes shone in the firelight. "But they wish for more, for the plentiful lands to the south. They want our food and water and wood, and will flock to whoever offers it to them."

Enala's stomach twisted with guilt as she thought of the struggles of her own people in Chole. But they had at least chosen to stay. Her family could have left for greener lands at any time, but Chole was their home and they would not abandon it. The enemy did not have the same choice.

"In truth, we gave Archon this army," May whispered.

Enala almost laughed at the harsh truth of May's words. She shook her head. "Maybe so," she looked around the room. "But if we win, this time things must change. We cannot let this happen again. If we win, we must find a way to put things right."

Eric nodded. "Agreed. But first, we have to win."

CHAPTER 11

Eric's chest heaved as he sucked in another breath and stumbled up the last of the stairs. His eyes teared in the salty air as he bent in two and gasped for another lungful of air. His muscles burned from the brief exertion and he cursed himself for making the trek to the outer wall. A single night of sleep had not been close to enough to restore him after the three days of flight, although it had certainly helped.

He felt the pommel of the Sword of Light against his neck and resisted the temptation to draw it. One touch and his weariness would flee, washed away by the fire of the blade's magic. The aches and pain would fade away to nothing before the thrill of its power.

Shaking his head, Eric straightened, chilled by the compulsion. The magic of the Sword was addicting, but he did his best to fight its temptation. Straightening, he looked across the ramparts of the wall, surprised to see flakes of snow drifting in the air. He shivered, pulling his woollen cloak tighter, glad for the gift Angela had made of it. It was far warmer than anything he'd ever owned.

"Looks like you could use a bit of exercise, sonny," a ruff voice came from nearby.

Eric scowled as he caught the eyes of the speaker. The man stood nearby, his broad shoulders and massive arms dwarfing Eric's small frame. Lines stretched across the man's face as he flashed Eric a smile, humour showing in his amber eyes. A massive war hammer hung across his shoulders and must have weighed at least ten pounds, though he did not appear to notice its weight. He was a monster of a man but his greying hair and the speckles of white in his beard suggested he must be at least sixty years of age.

"It was a long journey," Eric wheezed, walking over to join the man at the battlements. "I'm Eric, I only arrived yesterday."

"Alan," the giant offered his hand. "Welcome to Fort Fall, sonny. What brings you here? You look a little young for this business."

Eric grimaced, thinking of the path that had led him here. "That is a long story," he glanced at the soldier and grinned. "What about you, you seem a little old for this business."

To his surprise, the man threw back his head and unleashed a booming laugh. "Ay, ain't that the truth!" he wiped a tear from his eye. "You've got some nerve, sonny. No, I volunteered when I heard the news. Got here a few days before the first attack," he shook his head. "Sixty-six and still at the business of war. Who would have thought. But what is a man to do when evil knocks on his door?"

Smiling, Eric found himself taking a liking to the old warrior. "Why the hammer?"

Alan chuckled again, the sound ringing across the wall. Reaching up, he lifted the hammer from his shoulders and hefted it as though it weighed no more than a sword. "Old *kanker* has been with me since the beginning. We've won our fair share of fights, she and I. Wouldn't go to battle without her. And certainly not my last."

Sadness swelled in Eric's chest. "You think we'll lose?"

Alan stared out at the wasteland and then looked back to Eric. "Perhaps, sonny. That will be up to you young folk; whether you have the strength to hold them. As for myself, I know when I've come to the end. I can feel it in here," he patted his chest. "It's time I left this world, time I surrendered my place to the young. But at least I know my passing will have meaning, that my death might give others the chance to live."

Eric stood stunned, unable to find the words to answer the man's honesty. The moment stretched out, the silence punctuated by sadness.

"We will," Eric said at last. "We will hold them."

Eric met the amber glow of Alan's eyes and the old warrior smiled. "Ay, I believe you," he laughed then, and the sadness left the air, passing like an autumn cloud. "And what of that fancy sword of yours, sonny? You know how to use it?"

Eric's cheeks flushed. "I've won a few fights... Sort of," he replied. "Truthfully, I'm a Magicker, though I'm still learning that too. I usually use my magic instead of a sword."

Alan nodded. "That's all well and good. But from my experience, a Magicker is only as good as his stamina. More than a few rogue Magickers fell to my hammer when I was younger. I would suggest holding back your power until you really need it."

Eric sighed. "The Commander already mentioned that. We're to save our strength for the enemy Magickers and the beasts, if they come."

"Well keep close to me then, sonny," he reached down and picked up his hammer from where he'd leaned it against the ramparts.

"What?"

Alan nodded out towards the wasteland. "Here they come."

Eric stared as men began to emerge through the falling snow, their black cloaks staining the white ground below. They slid across the wasteland, silent as death, swords and axes held at the ready. Their eyes flashed as they looked up at the defenders, catching in the light of their torches.

Along the wall, the first blast of the trumpets rang out, sounding the call for the defenders to stand at the ready. The outer wall was already fully manned, but they would need the reserves soon enough.

Glancing to either side, Eric watched as the guards drew their weapons and strapped on their helmets. The red, green and blue cloaks of the Three Nations stood out crisp and clear amidst the snow. Eric felt a surge of pride at the sight, though the Lonian green outnumbered the others two to one. That would soon change once the other armies arrived.

Together they stood atop the wall and waited for the horde to descend.

Swallowing his fear, Eric reached up and drew the Sword of Light. Its fire flared at his touch and its power surged down his arm, but he pressed it back, fighting the rush of desire that came with it. He knew its power could decimate the enemy below, but May had warned him against using its magic too soon. If Archon sensed the Sword he might be provoked to attack with his own power, and they were not ready for that. Not yet.

The flames died away, though there was no stopping the white glow seeping from the blade.

"So, the rumours are true. The Sword of Light has returned," Alan grinned and winked at Eric. "Well, it's no *kanker*, but extra swords are always welcome up here."

"I'll do my best," Eric replied, heart thudding in his

chest. His legs shook and a voice in his mind shouted for him to run, that he had no place amongst these warriors. Gritting his teeth, he stood his ground.

Alan laughed. "Like I said, stay close to me, sonny. I'll keep you safe," he eyed the men below. "Don't worry how many of them are down there. It's the ones who make it up *here* that matter," he hefted his hammer. "I'll try to save some for you."

Eric grinned. "Hope I can keep up with an old fella like you."

"Don't you worry about that, sonny," Alan replied. "You just focus on whoever is trying to cut ya."

Eric swallowed, the big man's words slicing through his bravado. Beneath them the men were closing on the wall, and now their shouts and curses carried up to them. He spotted a dozen ladders amongst their ranks and cast a nervous glance at Alan.

Along the wall the first volley of arrows rose into the sky and plunged down into the enemy. Dozens fell but the rest came on, fresh men quickly taking the place of the fallen.

Alan pulled him back as the enemy returned fire. Their arrows clanged on stone as they retreated below the crenulations. A few seconds later there came a crash as the first ladder struck the wall. Eric made to grab for it but the larger man held him back.

"Don't bother. There's already enough weight on that thing that neither you nor I have the strength to push it back," he reached down and removed a length of rope from his belt.

Before Eric could ask its purpose he tossed the looped end over the top of the ladder and moved to the side. Flashing Eric another grin, he gave two massive heaves on the rope. On the third pull the ladder shifted, the wood scraping on the rock as it slid across the battlements. Then suddenly it was gone, disappearing sideways as it toppled back to the ground. Screams carried up to them as the climbers fell.

Puffing slightly, Alan returned to his station. "That's how you do it," he answered the unspoken question. "Though soon they'll be coming too quick and fast to have time for that."

Even so, Alan managed to dislodge two more ladders before the first of the enemy reached them. Eric shuddered as he imagined the slaughter below as the enemy waited to gain a foothold atop the wall. The walls of the fortress curved in towards the keep, leaving the men below exposed on all sides to the defenders' arrows.

But then there was no more time to think of those below. Summoning his courage, he leapt to aid the aging warrior as the first of the enemy reached the battlements. Not that Alan showed any sign of his years.

As the first man leapt from a ladder and sprang across the crenulations, Alan surged forwards. Their foe hardly had time to raise his sword before *kanker* struck, smashing in his chest with a sickening crunch. The man collapsed to the cold stone, blood bubbling from his mouth to stain the snow.

Eric shuddered at his fate, but there was little time to spare the man a second thought. Another ladder crashed onto the stone beside him and he forced himself to focus on the battle. Crouching low in the forward stance Caelin had shown him so long ago, he waited, the Sword of Light poised to strike.

His first opponent surged into view, rolling across the stone to land on his feet in a single movement. His sword was already in motion as Eric stepped up to meet him, arcing towards his head. Instinct alone saved him, the Sword sweeping up to deflect the blow as though directed by a mind of its own. Then he was moving, stepping sideways to avoid the next attack and slicing out with the Sword in a clumsy strike.

The warrior laughed as he deflected the blow, then his eyes widened. Eric stumbled back as the man crumpled, the back of his helmet caved in by a casual sweep of Alan's hammer. The big man nodded in Eric's direction and then turned back to his ladder.

Returning to his position, Eric took a deep breath, then threw himself at the next enemy to appear. This time he was prepared, and his blade caught the attacker in the chest before he could even raise his weapon.

As he fell, Eric caught the sound of a boot on stone and spun, deflecting the sword of another attacker. The defender to Eric's left lay dead, the ladder beside him unguarded. A second attacker was already clambering onto the ramparts, but Eric had no time to act. The warrior facing him growled and surged toward him.

Eric slid backwards, using a forward stance to maintain his balance, and caught the blow on the hilt of the Sword. Teeth gritted, he pushed forward so their blades locked together, leaving them face to face, each straining to overpower the other. Despite his small size, Eric remembered Caelin's training and came in low, using his lower centre to push the man off balance.

The man cursed and retreated back a step, then cried out as he tripped against the edge of the crenulations. The man's arms windmilled as he fought to regain his balance. Seeing his chance, Eric quickly stepped up and kicked him in the chest. The man toppled backwards off the wall and vanished from view.

Taking a breath, Eric stepped back and turned where the man had forced his way through their defences, but reinforcements had already plugged the gap.

Gasping in the cold air, he struggled to hold down the

sickness of utter exhaustion. His vision swirled and he stumbled for a second. Only a few minutes of battle had passed, and he was shocked by the fatigue already gripping him.

But still the enemy came on, clambering up the ladders in an endless tide. Eric straightened as the next appeared. Panting, he allowed the man to come to him now, hoping the Sword of Light's long reach would give him an advantage against the man's axe.

The axeman grinned as he dropped to the walkway, seeing only an exhausted boy opposing him. Eric swallowed and gripped the Sword tighter, prepared to summon its magic if necessary. The screams of the dying came from all around, but Eric's vision narrowed now to a single point, focused only on the axeman. He glimpsed the slightest movement of the man's boot and leapt forward, even as the man raised his axe and charged.

The man's eyes widened as the Sword of Light lanced up into his unprotected chest. The axe clattered to the pavement as Eric pulled back his blade, allowing the man to topple to the ground. His blood streamed across the snow, one more body to add to the mounting pile atop the wall.

"That was well done," Alan observed. "Told you I saw a fighter in you, sonny."

Eric nodded back, unable to find the breath to reply. He could not begin to understand how men fought for hours in battle.

Alan laughed at the expression on Eric's face and stepped back from the edge, allowing other men to take his place. "Rest, sonny, you've earned a break. The reinforcements have arrived," he gestured with his hammer to indicate the stream of men now bolstering their ranks.

Looking around, Eric felt a wave of relief to see their forces holding strong. The defenders were disciplined and well-armed, waiting out of sight of the archers below before dispatching the enemy as they reached the top.

"They won't take the outer wall today," Alan observed. "We're still fresh; it'll take a few more days to wear us down."

"How long do you think we have?" Eric asked over the ring of steel, staring at the mounting dead.

Despite their advantage atop the wall, Eric counted far too many of their own amongst the dead. From what he'd seen the day before, the enemy numbered in the tens of thousands. Fort Fall only had a thousand defenders; they could not afford to lose a single soul.

"A few days, a week. It depends how often they attack and when the reinforcements arrive. So far we've been lucky. They've only launched a handful of assaults each day. But they're just probes, from what I've seen. When the real assault begins, we'll struggle to find time for a jug of ale between the fighting."

Eric swallowed. He was about to reply when a roar came from behind them. The hairs on Eric's neck prickled with warning as Alan swore. Spinning, Eric raised the Sword of Light and reached for its magic, ready to unleash it against whatever foul creature Archon had sent.

Instead, he found himself staring in wonder as gold dragons dropped from the southern sky. He lowered the Sword of Light and released its power, watching as the beasts swept past and dove towards their foes.

Below the enemy had also seen the beasts, though they seemed unsure of their allegiance. The uncertainty did not last long. As one the dragons turned in the sky and roared. Columns of fire erupted from their massive jaws, streaming down to burn through the massed ranks below. A barrage of arrows followed, and Eric saw that men and women in Plorsean green clung to the dragons' backs.

Alan and Eric moved to the edge of the wall and stared

down at the devastation. The enemy were in full flight, the flames dancing amongst them like a living thing. Streaks of black marked the land below, growing as the flames spread through the black-garbed ranks.

Atop the wall, the defenders burst into applause, cheering as the dragons swept by for another pass. Men embraced, their eyes lit by the glow of hope.

As the last of the attackers vanished into the snow, the dragons swung around and headed back towards the land south of the fortress. All but one. Overhead the crack of wings drew Eric's eyes up, catching on the descending dragon. Somehow he knew the dragon, though it had been many long weeks since Malevolent Cove.

Eric, my eyes did not deceive me, he heard Enduran's voice in his head.

Grinning, Eric sheathed the Sword of Light and raised his arm in greeting. His heart surged at the sight of the familiar dragon, already seeing the happiness on Enala's face when she heard the news. Around him the soldiers retreated to make room for the dragon. With casual ease the great body settled on the battlements, its golden tale draping over the edge like a discarded cloak.

Folding his wings, Enduran lowered his head to inspect Eric. *You are looking well, little one. Your power has grown,* a rumble rose from Enduran's chest and Eric recognised the sound as laughter. *Yes, yes, get down then,* the dragon eyed Eric. *I believe you know my passengers.*

Eric's eyes slid to the figures who sat atop the dragon's back. One was already sliding down the dragon's side, clambering onto its knee and then dropping to the battlements.

Eric glimpsed a flash of scarlet hair and a long bow clenched in a pale fist. Then he was moving, racing across the short distance between them, his eyes blind to everything but her face. The icy stone slid beneath his feet but he did not slow. He watched as she turned and her eyes found his, and he knew he was right.

Inken managed two steps before he reached her, his arms wrapping around her, drawing her to him. Her lips pushed against his and warmth surged through his chest. Her body pressed against him, her fingers twining in his hair, her tongue dancing with his to a music only they could hear.

They clutched each other close, as though they would never let go, as though their very lives depended on it.

And in Eric's mind, a single word repeated itself, over and over.

Hope.

CHAPTER 12

Inken lay on the soft bed, eyes closed, listening to the gentle in, out of Eric's breath. Reaching down, she entwined her fingers with his and felt a gentle squeeze in return. She smiled, a tingling warmth spreading from her heart to her head, washing away all thought of the world outside.

It didn't matter. Tonight was theirs and the world could wait until the light of morning. For now, she wanted nothing more than to lie there with Eric and enjoy the miracle of their reunion.

Eric gave her fingers another squeeze and she looked over to see his blue eyes on her. Reaching over, she ran a hand across his brow and up through his hair. He closed his eyes, the creases of worry falling from his face.

"You're awake," she breathed.

Their only light came from the dying embers of the fire, though with Eric beside her the darkness no longer held the same terror. Even so, she would have to get up and add more wood soon. A storm had descended over the fortress and the temperature had plummeted.

"I am," he smiled. "Sorry I drifted off. It was… a long day before you arrived."

"From what I hear, you fought well," she leaned across and kissed him. "Caelin taught you well."

A shadow passed across Eric's face as she pulled away. "It was not the first time I've had to fight since…" he shook his head. "So much has happened… since I left you."

"You did not leave me, Eric. You did what you had to do. We all did," she embraced him. "You cannot second guess what happened. It was the only way. If you had not run with Enala, none of us would be here right now."

A tear spilt down Eric's cheek but he nodded. "It's been a long couple of weeks."

"Agreed," Inken shuddered, then pressed the memories down. There was no place for sorrow now. Grinning, she gave Eric a jab in the side. "So, how did *you* end up being the one wielding the Sword of Light?" she nodded to the blade leaning against the foot of the bed.

Laughing, Eric grabbed her hand and pulled her close. Before she could squirm free, his fingers began to tickle her side and she burst into laughter. "*Stop!*" she gasped.

Eric refused to relent until there were breathless tears in her eyes. He grinned at her, his smile infectious. "You'll pay for that," she threatened.

Eric only laughed. Finally he took a deep breath and answered her question. "Enala… is my sister. Antonia showed me a vision, from her prison within the *Soul Blade*. Enala and I are twins, but Aria's descendants took on a tradition of separating siblings at birth, so our family would survive even if Archon's hunters found them. Who knows how many other descendants of Aria there are now, lost on secret branches of our family."

Inken's eyes widened and her hand drifted to her stomach. She could not imagine the strength it must have taken

Eric's parents to give up their child. It had only been three days since Enduran had broken the news to her, but even so...

Fortunately Eric did not notice her unconscious gesture. She had not told him yet, though she could not explain her hesitation.

"Incredible," she whispered, then hesitated. "What... what is it like, the Sword?"

Eric shook his head and she saw a shadow cross his face. "It's... like my own magic, but stronger, fiercer. It fights me every time I use it, flooding me with its power, searching for a weakness. Only my own magic keeps it in check."

Inken shuddered. Eric had already told her what had happened to Enala. It seemed clear to her that the powers of the Gods were not meant for mortals. It terrified her to imagine Eric lost to the Sword's magic; that it might burn away his soul and reduce him to an empty shell. She remembered the demon Thomas had become, the empty darkness in his eyes, and prayed Eric had the strength to resist the pull of the Sword.

"What about you?" Eric interrupted her thoughts. "What happened to you and the others?"

Inken bit her lip, staring up at the stone ceiling. Memories raced through her mind and it was a minute before she found her voice. Eric's eyes did not leave her face as she recalled their escape from Sitton and their strange reception by the king in Ardath, nor as she spoke of the arrival of the gold dragons.

But as she spoke of their imprisonment in the black cells beneath the lake city, he reached across and drew her into his arms. She cracked then, the tears coming hot and fast as she struggled for breath. A groan rose in her throat and she sobbed in his arms, the horror of the darkness returning. The fear came rushing back, the helpless terror of their imprisonment.

Eric rubbed her back, his silent presence giving her comfort, and slowly her sobs subsided. At last Inken drew in a deep breath and wiped the tears from her eyes. She flashed Eric a smile, giving him her silent thanks.

"I'm here, Inken," Eric smiled back. "I won't leave again."

Inken suppressed another sob, still trying to get a hold of her emotions. "Sorry," she whispered. "I… I've never felt so helpless."

Eric squeezed her arm but said nothing.

Together they lay back on the bed and held each other close. Inken rested her head on his chest, listening to the steady thump of his heart and feeling the rhythmic rise and fall of his chest.

Closing her eyes, Inken released her fear. The painful throb of her heart slowed and exhaustion spread through her aching limbs. She fought the lure of sleep, unwilling to let the moment slip away. But its call was irresistible and within minutes she had slipped into a dreamless slumber.

GABRIEL COULD NOT KEEP himself from staring, still unable to believe his eyes. Enala sat across the table from him, her blond hair aglow in the light of the torches. Her single lock of scarlet hair drooped lazily across her face, begging him to reach out and tuck it behind her ear. He resisted, contenting himself to watch her eyes as she recounted her journey with Eric.

It was late now and the dining hall was all but empty, the other benches and tables vacant but for a few stragglers. He had hardly noticed the others leaving the hall, so intent had they been on their conversation.

Even the voice in his head had quieted, reduced to faint whispers in the back of his mind.

He shivered though at Enala's tale. It seemed her journey had taken her through more strife than even his own ordeal. She had almost died a dozen times. He could hardly believe her courage to sit here now, ready to face the might of Archon and his armies.

Most surprising of all, she now possessed magic. He would not have believed it had she not shown him, had he not seen it with his own eyes.

Now her voice shook as she described falling under the spell of the *Soul Blade's* power. Silently he reached across the table and grasped her hand. She broke off her story and gave a soft smile, squeezing his fingers tight.

"Thank you, Gabriel," she breathed.

He smiled. "I'm sorry I wasn't there," he paused, struggling to get the next words out. "I'm glad Eric was there for you though, truly," it surprised him to realise it was the truth.

Enala let out a long breath. "He's my brother, Gabriel. My twin."

Gabriel was surprised to find himself smiling, sharing in the joy on Enala's face. It warmed him to hear she had found family, even after the tragedy that had befallen her parents. Then sadness touched him as an image of his own parents and fiancée drifted through his thoughts.

Revenge, the angry whisper rose from the back of his mind.

He shook it off, ignoring the voice and looking back to Enala. "What happens now then, with Eric wielding the Sword? Will you leave, now that it is no longer your 'destiny'?"

"No," Enala sighed. "No, I think I have a different 'destiny' now. If they cannot free the Gods from the *Soul Blades*, it may…" her voice broke and she shook her head, unable to finish.

"Enala?" Gabriel stood and moved around the table to sit beside her. He pulled her into his arms, smiling as he felt her head nestle beneath his chin. "What is it?"

"I may have to use it again, the *Soul Blade*," she shuddered in his arms. "Last time… Last time it *destroyed* me, Gabriel. If not for Eric…"

"Why?" he could not believe anyone would ask such a sacrifice of this girl, not after everything she had been through. "Why you?"

"Because I have already used it. We know it will not kill me, that my magic is powerful enough for that at least. The Magickers in Kalgan thought that it was only my inexperience that allowed the God magic to possess me. Now… now I might at least stand a chance of controlling it."

"What if they're wrong?" Gabriel whispered, terrified for the girl in his arms.

Enala stiffened and push away from him. Fire flashed in her eyes. "Do not say that, Gabriel," she growled. "I don't need any more doubt, I have enough of my own. Don't you see, I'm *terrified*," tears sprang to her eyes. "But I don't have a choice; I have to do this. I can't let Eric face him alone!"

"Surely another Magicker –"

"*No*," Enala snapped. "If it comes to it, I won't let someone else risk death because I was *scared*. I can do this; I *will* do this."

"Okay, I understand," Gabriel held up his hands in surrender. "But what about the other one, the *Soul Blade* with Jurrien's magic?"

Take it! The whispers in his mind suddenly turned into a roar. *Take it and embrace your destiny!*

Gabriel shuddered as shadows danced just beyond his vision. The voice was stronger than he'd ever felt it before, drilling its way deep into his mind. Groaning, he slumped on the bench, his hands clutching at his face.

"*No!*" he ground out through clenched teeth.

"Gabriel?" panic rose in Enala's voice. "What's wrong?"

But her words were a whisper now, carrying to him from some great distance. He could hardly hear her over the screeching in his ears.

Take it! Take it and you will have more power than you could ever have dreamed.

He pressed his hands to his ears and shook his head, but it made no difference. The voice came from within, seeping through his conscious, reaching down to the darkness within him. A shadow stirred in his soul, claws reaching up, desperate to be free.

"Gabriel!" Enala shook him. "Gabriel, what's happening?"

Gabriel tasted blood as his teeth clenched on the inside of his cheek. Slowly, he pulled back from the edge of the abyss and the voice retreated to a whisper.

He looked up into Enala's sapphire eyes, saw the concern there, the fear.

"It's back."

$\approx$

"YOU'RE LOOKING bright this morning, Commander May," Caelin grinned as the woman moved through the dining hall and sat across the table from him.

"Yes, well I'm enjoying my good mood while it lasts," she waved to a server, who nodded and raced to bring her food. He caught her eyes on his plate and pulled it out of reach. May raised an eyebrow. "You know, it would be polite to offer your food to your superior."

Caelin laughed and scooped a spoonful of beans into his

mouth. "Not on your life," he swallowed. "Flying on a dragon's back may look like fun, but it gets uncomfortable after a few days. And we didn't exactly stop long enough for hot meals along the way."

May waved a hand, grinning as the servant placed a plate of food in front of her. "Just in the nick of time," the plate was heaped with beans, bacon and eggs.

Grinning, Caelin shook his head. "I'm glad you're the one in charge here, May," the woman had been a legend even when he'd been training to join the army. He doubted there was anyone he would trust more with the defence of the fortress. "How are the defences looking?"

May finished chewing her mouthful before answering. "Better than a few days ago, that's for sure. The Lonian army arrived not long after your somewhat eventful entrance. That gives us another five thousand swords. The Trolans are still a few days out, but their birds say they have another ten thousand. And we now have the Sword and forty dragons."

"But you don't wish to use them?" he was still confused by May's decision.

"Not yet," she shook her head. "Archon's army may outnumber us, but his human forces alone are not likely to take even the outer wall. Now that we've been reinforced, they will not break us. But his beasts are another matter. I don't want to lose a single dragon before they are needed, and make no mistake, we will need them if we are to hold back Archon's creatures. The last time Archon came, those beasts swept us from the outer wall like we were no more than children."

"And what about the Magickers?"

"I have them stationed on the walls in case they are needed, but they are under strict instruction not to use their magic unless they absolutely must."

Caelin nodded and suppressed a yawn. He had spent

much of the night surveying the fortress' defences for himself, and couldn't help but agree with May's plan.

Looking around the dining room, he spotted Eric and Inken moving towards them. He smiled, warmed by the sight of their reunion. Joy radiated from their faces as they joined them at the table. Gabriel and Enala appeared next, but Caelin was disappointed to see the haunted look still darkened Gabriel's face. If anything, he seemed to have lost more colour.

Looking around the table, he took stock of their reunited company. He smiled, though a sadness stirred in his heart as he remembered those they'd lost. The gap left by Michael and Alastair was plain, but they would never be forgotten. Their sacrifice spurred them on, giving them the strength they needed to face the challenges still to come.

"It's good to see you two again," Caelin nodded at Enala and Eric. "You seem to have gotten yourselves into quite a bit of trouble since you left us."

Eric grinned. "I heard you got yourself thrown in prison, Caelin, and had to be rescued."

"It was all part of the plan," Caelin laughed. "But what's this I hear about you two being siblings now?"

"Believe me, it was just as much of a surprise to us," Eric looked around the room. "I'm glad to see you too, all of you," his eyes lingered on Gabriel.

Gabriel looked away and his face darkened. Caelin raised an eyebrow. He'd thought Gabriel might have finally forgiven Eric, though he understood the young man's pain. To Eric's credit, he let the slight pass.

Enala did not. She reached out and squeezed Gabriel's wrist, then turned to the room. "He's glad to see you too, Eric. But there is more here, something Gabriel has kept from the rest of you."

Gabriel shuddered and Caelin glimpsed the gleam of

tears in his eyes. "It won't leave me alone," he hissed. "It won't stop."

A shiver raised the hairs on the back of Caelin's neck. "What won't leave you alone?"

"The demon," Gabriel hissed. "The thing that came to me in the forests of Oaksville all that time ago."

"Demon?" May half-rose from her seat, her hand going to her sword.

Gabriel nodded. "That's what I've always thought it to be. It… it came to me after my men were slaughtered by the Baronians outside Oaksville, when I'd come so close… to killing you, Eric."

Eric swallowed, clearly uncomfortable with the memory, but Gabriel continued.

"I knew it was evil. It appeared as a shadow in the forest, cloaked in the spirits of the dead. Somehow, *somehow*, it convinced me to listen to it, to take its gift. It offered me resistance to magic, though I never tested it. Not until Ardath," quietly he explained how the dark magic cast by the false king had slid from him like butter.

"But its gift came with a price. It stole my thoughts, my memories, my very soul, until I had nothing left but hatred. Only my encounter with Enala broke the spell, when it told me to kill her."

"I thought I had rid myself of it then, but in the cell it returned. It has been with me ever since, whispering in my mind, driving me towards the darkness," Gabriel hung his head as he finished.

Caelin stared, mouth open in shock. He'd thought it had been madness haunting Gabriel, but now he shuddered at the memory of the darkness in their cell. An evil presence had hovered over them, drawing away their strength. Could it have been Gabriel's demon all along?

"What –?" the ring of trumpets cut May off before she could finish the question.

A shadow swept over the dining hall. Caelin's heart sank as he glanced down at his half-finished plate. Then he stood, lifting his sword belt from his chair and strapping it around his waist.

His eyes found Gabriel's. "We will speak of this after the battle, Gabriel. For now though, I think it's best if you sit out this fight. Afterwards, we will find a way to help you," he reached down and squeezed Gabriel's shoulder. "I swear it."

Gabriel nodded back, the despair in his eyes unmistakable. But there was no time to offer the young man further comfort now.

The evil at their gates would not wait.

CHAPTER 13

Adrenaline swept through Inken as she picked up her bow and followed the others from the hall. This was why she'd first become a bounty hunter: the thrill of combat, the exhilaration as she tested her skill against another's. Her strength had returned over the last few days and she was eager to prove she had lost nothing to the darkness of her imprisonment.

She had already decided she would not back down from the battle. Every sword and bow was needed now, and if Fort Fall was lost, the Three Nations would soon follow. There would be nowhere for her to run, no place left to keep a child safe. No, it was all or nothing, and if she had to give her life so others could raise their children in peace, so be it.

Their boots cracked against the brick path as they raced for the outer wall. The mess hall where they had been eating adjoined to the outermost barracks between the middle and outer wall, so it did not take long for them to reach the staircase leading up to the front line. Behind them others were rushing to their respective stations, ensuring the other two walls were manned in case the first fell.

But that would not be today, not if she had anything to say about it.

May led the way, striding up the stairs while keeping her pace in check. Inken smiled at the woman's self-control. It would not do for the defenders to see their commander panicked, but May seemed to have little difficulty maintaining an outward calm.

At the top May moved off along the wall, her voice bellowing out as she gave orders for the archers to form up. Inken slid her bow off her shoulder and strung it, then stepped into the front line. She sensed the presence of her comrades as they moved in behind her, but she only had eyes for the enemy now. Looking down, she searched for her first target.

Below, a wave of men surged towards the wall, weapons raised in defiance. The snow had cleared during the night but the ground remained frozen white, slowly giving way to the incoming tide of black. The screams of the enemy and the banging of shields carried up to the defenders, breaking on the steel of their courage.

Inken smiled, proud to stand amidst the best of the Three Nations. But as the sunlight glinted off the weapons of the enemy, Inken felt a trickle of fear slide through her chest. Her hand drifted to her stomach and she found herself retreating a step before she caught herself. She bit her tongue, struggling to find the nerve to step back to the edge. Within, a voice was screaming for her to flee.

"There's more of em today," an old warrior stepped up beside her, his amber eyes looking down at the oncoming enemy. He held a massive war hammer casually in one hand.

"Seems that way," Inken swallowed.

"Won't matter much, so long as they stay down there," the giant commented.

Inken found herself grinning, her fear falling away. Reaching up she drew an arrow from her quiver.

"That's what you said yesterday, Alan," Eric muttered from behind her. "And my arms are still hurting."

Inken jumped as Alan's laughter boomed out across the wall. "You'll get used to it, sonny. I expect they'll be throwing the anvil at us now, after yesterday. And whatever else they can get their hands on."

Caelin nodded. "Ay, they'll want a win after yesterday's slaughter."

"Well, sonny, they won't have any luck while I still stand," Alan grinned. "*Kanker* here and I have never lost a fight, and I don't intend to start today," he hefted the great hammer in both hands.

"Is that so?" Caelin grinned at the older man. "Well, just see if you can keep up with me then, old man."

Inken chuckled as Alan replied with a toothy grin. She eyed the older warrior with a professional eye, and guessed Caelin might find himself outmatched on this occasion. Despite the greying hair and lines on his face, Alan held the war hammer seemingly without effort and he moved with the natural grace of a fighter.

"Here they come," Enala commented.

Turning back, Inken swore and nocked her bow.

From down the line she heard the call from May. "Archers: draw, *loose!*"

Sighting down the arrow shaft, Inken found a man at the forefront of the charge and fired. Along the wall the other archers did the same and a volley of arrows swept out to meet the incoming tide. The enemy ranks faltered as it struck, the front line disappearing beneath the deadly rain.

Screams carried up to the wall, but despite the devastation at the front, the men behind came on.

"Archers, nock, draw, *loose!*" May's voice rang out again.

Inken drew a breath and released it, losing herself in the rhythm of the bow. With each volley she reached for her next arrow before the last had even found its target. They managed a dozen volleys before the first of the enemy reached the base of the wall.

"Fire at will! Fighters, at the ladders!"

Then the enemy were firing back and Inken hardly heard May's words as she ducked beneath the crenulations. The hiss of an arrow's passage raised the hairs on her neck and she swore, rolling sideways to come up in a new position. Leaping to her feet, she quickly sighted on an enemy archer, loosed, and ducked back out of view.

Glancing around, she saw the first of the enemy had reached the battlements and were leaping from their ladders to engage with the defenders. Their shaggy coats and black leather armour stood out in stark contrast to the red, blue and green of the defenders. So far, none had managed to gain a foothold on the walkway.

Yet there was no stopping the flood of men racing up the ladders.

A crash came from nearby and she looked up in time to see a man climb into view. Without thinking she drew back her bowstring and loosed her arrow. The bolt struck the man in the chest and flung him backwards. He toppled out of view.

Inken reached for another arrow and found her quiver empty. Cursing, she realised they had spilt from the quiver as she rolled. Tossing aside her bow, she drew her sabre. The next man to clamber onto the parapets was met with steel, his skull shattered by her first swing. As he fell, Inken took up position to the side of the ladder and waited for the next attacker.

A roar came from her left and she looked up in time to see Alan charge into a cluster of three black-garbed enemies. She turned to help him, but quickly realised there was no need. The war hammer caught the first man mid-charge, smashing him from his feet, even as the giant's fist crashed into the face of a second man. The man's head bounced backwards into the stone with an audible *crack*. Panic swept across the face of the last man and he turned to run.

Dropping his hammer, Alan leapt after the man. Grabbing him by the neck, Alan hoisted the man over his head and tossed him at two enemy warriors who had just gained the battlements. The man screamed as he flew into his comrades, knocking them backwards off the wall.

Alan swept up his hammer and turned to see her staring. "Watch yourself, missy," he nodded to another enemy who had just appeared.

Inken grinned back, pleased her assessment of the old warrior had proven true. She doubted even Caelin could keep up with such a man. His strength was prodigious and with that war hammer he appeared to be all but unstoppable.

The enemy approaching her had no such skill and in two breaths she had speared him through the heart. Stepping back, she swung to check on Eric. A tingle of fear went through her as she saw him facing two men.

Before she could move to his aid, Enala leapt in from the side, her short sword stabbing out to catch one of the men in the stomach. As the other turned towards her, Eric surged forward and the Sword of Light crunched through bone. The man crumpled beside his comrade.

"Well done," Inken commented as she joined them.

"Thanks," Eric panted, flashing a weary smile.

As the next wave of enemies swept over the battlements they leapt together to meet them, swords flashing in the morning sun. Inken's heart thudded hard in her chest, strength warming her arms as another enemy fell to her blade and she ducked beneath a swinging axe.

Yet even as she fought, regret touched her. This had been her life as a bounty hunter, an existence filled with excitement and danger. But that life seemed a thousand years ago, and it felt now as though she were reaching back to a past long gone. Sadness stirred in her stomach as she realised how empty that existence had been.

She had been drifting through life before, living each week for the thrill of the hunt, but now she had finally found her purpose. Not for the first time, she thanked the Gods she'd made the right decision all that time ago, when she had sided with the company and joined their quest, when she had joined the fight to save their world from Archon.

And as she slashed past another enemy, she realised with a smile that this war would be her last fight. Not because of the life growing within her, but because she knew she could not return to her old life. After this, she could find no joy in such an existence.

No, there had to be more. Glancing at Eric, warmth rose in her throat at the thought of starting a life with him. It would be an adventure all of its own.

She swore as a blade sliced past her face, coming far too close, and then brought her sabre around to block the next attack. The hilt rung in her hand, but she did not flinch back from the power in the blow. Reversing her swing, she hammered her blade into the man's skull. Wrenching her sword back, she kicked the man through the gap between the crenulations.

Swinging around, Inken surveyed the wall, ready to aid her friends if necessary. A tingle of panic started in her stomach as she saw the enemy were beginning to gain the upper hand. The black-garbed warriors had won purchase atop the battlements in several places and now more were pushing up the ladders behind them. Around them the defenders were falling in greater numbers, their coloured cloaks dotting the walkway amidst the hordes of fallen enemy.

Then she saw the old warrior Alan, still standing his ground amidst the slaughter, a calm centre amidst the storm. Where others were being forced back he stood like a boulder, immovable as the enemy pressed forward around him. Black-cloaked bodies lay strewn about him.

Yet Alan's defiance also threatened to cut him off from the other defenders as they retreated beneath the enemy's weight.

Seeing the threat, Inken screamed to the others. "Follow me!"

Knowing Eric, Enala and Caelin would not let her down, she charged into the ring of men gathering around the old warrior. She took the first one in the back, bearing him to the ground as her momentum carried her forward. Pulling back her blade, she leapt to her feet, her steel finding a second victim before the others could turn to face her.

Then Caelin was there, his sword like lightning, dancing amidst the enemy, too quick for thought. His foot lashed out, knocking an axeman off balance as he parried the sword of another. Eric followed him in, the long blade of the Sword of Light cleaving into the enemy ranks, and Enala too, her short sword stabbing low beneath the enemy's guard.

In seconds the fight was over, the enemy overwhelmed before they had a chance to regroup.

Together they re-joined with Alan, helping him to dispatch the last few enemy on his other side. As one they faced the next wave of attackers, their weapons red with the blood of the fallen.

Inken's heart raced, her movements beyond reason now,

beyond thought. She attacked with a primal instinct, developed from her years of combat. The enemy fell like autumn leaves before their fury, and though her lungs heaved and she could hear the laboured gasps of her comrades, Inken knew not one of them would back down.

Around them the other defenders took courage from their defiance and began to press back against the enemy, making them pay for every inch of bloody stone. Where the enemy had gained footholds their numbers quickly shrank, falling away beneath the fury of the defenders' blades. Together, the men and women of the Three Nations stood atop the wall, and defied the might of Archon.

Inken heard May's roars of encouragement from further down the wall. Bit by bit, the defenders drove the enemy back.

Slowly the tide turned and the anger in the eyes of the enemy turned to fear. They had been winning, had been within an inch of claiming the wall, but now that triumph was slipping through their fingers.

Inken smiled as panic spread through the enemy ranks and they began to retreat back towards their ladders. But with men still surging up from below, they had nowhere to go, and there on the battlements they were slaughtered.

It took a few minutes for Inken to realise there were no more enemies left to fight. Blinking in the bright sun, she looked around and saw the last of the enemy had fallen to the defender's blades. Below, the black tide was retreating and men were leaping down from the ladders in panic, desperate to escape the fury of the defenders above.

Her friends stood around her, wide smiles on their faces.

"We did it," she laughed.

"Ay, we did," Alan smiled. "But I am afraid this is just the beginning."

GABRIEL WATCHED from a distant window as the defenders began to clean up in the aftermath of the battle. They started with the enemy, with defenders taking it in turns to lift the lifeless bodies between them and toss them back out into the wasteland. There were more than he could possibly count, though he knew in his heart it was still not enough. Archon had countless warriors at his disposal, along with whatever nightmarish creatures waited out in that vast wasteland.

When the defenders started with their own fallen, Gabriel could hardly watch. They brought them down one by one, carried solemnly on stretchers to be laid out on the ground below. There a great pit had been prepared, although men were already working to make it larger. The losses today had far exceeded anyone's expectations.

Yet even that was not the worst of it.

Screams echoed up from below him, the cries of the injured and dying rising through the floorboards. They had been carrying them down throughout the battle, clearing the wall for fresh defenders. Some had even brought themselves, hobbling down on shattered legs or cradling broken limbs.

They had set up a makeshift hospital in the large hall beside the mess hall to treat the worst of the injured, to stabilise them before moving them to the main infirmary inside the keep. Gabriel had stumbled down earlier, desperate to make a difference, but the cacophony of sound and smell had driven him back.

Never before had he felt so powerless, so helpless to aid his friends.

And still the whispers would not stop.

You can help them, Gabriel, the voice came from the shadows. In the corner of his eye, Gabriel could glimpse the demon, the flickering of ghosts whirling around it. But he refused to face it, to acknowledge its presence. *You could be more powerful than you ever dreamed.*

Gabriel closed his eyes, struggling to ignore the words. They clawed at him, dragging hooks of guilt through his soul. Could he truly help them? Could he use that sword and use it to drive back the enemy?

"No," he growled to himself. "It lies. You know what it is, *what it wants!*"

I want nothing, the demon's voice came again. *You are my child, Gabriel, do you not see? I only wish to free you.*

"I am no child of yours, demon!" Gabriel finally swung to face the creature.

The demon emerged from the shadows, its slow, gliding movements revealing its insubstantial form. The strength fled Gabriel's legs as he watched it approach. He sank to his knees and looked up into the pale face of the demon. Death hung around the thing like a cloak, drawing the life from him.

It seemed more solid now, more powerful. As though it had fed, had grown stronger.

I only wish to help you, Gabriel, to give you strength. Do you not wish to aid your comrades?

Gabriel shuddered as the creature reached down and grasped his shoulder. Its touch felt like ice, its chill spreading out to engulf him. Tears ran down his face and he felt the darkness inside him rising from where he had banished it. This time, desperate and alone, he could not find the strength to fight it.

The shadow leaned closer, until the deathly lips were an inch from his ear. *You know who you are, Gabriel, what you must do. Return to the girl's room and take up the Soul Blade. Only it can give you the strength you need. Go!*

Hot tears burned in his eyes as Gabriel found himself standing. The darkness spread out within him, pushing him back, swamping him. He faced the creature one last time, looked into the infinite depths of those black eyes. But there was no breaking its spell now, and with a twist of terror he found himself turning and walking from the room.

Somewhere below, the *Soul Blade* waited for him.

CHAPTER 14

The slow thump of Gabriel's boots on the wooden stairs echoed in the narrow space. The descent seemed to take an age, though less than a minute had passed since the demon had come. Gabriel's head burned as he struggled to stop himself, but each thump brought him one step closer to the *Soul Blade*, closer to some dark fate he could only imagine.

The darkness within him swirled, rejoicing at its triumph, and Gabriel felt himself slipping away. He struggled against the emotions rising within him, the rage and hate he had thought long buried. Greed coloured his thoughts, and a desire rose in his chest, a craving for the power offered by the *Soul Blade*. He closed his eyes, trying to deny the darkness within.

But he could not close it off any longer, could not control it.

Then he was standing within Enala's room, crossing to where a burlap sack lay carelessly discarded at the foot of the bed. He could feel the power radiating from within the sack, the aching taint of the *Soul Blades*. Reaching down, Gabriel upended the contents onto the floor.

The *Soul Blades* tumbled out, their blue and green glow spilling across the room. Gabriel staggered backwards as a tingle of fear caught him, cutting through the hate and greed. For a second he stood frozen, the dark and the light warring within.

But fear alone was not enough. The darkness roared and his soul shrank, retreating back to the depths of his conscious. With a long sigh, he straightened and stepped towards the swords.

The blue glow of Jurrien's *Soul Blade* washed across the room, beckoning him. Voices whispered their warning in his mind, but the call of the blade was everything now. He was beyond reason, beyond thought. He shivered, his skin tingling with the power of the sword.

All the power of the Sky lay at his fingertips; the very magic Eric had used to destroy his life.

A dark grin crossed Gabriel's lips as he reached for the *Soul Blade*.

"*Gabriel!*" Enala's shriek pierced the mist around his thoughts.

Gabriel looked up, eyes widening to see Enala standing in the doorway. Blood stained her clothing and her hair hung limp across her eyes. Brown and red streaks marked her skin, but there was no mistaking the fear on her face.

"What are you doing?" she stared, mouth agape, fingers hovering on the hilt of her sword.

"I – I –" Gabriel looked from her to the *Soul Blade*, but whatever hold the demon had over him, Enala's presence had not freed him. He felt tears sting his eyes. "I'm sorry," he breathed.

Then he lunged forward and wrapped his fingers around the hilt of the *Soul Blade*. A surge of energy raced up his arm as he lifted it. He stiffened as the power reached his chest, the blue fire burning down to his very core. His fingers clenched tight to the hilt of the *Soul Blade*, locking it in an iron grip. From somewhere far away, he heard a girl scream.

A grin pulled at Gabriel's lips as the power spread and a euphoric joy lit his mind, banishing doubt and fear. He had never felt such power, such strength.

His eyes opened and Gabriel found himself looking out at the world through a haze of blue. Energy crackled in the air, the raw potential of the Sky begging to be unleashed. He had only to wish it, and he could use its power to wipe the fortress from existence. Winds would tear the stones from the walls and lightning would fall from above, burning rock and steel alike to ash.

A mad smile split his lips. Reaching out, he touched a swirling ring of light. Thunder boomed as lightning materialised within the room. The blue threads of power crackled and danced across the wooden floorboards. A shriek came from somewhere and he turned to see a figure flee through the open door.

A trickle of regret touched him, quickly gone, and then there was only the magic of the *Soul Blade*, the thrill of its power.

Gabriel, the voice was so soft, so faint he would not have heard it if not for the shiver it sent through his soul. He shook his head, trying to dismiss the whisper, but a part of him clung to it, to the comfort of the voice. It hung in stark contrast to the demon's whispers.

Yet the room was empty, his only company the roar of lightning and the crackle of flames now licking the walls. Slowly, the feeling fell away, tumbling back into the depths within. A dark joy throbbed in his head as the magic filled him. It raced through his mind, burning away thought and reason, and Gabriel felt himself slipping away.

Looking down, he watched lightning take form in his hands, crackling between his fingertips. His fingers clenched as though by a will of their own, and Gabriel suddenly felt like a spectator in his own body. His throat quivered as laughter filled the room.

Gabriel, this is not your destiny, the voice came again, stronger now.

A growl rose from Gabriel's chest as his eyes searched the room. He spun, throwing out his arms. Lightning leapt outwards, catching on the bed, the wardrobe, the walls. It raged around him, burning away the meagre contents of Enala's room.

"*Where are you?*" he raged.

Someplace you can never harm me, sadness touched the voice.

The voice cut through the power, finding Gabriel deep within his conscious. A tingle of recognition touched him and he clung to the words, pulling himself back towards the light. He struggled to remember the speaker, but his memories came in bursts now, burned away by the throb of magic.

"*Who are you?*" words grated from his mouth in a metallic screech.

Gabriel's eyes slid to the *Soul Blade*, fighting the pull of the magic. The veins of his arm stood out stark against his skin, glowing blue in the light of the sword. But he saw now the colour of the *Soul Blade* had changed, the blue of the Sky tainted by darkness.

And still the power raced up his arm, crashing upon his consciousness, pushing him down.

What is happening to me? He screamed in his mind, his jaw clamped shut, locked by the forces surging within him.

It will take you, Gabriel, the voice came again, a desperate edge to its tone. *Unless you let me help you.*

How? Gabriel could feel himself teetering on the edge, an infinite precipice dangling beneath him.

Relax your mind, and let me in, the voice demanded.

Gabriel swallowed, struggling to breathe as energy crackled in his chest. The God magic was everywhere now, burning, crackling, overwhelming. He fought it still, desperate to break free. Slowly the voice's command seeped through to him.

No, Gabriel cried into the emptiness within. *I will be lost.*

It is the only way.

Shuddering, Gabriel felt the magic welling again, the power gathering to sweep him away. Unable to fight any longer, Gabriel succumbed to the voice's command, and let go.

As his mind relaxed, a brilliant flash erupted behind his eyes. He felt the God power flee before it, racing back into the darkness of the *Soul Blade,* and then the world turned white.

For a long time Gabriel drifted, his mind afloat on the empty white. He knew he was lost, adrift in a foreign land, but somehow he could not find the will to care. He felt no worry, no dark touch of emotion to colour his thoughts. There was only the light, the unending space. It had been a long time since he'd felt such peace.

Closing his eyes, Gabriel gave himself to the feeling.

"Gabriel," it was the voice again, calm now, the panic gone.

Reluctantly, Gabriel opened his eyes to search out the source. The absolute white still stretched out in every direction, but he was no longer alone. A man walked towards him, striding through the emptiness as though a bricked path lay beneath his booted feet. He wore a blue shirt and tight black pants in the fashion of a sailor, though his white hair was well kept and his face clean-shaven. His ice blue eyes found Gabriel's, and held them.

"Jurrien", he whispered, remembering the God from the battle in Sitton. "What happened? How are you here?"

Jurrien's face darkened. "What one might expect, when someone without magic tangles with such an artefact. You have no power of your own, Gabriel, not even a touch of magic waiting to be born. Without it, your body had no defence against the magic within the *Soul Blade*."

Gabriel shuddered. "Enala… the same thing happened to her when she touched the other blade. But Antonia did not come to her. Why?"

Jurrien frowned. "I do not know. I cannot sense much of the outside world; only what the wielder of the *Soul Blade* allows. But I have been saving my strength, preparing myself for a moment when I might be needed. When I felt the God magic taking you I thought it would be best to intervene. But my power is all but spent now…"

"Antonia had already come once, for Eric," Gabriel breathed. "She had nothing left to save Enala."

"Ay, my sister has always had a soft spot for the descendants of Aria's line. I cannot imagine her willingly sitting by while one of Aria's children was lost to her God magic."

Gabriel smiled. "Thank you, Jurrien. I hope you don't come to regret using your strength to save me. But you will not be in here much longer. The fortress' Magickers are working on a way to free you from the *Soul Blade*."

"They will not succeed. Not unless…" the God trailed off, then waved a hand. "No, our bodies have been destroyed, returned to the earth as we have returned to spirit. We are Gods no longer."

Despair touched Gabriel then, seeping up from wherever his body lay back in reality. "But we need you, Jurrien. We cannot defeat Archon without you."

"You will find a way. You humans have never ceased to amaze us, even when we watched you only as spirits."

"How?" Gabriel shook his head. "Archon is too powerful."

Jurrien only smiled. "Together. You will defeat him together, Gabriel. The Three Nations joined as one."

Gabriel's shoulders slumped as he looked into the God's icy eyes. "We cannot leave you here, trapped forever," he looked around "Wherever here is."

"This is the spirit realm, of sorts," Jurrien answered. "Though it has been warped, a part of it twisted and broken off into the *Soul Blade*, ensuring a spirit can never truly depart."

"Am I trapped here too then?" Gabriel swallowed at the thought.

"No," Jurrien shook his head. "You are not truly here. Your body still waits for you back in Fort Fall. I only brought your spirit here to protect it from the God magic."

Gabriel breathed a long sigh. "Thank you, Jurrien. Thank you for sacrificing the last of your strength to save me," he paused, sensing the God still held something back. "Are you sure we cannot free you?"

Jurrien smiled. "Forget us, Gabriel. Our time is done. We cannot return, not without sacrificing more than I am prepared to ask. I will offer you only this: if the time comes when you have nowhere left to turn, nowhere to run, look again to the *Soul Blade*. The answer will come to you then," the God raised his hand. "Farewell, Gabriel."

Gabriel opened his mouth to argue, but Jurrien was already fading, the white world falling away.

ENALA'S HEART raced as she fled the room, the mad laughter

of her friend chasing after her. A boom came from behind, followed by a wave of heat. She spun around a corner and leapt for the stairwell, thumping down the wooden steps as flames licked at her heels.

Another boom shook the air and a wave rippled down the stairs, shattering the boards beneath her feet. She stumbled on a jagged edge and went tumbling down the last flight, arms raised to protect herself. Then she was up, swinging herself into the corridor and racing for the outer doors.

Other men and women filled the hall, stumbling towards the exit, the healthy carrying the injured. Most of the army remained on the wall awaiting the next attack though, and Enala realised there were not enough able-bodied to carry all the wounded. Panic gripped her chest as another roar came from overhead.

Racing outside, Enala spun to face the building. Flames poured from the upstairs windows and thick smoke stained the sky. A crash came from inside as walls began to collapse. The blaze was spreading far too quickly – the building would collapse long before it could be evacuated.

Enala cursed her hesitation when she'd seen Gabriel standing over the *Soul Blades*. She should have grabbed him, tackled him, done whatever it took to stop him. But she had not even had time to grab the other *Soul Blade*. Now they had lost the God power it contained, and only the Sword of Light could match the power flooding through Gabriel's body.

Overhead the noonday sun streamed down on the clearing between the walls, but its heat was nothing compared to that of the burning building. Screams came from within and Enala knew she could not hesitate any longer. Something had to be done, or innocent lives would be lost.

As people streamed past her, fleeing the burning building, Enala reached down to the power burning within her. Its red light rose at her touch, snapping at her mind, but she had no patience for its wilful nature now. Clenching it with a will of iron, she released her mind and opened her spirit eyes.

Staring at the building, she saw the eerie glow of the flames and reached out for it with her magic. Taking a firm grip of her power, she soared closer. Lines of magic stretched out from her, wrapping around the flames and binding them to her will. They fought against her, desperate for freedom, to feed their ravenous hunger, but Enala refused to give in. Gritting her teeth, she pulled the ropes tighter, and hurled them skyward.

Screams came from around her as flames rose from the barracks and took to the sky, soaring over their heads towards the wall. Embers drifted down and the crowd flinched back as one, panic spreading through their ranks. But the flames did not fall, and a moment later they disappeared beyond the curve of the wall, tumbling into the wasteland beyond.

"What's happening?" Eric's shout came from beside her.

Enala drew back to her body. "It's Gabriel," she gasped, her thoughts still half with her magic. "He picked up the *Soul Blade.*"

Eric swore and reached for the Sword of Light. Flames lit the blade as he drew it, sizzling in the air, and she raised an eyebrow. "I don't think we need more of that," she offered.

Shaking his head, Eric closed his eyes and the white fire died away. Beads of sweat sprang out on Eric's forehead and his breathing quickened.

"Are you okay?" she sensed the tingle of power from the building and knew the flames were growing again.

Eric shook his head. "No. I… I'm still exhausted from the fight. But I have it under control. It's just a good thing I didn't use my magic in the battle."

"Can you help?" Enala asked, nodding at the glow of fire coming from the upper windows.

Eric flashed a smile. "We'll find out soon enough."

He lifted the Sword and pointed it at the building. Enala closed her eyes and released her spirit again, pulling her magic with her. The fire leapt as her magic touched it, hungry to devour everything within reach. She sensed the surge of magic thumping in her ears and knew Eric was using the Sword's power to do the same.

Together they wrapped their magic about the fire. A muffled roar came from the building as the roof collapsed and the flames rushed outwards, breaking free of their grasp. Enala raced after them, flinging out hooks of energy to pull them back. Slowly the flames began to calm, surrendering to their will.

As one they pulled the flames skyward and hurled them across the wall. As they disappeared beyond the wall the air grew still. Voices whispered around them as the injured continued to be carried from the building. Then another boom of thunder came and Enala sensed fresh flames take light.

Sweat beading her forehead, Enala threw her spirit back into the conflict. Beside her she sensed Eric's own determination, but worried for his soul. Whatever he said, using the Sword clearly cost him. And her own strength was already wavering. They could not keep this up forever.

Still they kept on, determined to save the injured souls still fleeing the building. Overhead a river of fire streaked the sky, rising from the barracks to fall on the desert beyond the wall. Enala panted for breath, desperate for water in the sweltering heat of the flames. The air was growing thin and her muscles burned as though she had run a hundred miles. Her mind swam, crying out for relief.

Then with a final boom, the lightning died away to nothing. Silence fell as the last of the flames disappeared and a hush fell across the crowd. As one they turned to the building, waiting to see what would come next.

Enala sank to her knees, swallowing a mouthful of air, her throat like sandpaper. Eric sat down beside her, his fingers clenched on the dry ground. He gasped, his face pale and his eyes ringed by shadow.

"What happened?" Inken appeared beside them, sweat running down her forehead.

"Gabriel," Enala croaked.

Before Inken could reply a whisper spread through the crowd. Enala turned, seeking out the source of the disruption. They sat at the front of the gathering, nearest to the barracks, so it only took Gabriel two steps to reach them. His eyes were clear now, empty of the darkness from earlier, though they were ringed by exhaustion. His clothes had all but burned away and his skin had bubbled in places, unprotected against the fire.

He stumbled as he reached them, almost falling before staggering to a halt. He looked down at them, his eyes filled with fear and wonder.

"Jurrien," he murmured. "I saw him."

CHAPTER 15

I nken strode down the empty stone corridors of Fort Fall, shivering as a cool breeze swept through an open window. Three days had passed since Gabriel had picked up the *Soul Blade,* and the mood of the fortress was now teetering on a fine balance. Hundreds had witnessed the power wielded by Eric and Enala to save the barracks and those inside from the fire, but others whispered about what had happened afterwards, of the man who had been last to stumble from the building.

Even May had taken some convincing just to keep Gabriel from the hangman's noose. As it was he had been locked away until the Magickers could confirm the dark magic had truly left him. Eric and Enala had not had the strength for the task. The magic they'd spent saving the infirmary had cost them dearly and the two had spent the last few days confined to their beds.

For the rest of them though, the last three days had been filled with the ring of blades and screams of combat. Archon's forces hardly paused for breath now, the enemy coming night and day to climb the walls and die beneath the defenders' blades. Each attack would continue for long, gruelling hours. And each time the enemy would be fresh, while Inken struggled to find the strength to lift her blade again.

Exhaustion clung to her very bones now. They fought in shifts, rosters of men and women taking turns to hold the wall, but even so the defenders were lagging. Even with the extra soldiers from Lonia, there were only so many of them, and the long hours of battle sucked the strength from her soul.

Their only source of hope was the impending arrival of the Trolan army. The ten thousand swords they brought would provide a welcome relief, and the Trolans were renown throughout the Three Nations as fighters. Word from their army said they would arrive tomorrow.

Until then though, it was up to their weary arms to hold back the black tide outside. Inken clenched her bow tight, drawing comfort from the firm wood. Her sabre slapped at her side as she moved. She had lost count of the number of men that had fallen to her blade. It was all a daze now. All that mattered was staying alive, keeping out of reach of the swords and axes of the enemy, and the arrows flashing up from below.

In truth, even with her skill she would have fallen long ago without Caelin and Alan. They fought together as a unit, smashing through any resistance the enemy could mount, the big man's strength providing them an anchor in the chaos.

She saw him now, a wide grin spreading above his greying beard. Caelin stood beside him in the gates from the citadel, waiting for her arrival. It was their shift again, their turn to hold the fortress against the evil of the north. Feeling the weight of her bow in her hand, Inken hoped she had enough strength left to survive the day.

"You okay, missy?" concern edged Alan's voice as his soft eyes inspected her.

Inken shook her head and straightened. "Only tired. I hope the Trolans arrive early; it's about time they had a turn against the buggers."

She felt a hand on her shoulder. She looked up, expecting Alan to dismiss her back to the citadel. But the big man only smiled. "Just remember, stay close, missy."

Inken opened her mouth and then closed it, fighting back tears. There was such a kindness in Alan's eyes she found herself lost for words, unable to respond to the compassion there. Choking out an unintelligible response, she pushed past them, wiping tears from her eyes when she thought they would not see.

Where did that come from? She cursed her weakness and swallowed the emotion. Turning, she called back to them. "Well, what are you waiting for, boys? Don't tell me the years are catching up to you?"

Alan's booming laugh chased after her, bringing a smile to her face. Together they marched through the gates of the first two walls, glancing up at the men stationed on each. All three were manned now, ensuring if one fell there would be enough to hold the others from a sudden rush by the enemy.

At last the outer wall loomed ahead. Inken's eyes lingered on the ruined barracks as they moved past, remembering the stream of flames that had leapt from the building into the sky. Not even Enala and Eric's best efforts had been able to save the barracks, but hundreds had been able to escape in the time they'd bought with their magic.

When the building had finally collapsed, the company had made their way into the ruin. The stench had been overwhelming, sending rescuers staggering back into the open air. But there was something they needed to retrieve, though Inken would rather have left the cursed things where they lay.

The *Soul Blades*.

She shuddered as she remembered uncovering them, finding them untouched amongst the wreckage. The blades still glowed with the eerie colours of the magic trapped inside, bathing her with their power. But she felt no desire to wield that power. It was a curse she was glad to avoid.

Gabriel had passed on Jurrien's words, that the Gods could not be returned to this world. Enala had paled then, stumbling away, open terror on her face. The rest of them stood in silence, unable to find an answer to the news. From this point on, the Three Nations stood alone against the might of Archon.

Shaking her head, Inken turned her thoughts back to the task at hand. There was no point stewing over matters beyond her control. She did not have the power to face the dark magic wielded by Archon, but she had her bow and her sword. War at least she excelled at, and she did not intend to lose that battle.

Silence carried down from overhead as they began their ascent to the ramparts. Inken breathed a sigh of relief, glad at least that the fighting had not yet started. Determined as she was, a few extra moments of rest would be welcome.

As they reached the top they moved quickly to their station and sank as one to the cold ground. Inken leaned back against the crenulations and looked up. The sky was an endless blue and the air was crisp and dry. A cool winter breeze blew across the wall, but in the shelter of the battlements they remained warm. Any other day and she would have called it beautiful. Today though she could think of little else but death. Blood stained the stones around them, reminding her all too vividly of the violence to come.

"Another lovely day at Fort Fall," she commented wryly.

Caelin laughed, stretching in the sun. "Almost makes me wish for a swim," he said, nodding towards the distant surf. "Although it looks a little rough."

"Little man," Alan chuckled. "You don't have the stones for that water."

Caelin grinned back. "That sounds like a challenge, big man."

"Oh the arrogance of youth," Alan shot Inken a wink and she smiled back. "You think the wolf worries when the puppy barks?"

"A challenge it is then," Caelin slapped his hand on his knee and pointed to the far off water. "When this business is done, we'll see who lasts the longest."

Alan raised an eyebrow. "Five silvers say you don't last five minutes."

"Deal!" Caelin held out his hand and they shook.

Inken grinned at them. They had spent most of their spare time over the last two days in similar debates and she had already lost count of their wagers. The contests between them would be something to look forward to after all this; if any of them survived. She had joined in more than a few bets herself, but today she could not find the energy. Weariness gripped her soul, and she yearned to return to the citadel and Eric.

She still hadn't told him; told anyone but the king for that matter. She was not sure why she hesitated, but the knowledge felt personal, a secret she was not yet ready to share. Perhaps because when the truth came out, it would become all too real.

And despite her trust in Eric and Enala, she struggled to find hope for their future. Even without his army, Archon was just too powerful. Antonia and Jurrien, with all their knowledge and power, had not been able to stop him last time. Archon had crushed them like insects beneath his boots.

Even with the Sword of Light, the Gods had only had the strength to banish him.

Horns sounded along the wall and with a long sigh Inken forced aside her doubt. There would be time for that later. For now, she had another battle to survive. Putting her hands beneath her, she pushed herself to her feet and hefted her bow.

From below came the familiar screams of the horde as they rushed forward to meet their deaths. Closing her eyes, Inken let the sound wash over her, trying to calm her racing thoughts. How she longed for the peace and quiet of the forest, to return to the glade in Dragon Country where she and Eric had first made love. If only they could leave all this behind.

But it was not to be. Biting her lip, Inken reached down and strung her bow. The familiar call went out along the line, ordering the archers to the fore. Below, the enemy dead covered the ground, marking the range of the defenders' arrows. Then the order to fire came and the first wave of arrows rose into the sky.

Inken could not have said how long the assault continued, only that her arms and legs were aching and that a dozen men or more had fallen to her sword by the time the enemy horns sounded their retreat. The whole time Alan and Caelin had stood strong beside her, their contrasting styles of brute force and subtle skill unstoppable. Together they held the centre of the line, their courage providing the backbone of the defenders.

As the last of the enemy fell Inken stepped back from the edge, her breath coming in heavy gasps. The blade was heavy in her hand and she knew she was close to the end of her strength. Turning away, her stomach lurched. Unable to hold the nausea down, she stumbled to the backside of the wall and hurled her breakfast over the edge. An acrid sting burned in her throat as another convulsion shook her. The strength fled her legs and she slid to the ground, gasping as she leaned against the cold stone.

"Inken!" Caelin was at her side in an instant. Alan was not far behind.

She waved a hand to show she was okay, but another wave of sickness swept through her and she found herself too preoccupied to reply. Tears stung her eyes as she struggled to breath between heaves.

"I'm okay," she croaked at last.

"What's wrong?" Caelin gripped her by the shoulder and forced her to look at him.

She saw the concern in his eyes and tried not to look away. "Not now," she whispered. Taking a hand from Alan, she struggled back to her feet. "Are they done?"

Caelin nodded. "For now," but even as he spoke, the horns began to sound again.

Around them, murmurs of fear came from the defenders.

"They're attacking again, already?" Inken groaned. She searched deep inside for some forgotten store of strength, but she had little left to give. Her energy was spent, stripped away by the endless days of combat.

"Ay," Alan stood at the edge of the ramparts, staring out at the enemy. "They're coming. But not men. Beasts."

Pain twisted in Inken's chest as her heart fell to the pit of her stomach. "The beasts?" she breathed.

She moved with Caelin to stand beside Alan, her eyes sweeping out to search the plains below. Far in the distance, but closing at a frightening speed, came a host of creatures born from the pits of their worst nightmares.

The Raptors led the charge, their razor sharp teeth glinting in jaws wide enough to swallow a man's head whole. Thick black tails stretched out behind them as their massive feet carried them across the open ground. Behind them

Inken glimpsed flashes of fur and scale, teeth and claw, but a cloud of dust obscured the details of the other creatures.

They carried no ropes or ladders – they did not need them. Tales from Archon's war told of how they'd scaled these walls, how their claws had dug deep into the mortar between the stones and carried them up to the defenders above.

"Where are the dragons?" Inken whispered.

Before the others could reply the horns sounded again, three long blasts echoing back to the citadel. Beyond the dragons had nested these last three days, lying in wait for when they were needed most.

Inken's heart soared as the first roar carried to her ears and the golden beasts rose into view, wings beating hard in the frigid air. She grinned, turning back to the oncoming horde. Let the beasts come; the dragons would burn them where they stood.

The crack of wings came from overhead and a shadow fell across the wall. Inken looked up in time to see the golden body of Enduran swoop past, the rest of his tribe following close behind.

Rest easy, little one. We will take care of these creatures. The great globe of the dragon's eye found her as he spoke in her mind. Then the dragons rose higher into the sky, sweeping out towards the oncoming beasts.

Inken grinned and a desperate longing rose in her chest. She wanted to be with them, soaring into the sky on the back of a dragon, ready to rain death down on those below.

The dragons soared past the first ranks of black creatures, then spun in the air, their wings folding as they dived towards the beasts below. They fell like darts, flames billowing out ahead of them as they unleashed death on Archon's creatures. An inferno ignited below them, roaring through the horde, consuming all in its path.

A cheer rose up from the defenders as Archon's beasts

disappeared into the firestorm. Along the wall, men and women embraced and raised their swords in salute. Inken watched with quiet joy as the dragons rose back into the sky and wheeled about, preparing for another attack.

Then she frowned as beasts started to leap from the inferno. From the distance she could not see what had happened, but it appeared as though the following ranks of creatures had already overtaken their fallen leaders.

The dragons dived again, catching the next wave in the white hot heat of their fire, and again the defenders cheered. But Inken watched closely now, a tingle of alarm racing down her spine. The beasts were closer now, and her stomach twisted as Raptors exploded from the columns of fire. Flames licked at their scales but they appeared unmarked.

Inken clenched her bow tight as the rest of the creatures followed, leaping through the inferno in an endless flood. Smoke clung to the plain below, obscuring the horde beyond. But the vanguard was in full view now, the Raptors leaping across the bodies of the enemy, their eyes locked on the defenders above.

The dragons' fire had done nothing. Somehow Archon had outmanoeuvred them, casting his dark magic over his creatures to protect them from the flames. And now they were closing on the wall, already within bowshot, and still the defenders stood frozen.

Inken looked up as the dragons roared and came again. But a flash from the enemy camp drew Inken's eyes. Beyond the columns of smoke, a ball of power gathered in the air. She opened her mouth to scream a warning, but it was already too late. The ball raced upwards, accelerating as the dragons whirled to avoid it. One lagged a second slower than the rest and the ball of energy caught it in the chest.

Darkness exploded outwards, enveloping the dragon in a shroud of black. Within the cloud the dragon stiffened, its wings locked in place, and without so much as a sound, it plummeted to the earth.

Along the wall, the defenders heard the sickening crunch as it struck the ground.

Howls of sorrow came from the sky and as one the dragons turned and retreated beyond the walls of the fortress.

I'm sorry, little one, Enduran's voice was heavy with despair. *His power is too great; we cannot stop them.*

Thank you for trying, Enduran, Inken thought back. *Join us on the wall. We will fight them together.*

A roar of agreement carried down and then the defenders were crowding backwards to make room for their allies to land. Only ten could fit atop the outer wall; the rest took up stations on the other battlements or the citadel itself.

Even with their support, Inken could sense the fear of the defenders, spreading like a sickness through their ranks.

Then May's voice carried over the whispers. "Archers, to the fore. Nock arrows!"

The calm in her voice cut through the panic and steadied their courage. Inken stepped up with the other archers, shaking off Caelin's arm.

"We have to stop them, Caelin. It will take everything we have to hold them back," she reached down and swung a fresh quiver of arrows onto her back.

Drawing an arrow, Inken nocked and sighted at the nearest Raptor. As May's cry to fire rang out she loosed, watching with satisfaction as her arrow found its mark. But the Raptor did not even stumble as the shaft embedded itself in its shoulder. It came on, black scales shining in the light of the flames behind it.

Inken nocked again but did not wait for May's command – volleys would not stop these creatures. Her next two arrows found the creature's neck and shoulder again, and finally the beast slowed. Its head swung around, the great jaws tearing the shaft from its neck.

Sighting, Inken put another arrow through its neck. This time as it struck, the Raptor tripped and went tumbling across the rocky ground. It took a long time to get back up and Inken prayed it would no longer have the strength to climb.

She emptied her quiver into two more Raptors before the first beasts reached the wall, and then tossed her bow aside. Drawing her sabre, she stepped back between Caelin and Alan, and waited.

"Up for this, missy?" Alan asked softly.

Inken nodded. "Ask me again after we see the damn things off."

"Just stay between us, Inken," Caelin grunted. "Eric will have our heads if we don't bring you back safely."

"You two concentrate on keeping yourselves alive," Inken replied, though fear flickered in her chest. "I can take care of myself."

She saw her own fear reflected in Caelin's eyes as he nodded back.

"Right then," Alan raised his voice so those around him could hear. "Let's show these beasts what we're made of!" Alan raised his war hammer and a ragged cheer went up from around them. Inken could see no fear in the big man's eyes, only the same steady determination she had seen in the last few days, and drew strength from his courage.

Silence fell then as they stood together, listening to the scrambling of claws on stone.

The Raptors appeared in a rush, surging over the crenulations to fall on the ranks of defenders. Along the wall the dragons roared their defiance and the defenders rushed forward to meet the beasts.

Inken dove backwards as a Raptor's claws slashed for her

throat. She stumbled on the bloody bricks but Caelin hurled himself into the fray, his sword slashing for the beast's head. It bounded out of reach, then the thick black tail swung round to catch Caelin in the chest. He staggered back, the breath wheezing from his lungs.

Recovering her balance, Inken lunged in. Her sabre lanced towards the creature's midriff, point poised to strike, but the Raptor leapt to the side and sparks flew as her blade struck stone. She flinched as the Raptor attacked then, the giant jaws stretched wide to tear off her head.

A strong hand grasped her by the collar and jerked her backwards, then Alan charged into the fray, his hammer crunching into the Raptor's jaws. It roared, staggering sideways and then leapt to avoid his next blow. The beaded eyes followed Alan as he turned. Charging in, the creature snapped at Alan's face, but his fist swung round to catch the creature's chin. To Inken's shock, the blow staggered the Raptor and Alan stepped clear.

Before it could recover, the big man turned back, hammer raised, and charged. The Raptor growled, swinging to meet him, but the slick stone slipped beneath its claws. Alan raised *kanker* high as the creature struggled for balance, and brought it down on the Raptor's skull with a crunch.

Black blood splattered the bricks as the beast collapsed beneath the blow and started to thrash. Alan retreated out of range as the wicked claws tore blindly at empty air.

Inken sucked in a breath and joined him as another Raptor hauled itself into view. Caelin was back on his feet too, standing on Alan's other side. Together they attacked, weapons slicing for the creature's stomach. It scrambled to face them, its claws flicking out to turn aside Inken's blade. Its other talon swept past Alan's guard and sliced through his jacket.

Alan staggered backwards but Caelin leapt in, dancing

past its claws to bring his sword down on its neck. The blade cut deep and the Raptor roared, turning to crush the foe that dared to harm it. As it turned, Inken darted in and drove her sword down into the same place Caelin had struck. It roared again and spun, but she was already retreating out of range.

A final blow from Caelin finished the creature.

As it collapsed, Alan stepped up and crushed its skull with his hammer. Looking around, he swore softly under his breath.

Inken followed his gaze and swallowed hard. The beasts swarmed across the wall, leaping from the crenulations to swamp the defenders. The climb did nothing to slow them, and only the pockets of men around the dragons were holding their own. But one of the golden creatures had already fallen, brought down by a mass of black-clawed beasts. The others fought on, their massive claws and teeth smashing the creatures from the wall.

Even so, the odds were quickly turning against the defenders as the flood of dark beasts continued unabated. In places their people were in open retreat. They fled down the staircases, their exposed backs easy pickings for the beasts above.

"The wall is lost," Caelin roared. "We have to retreat," a trumpet sounded with his words, the long, drawn out note of defeat. It was the first time Inken had heard the call, but she knew its meaning well enough. May had echoed Caelin's thoughts and sounded the retreat.

Inken looked at the wide open space between them and the next wall. It was a long way. How long would the gates stay open for them? Could they make it?

A growl came from behind her and she swung around. New creatures were pulling themselves onto the battlements, catching up with the vanguard of Raptors that had led the charge. Two crept towards them now. The first wore the black fur coat of a feline, its bright yellow eyes staring at them with hunger. The other was a lizard, its grey scales gleaming in the sun. It scrambled on all fours towards them, razor sharp rows of spines rippling along its back. The beasts growled, jaws opening to show rows of dagger-like teeth.

Inken raised her sabre, prepared to throw herself at the creatures, but Alan stepped between them.

"Go," he said calmly as he faced the beasts.

"*What?*" Inken yelled over the screams of the dying.

"Go, both of you," Alan spoke without turning, his eyes locked on the dark creatures. "I won't make the gates, but you two can," he risked a glance back. "Go, *live!* I never intended to leave this wall. I will not show these creatures my back. We part ways here, my friends."

Inken opened her mouth but could not find the words. Tears burned in her eyes as the weight of his decision fell on her shoulders. She could not let him do this, could not let him sacrifice himself for them.

"You don't have to do this!" a vice had closed around her chest but she managed to choke out the words.

Alan only smiled and turned away. "Go now, missy. *Kanker* and I have one last battle to fight, but you must live. I don't want to see you on the other side, not for a long time. *So go!*" he roared the last words as he charged, hammer raised high as the beasts leapt to meet him.

"Farewell, my friend," Caelin murmured.

"Farewell," tears streamed down Inken's face as Caelin grabbed her by the arm.

Together they turned and ran for the stairs.

CHAPTER 16

Caelin sat at the table, staring at his hands, his thoughts adrift on an ocean of sorrow. Another friend lost, another soul sacrificed so the rest of them might live. He could not stop the images from sweeping through his mind: Alastair lying on the beach, helpless beneath the sword of Balistor, Michael in Sitton, his eyes wide as the demon's *Soul Blade* took him in the chest. And now Alan, his life given to hold back the tide of Archon's creatures.

They had barely made it behind the second wall before the gates had swung closed. Inken and himself had been among the last of the defenders to reach safety, fending off a handful of creatures that had chased them across the killing field. The beasts had only turned back when they'd come within range of the defenders' arrows, allowing Inken and Caelin to turn and sprint the last fifty yards to safety.

There the men and women of Fort Fall had waited, breath held, and watched as the last pockets of defenders on the outer wall fell one by one. His heart twisted as he watched again the big man fighting alongside those others who had refused to retreat. Alan had mustered the last of the defenders around him, and together they had formed an island amidst the ocean of darkness.

They had fought longer than anyone could have imagined, dozens of the creatures falling beneath their blades. But there was no resisting the savagery of the beasts, and one by one the defenders had fallen. Alan had been the last, his hammer still raised in defiance as he was finally overwhelmed.

The council room was silent, empty but for May and the rest of their company. Their losses on the outer wall had been horrific and May's surviving officers were needed to command the defences in her absence. Their only relief had been the arrival of the Trolan forces yesterday evening. Their fresh soldiers had taken over the frontline defences, allowing the defenders a welcome respite.

Even so, morale was low. Yesterday Archon had shown them just how weak they truly were. In a single attack his beasts had swept them from the outer wall, and not dragon or sword or arrow had been able to halt their advance.

The silence stretched out, each of them sitting with heads bowed in respect for the ancient warrior and those others who had fallen. But Caelin knew they could not afford to brood long. The hopes of the living still rested on their shoulders. He did not intend to let them down.

"We need the *Soul Blades*," his voice cut through the silence, firm, desperate.

May nodded from beside him, lifting her chin from her hands. She had been unusually despondent, her sorrow clear for the men she had been forced to sacrifice, but she stood now and walked around the table.

"After Gabriel's discovery, I had the Magickers choose amongst themselves who would be best to wield Jurrien's blade," her eyes lingered on Gabriel, who had finally been freed after the battle. May had still argued against it, but there was no denying they needed every fighter they could get now.

"Have they chosen?" Eric spoke up.

"It seems so," May moved across to the door and leaned out.

A moment later a man appeared. He nodded as he entered, moving around the table to take an empty seat. He wore the blue robes of a Sky priest and his black hair was cropped short in the style of the army. Together they marked him as a battle Magicker, and the scars on his face suggested he was one of some experience.

His green eyes surveyed the table, lingering on each of them. "My name is Sylvander," he spoke in a soft, slippery voice. "I am a Sky Magicker, similar to yourself, Eric, but with only the power to control lightning. I hope I prove worthy of the challenge posed by the Storm God's magic."

Caelin's eyes slid to where the *Soul Blade* rested in the centre of the table. He had been trying to ignore its dark presence, but now the time had come to test its power. The dark blue glow shone across their faces, flickering in the eyes of his friends. Their fear hovered in the air, seeming to have a presence all of its own. The danger they faced was undeniable, but so was the fact they needed the power in that blade.

"Are you sure?" Enala asked. "You saw what happened to Gabriel. You know what happened to me. Are you sure you will be able to control it?"

A smile played across the man's face. "Reasonably confident. I grew up with this power. The Sky is a part of me, a part of my blood. It is as familiar to me as the back of my hand. The risk is low, for myself at least."

Caelin glanced at his hands and raised an eyebrow. "I hope you spend as much time practicing at magic as you apparently do studying your hands."

Sylvander chuckled and ran a hand through his hair. "A figure of speech, sergeant. Believe me when I say it was a unanimous decision amongst the Magickers to choose me."

"Very well then," May spoke with quiet authority, cutting through their hesitation. "Do it."

Sylvander nodded and reached across the table. His hand wrapped around the hilt of the *Soul Blade* and lifted it from the table. Light flashed from the black steel, glinting from the man's emerald eyes. Tension spread through the room. Caelin could almost taste the throb of power on the air.

The Magicker's eyes widened and his forehead wrinkled with concentration. Caelin gritted his teeth, holding his breath as he watched the battle playing out within the man. They needed this, needed all three God powers if they were to have a hope of victory.

Long minutes stretched out, the tension building within the council room as the lines on Sylvander's face deepened. He stood taut as wire, jaw clenched, veins bulging on his arm as the glow of the *Soul Blade* shone in his eyes.

Caelin jumped as the Magicker released his breath. Grinning, Sylvander looked around the room, and opened his mouth to speak.

But whatever he had been about to say never made it out of his mouth. A sudden crash shook the room and lightning exploded from the Magicker's chest. Blue light lit the room, blinding them all. The stench of smoke and burning flesh quickly followed, catching in Caelin's throat as he breathed.

Lightning danced around the room, narrowly missing them before dying to nothing, and Caelin silently gave thanks to Eric's magic, guessing the boy had protected them. Another boom shook the air, and then silence fell.

Ears ringing and half-blind, Caelin stumbled to his feet. He staggered across, desperate to see what had become of Sylvander.

He choked as he reached the spot where he'd last seen the Magicker. Acrid smoke clung to his nostrils and his stomach lurched. Where Sylvander had stood seconds before, only a pile of ash remained. The *Soul Blade* lay amidst the remains, its light dimmed back to a faint blue glow.

Gasping for breath, he turned away.

"What happened?" he croaked.

And then everything went black.

"WHAT HAPPENED?" Eric heard Caelin speak over the ringing in his ears.

He blinked, trying to find Caelin through the stars dancing in his eyes. The room slowly came into focus, but something about it did not make sense. Eric closed his eyes again, willing his vision to clear, then looked around the table at his comrades.

Fear touched him as he realised why they had not replied. Caelin stood where Sylvander had disappeared, staring across the table, his mouth open as though to speak. But he did not move, did not so much as twitch.

Eric glanced across at Inken and May and found them still sitting in place, their faces twisted in fear, frozen in place by some dark spell.

Then Enala moved, turning to stare at Eric. Her face was pale and her hands clutched the oilskin wrapped around her own *Soul Blade* in a vice-like grip.

"What's happening?" she whispered.

Gabriel reached out and grasped her shoulder, shaking his head, his mouth wide with stark terror.

"I thought we should finally speak. In person," a voice spoke from behind them.

Eric spun, staring as a man stepped through the doorway.

He moved without sound, his black boots touching down without so much as a thud on the stone floor. A cloak of grey and orange feathers hung about his shoulders, the orange shimmering in the smoky air, so that it almost seemed the man were aflame. He wore a white doublet beneath the feathers, the pale skin of his hands appearing almost to fuse with the cloth.

His face was absent of any discernible wrinkle or imperfection, and there was an ageless way in which his eyes looked on them, as though he had lived a thousand years and more. He carried no weapon, but Eric could feel the power radiating through the room and knew this was no mortal man.

The man's dark blue eyes surveyed them each in turn, ignoring their frozen comrades. A warning screamed in Eric's head as the man's eyes reached him and he leapt to his feet, reaching for the Sword of Light. The man only waved, and Eric found his hand frozen, his fingers still an inch from the Sword's pommel. No matter how he strained, he could not reach the weapon.

"Come, come. Sit, let us talk!" he waved again and an invisible force pushed Eric back into his chair.

Looking around he saw the fear on Enala and Gabriel's faces as they strained against the same force. They looked up at the man, the devil that had strode unopposed into the depths of their fortress. Fear swamped Eric's every thought as he reached for his power and found nothing but a wall of darkness. With horror he realised they were helpless before this man's might, and knew beyond doubt who stood before them.

Archon had come.

The man laughed. "Such a quick mind, Eric," Archon's voice was soft but clear, without hint of emotion.

Eric opened his mouth, but only a low whine came out.

Fear had frozen his tongue, his wit, his magic. He could not find the courage to think.

"*You!*" Gabriel gave a strangled cry.

"Hello again, Gabriel," the man smiled. "I am pleased to see you here. You have done well, my son. Exceeded all my expectations."

"You are Archon," Enala interrupted and Eric felt a surge of pride for his sister. "You murdered my parents," hate twisted Enala's face and he could see her straining against whatever force constrained them.

Swallowing, Eric searched for his own courage, trying to reason away his fear. Surely Archon had not come to kill them – else they would already be dead. He shuddered at the man's power, to have walked alone through all their forces to come so casually to this room.

Archon moved to stand over Enala. He reached down and brushed the strand of copper hair from her face, a faint smile on his lips.

"Oh my dear, Enala, how the world has hurt you."

Enala flinched back from his touch, a shiver running through her. "*No!*" her shriek was pure desperation, a helpless cry against the dark creature standing in their midst.

"I am sorry," Archon moved away. "Sorry you have all had to suffer so," he approached Eric, his power overwhelming, though he was not a large man. "That you have had to run and flee amongst these weak minded fools," he cast a hand at their frozen companions.

"Why are you here?" Eric somehow found the strength to speak, grating the question through clenched teeth. "It was you who made us suffer."

Archon only smiled. "It was the Gods who made you suffer, sweet child. They are the source of all our suffering. They are the reason my people cower in the desert, their children dying at the breast for want of sustenance. Since the birth of the Gods, the so-called Three Nations have cowered beneath their yoke, bowing to the power they created. Only I dared rebel, to speak out against their tyranny."

"You slaughtered thousands of our people!" Enala cursed him.

Eric's heart raced as he strained to break the force holding him. He reached again for his magic but found only darkness, an all-consuming fog lying between himself and his power.

Archon bowed his head, but he wore a smile on his lips. "They left me no choice. I wanted only to see the Gods fall; to free us all from their power. But your people stood against me, time and time again."

"Why?" Eric looked up at the fire in Gabriel's voice. "Why have you haunted me? What do you *want?*"

Eric shivered at the truth behind the words, as he realised it had not been a demon haunting Gabriel, but Archon himself. He had been with them from the start, twisting the strings of their fates to his own desire.

Archon's eyes softened as they looked on the blacksmith. "Gabriel, my child. I have only ever tried to help you, to free you from the bounds of your mortality. It saddens me so, to watch my own blood waft through life without magic, without power."

The blood in Eric's veins froze at Archon's words. *His blood?*

"*I am not your child!*" Gabriel growled, the veins bulging on his forehead.

Archon laughed. "Do you not feel blessed? To know the blood of my family courses through your veins? How else could you have survived my *Soul Blade*?" he waved a hand at the pile of ash that had been Sylvander.

"Jurrien protected me," Gabriel snapped back, a snarl on his lips.

"Of course, of course," Archon waved a hand. "The Storm God saved you from his God magic. But *that*," he pointed. "That is what happens when one without my blood attempts to use my *Soul Blades*," Eric shuddered as the man's laughter swept the room.

Then his stomach twisted with nausea at another thought. "Enala used the *Soul Blade*," he whispered.

Archon grinned, leaning down to run a hand through her hair. "She did," he smiled, stroking her cheek as she struggled to free herself from his touch. "My sweet daughter, so strong, so beautiful."

A primal growl rose from the depths of Enala's throat. Archon chuckled as he straightened. "And Eric, my son, your strength has surpassed every challenge I placed before you."

"*Why?*" Eric hissed through bared teeth. "*How?*"

Archon sighed. "The Gods would not have told you; they have never been good at truth. They would not have wished for you to know it was my brother, Artemis, who first knelt before them. For his fealty, they named him as the Trolan king."

Eric shuddered as Archon continued. "For the longest time I hated them, those descendants of my blood who stood against me. When I rose to power I sent out my creatures to hunt them down and their line was all but destroyed. Only Thomas and his sister Aria survived."

"And they did all in their power to destroy you," Enala grated.

"Did they?" Archon's cold laughter filled the room. "It was not enough. Thomas' line fell to my magic or turned to my side."

"But Aria's children survived," Eric countered.

"Ay. She and her descendants were clever, always a step ahead of my hunters. Whenever I thought the line had been snuffed out, a new branch sprang up. Gabriel, for instance, is a rather distant cousin of a cousin to you," Archon sighed. "Eventually I was forced to settle on a new plan – to destroy the Gods and take their power, ensuring your line's survival no longer mattered when I rose again."

"Then why did you haunt me?" Gabriel growled.

"Because as my plan changed, I saw an opportunity. I have no wish to rule your Three Nations alone, children. With the Gods destroyed, I need faithful souls to rule in their stead. And who better than my own blood?"

Eric shook with anger, with fear; but as he looked up into the blue eyes of Archon, the same eyes he shared with his sister, he found his courage. "Why do you hate them so?" he hissed, refusing to cower before the man's icy stare. "What could they have done to you, what could have been so awful to feed your hate for so many centuries?"

Archon stared back and for a second Eric thought he saw a trace of humanity in those empty eyes. "They took everything from me."

At the words, Archon raised his hand and black light flashed across the room.

Before Eric could so much as cry out, the world turned to black.

CHAPTER 17

E nala blinked as her vision returned and she found
herself standing atop a great canyon. Sheer granite
walls stretched down to a winding river far below,
while behind her the white peaks of snow-capped mountains
stretched up into the sky. A cold wind blew across her neck
and swept down into the ravine, bending the long grass on
the plains beside the river. The rumble of tumbling water
came from a nearby waterfall, the water racing over the edge
to fall to the stones far below.

Then the first echo of thumping boots carried to her ears
and she turned to look down. Men were marching around
the bend in the canyon, heading upstream away from her.
The blue of their cloaks marked them as Trolans, but there
were far, far more here than the host that had joined them at
Fort Fall.

Stumbling backwards, Enala searched the clifftops for her
friends, but found herself alone. She bit back a scream as the
world suddenly jolted and she was drawn backwards. For a
second she watched the ground shift beneath her feet, and

then with a thrill of fear she remembered the yawning drop behind her.

Diving to the ground, Enala threw herself at a nearby boulder, scrambling for purchase. But her hands sank through the rock as though it were empty air and then she was out over the edge, the five hundred foot drop stretching out beneath her.

Yet somehow she did not fall. Enala stared down at the canyon as she drifted in the open air. Picking up speed, she found herself racing towards the distant head of the army. Straining her eyes, Enala stared at the men as she soared over the never-ending mass of humanity. The canyon twisted and turned, the terrain below shifting from open grass, to swamp, to scattered fields of boulders and back. It made no difference to the soldiers. They marched on, eyes fixed on the distant peaks rising to the east.

Finally the canyon floor rose sharply towards a narrow pass between the cliffs. There, the green cloaked army of the Lonians waited, and she knew where she was.

And when.

Swallowing, Enala watched as the ancient army of Trola charged up the hill towards the Lonians. Somehow, she now found herself watching the Great Wars of a thousand years before, in the time just before the ancient priests of Lonia and Trola had joined their magic and given birth to the Gods.

The clash of steel carried up to her as the two ancient forces met, the roar of their voices drowning out the screams of the dying. The Lonians buckled before the ferocity of the Trolan charge, their line bending back into the narrow pass. Beyond, Enala saw thousands upon thousands of Lonian men waiting to join the battle.

Chaos enveloped the mountain pass as Magickers from both sides joined the fray. Enala shuddered as waves of fire tore through the helpless ranks of soldiers below. Caverns ripped through the earth, swallowing hundreds into the dark depths below, and lightning rained down from the blackened sky.

The destruction was beyond all imagining.

Yet Enala knew the worst was still to come. This could only be the final, catastrophic battle, when the best and brightest souls of the two nations had been lost to a great conflagration, to wild magic gone horribly wrong.

Slowly, inexorably, the Trolans pushed the Lonians back, until their blue cloaks filled the mountain pass. But even as they fell the Lonians refused to yield, stabbing out at their enemy's legs even as their lifeblood fled them. Enala could feel the hate radiating up from the soldiers, fed by the ancient enmity between the two nations.

Then she felt it, the pulse of a magic far stronger than anything she had sensed so far. She turned and saw the green cloaks of the Lonian Magickers on the ridge above the pass. Light shone out around them, blue and green hues mixing to form a sickly yellow light.

The Trolan Magickers saw it too, for she felt the throb of their magic rising in response. A brilliant white rose from their ranks, spreading out to envelop their army. A trickle of horror touched her as she saw darkness mixing with the light and realised the Trolan's had gone beyond the three elements. They were using dark magic now, such was their desperation to halt the Lonian attack.

The opposing magics stretched across the sky, tongues of power flicking out to clash with one another. Thunder roared within the canyon, echoing off the narrow walls, but this time there was no lightning. A grumbling groan came from all around, rising up from the pits of the earth itself.

Still the Magickers kept on, unrelenting. From her vantage point above, Enala watched as they began to collapse, blood gushing from their mouths and ears. Yet the magic continued unabated, thrashing in the sky overhead. Bolts of pure energy raced out, disintegrating rock and wood and flesh alike.

Then the groans coming from the earth rose to a shriek, and the sheer walls of the canyon tore loose of their bounds. The ground shook, sending the men of both armies to their knees. Terrified eyes looked upwards as they realised the doom approaching them. With another roar, the granite cliffs of the canyon began to close.

Panic spread through the armies below. Enala looked to the Magickers, unable to believe they would sacrifice their own army to defeat the other. But she saw then it was too late, that the Magickers had already fallen. Their broken bodies writhed on the ground, caught in the last throes of death.

This was not by design. This was wild magic, its uncontrollable intent on only one thing.

Death.

Enala wanted to look away, to close her ears to the screams below. But whatever spell Archon had cast would not allow it, and she watched the horror unfold below, her stomach twisting in knots as men raced to escape the death grinding towards them. Some leapt for the cliffs, but they stood no hope of scaling that five hundred foot climb. Even the most skilled of climbers would struggle to reach the top in an hour.

These men only had minutes.

Tears rushed down Enala's face as she watched on in terror. This was far worse than anything she had ever seen, had ever imagined.

Others were fleeing down the valley, down the ever narrowing gap between the canyon walls. They would never make it though. The valley had been some twenty miles long – only the rear guard stood a chance of escape.

The last of the men below simply sat, the blue and green of their cloaks mixing, a final show of peace before the inevitable. Anguish twisted their faces as they hugged men they had tried to slaughter moments before, the truth of their senseless war laid bare. Their hate had driven them to this, driven them to this doom.

A strangled moan rose in Enala's throat as she finally lost sight of the men below, as the ravine snapped shut.

Then there was only silence.

The image faded then, and Enala found herself instead in a tiny room. Three priests sat in the centre, their robes representing each of the three elements of Magic. The Light, the Earth, the Sky.

A tingle of recognition raced up Enala's spine. She had read of this fateful meeting long ago, the meeting where the head priests of the three orders had come together and resolved to end the slaughter between their nations. The cost of the wild magic had been beyond anything ever seen before. An entire generation had been wiped from the world, and they were determined to ensure their people never suffered such a fate again.

Leaning closer, Enala listened to their words.

"It has never been done," an old man in blue robes whispered. "Never been attempted. Even with all of our orders, would such a feat even be possible?"

"I am happy to listen to other suggestions," the man in white snapped back. He looked around at the other two but found only silence. Closing his eyes, he ran a hand across his face. Stress lined his skin, seeming to age him twenty years. "We must be reined in – there is no other way. Our people are not worthy of the gift of magic."

The woman in green nodded, the weariness showing on

her face. "We know; there is no argument of that. But how can we make the spirits a reality? There is no substance to them, no power. What can we do, trap them in an object? That would only serve to place even greater power in the hands of men."

The man in white rubbed his eyes. "Of course not," he shook his head. "The spirits possess thought, have purpose. We know that – our orders have studied their presence for centuries. They must have autonomy, the ability to use their power as they see fit. When we bring them forth, they must take human form. They will be our rulers, our Gods."

"They are already Gods," the old man in blue snapped. "Whether the people recognise them or not. They govern the rules of magic – their power is unlimited."

"And yet their influence is limited to the spirit realm," the woman replied. "That must change."

"How?" the old man growled.

"Sacrifice," the others replied in unison.

Enala's heart gave a painful lurch as the three priests faded away. Within seconds a great hall of people had replaced them, but questions still whirred through her mind.

Gods, what did they do?

She had never heard of the Gods' birth involving sacrifice. Was that how the priests had done the impossible? By slaughtering innocent people?

Enala floated through the throngs of people packing the hall, unable to control her path. Finally she came to a halt in the centre of the hall where a ring of priests stood in a circle. The blue, green and white of their robes told her all three orders were present, united in this great task. Each member held their hands raised and their eyes were closed. Magic throbbed through the room, stirring in Enala's chest as the priests sought their power.

"It is time," the voice of the woman from the secret

meeting rose above the whispers. "You who have volunteered, who have chosen, step into the circle."

Enala's gut churned as men and women threaded between the priests to enter the ring. There were dozens of them; people of all age and size and class. Men in the tattered rags of the poor stood alongside the rich garments of the nobility, and white bearded men held the hands of young women, offering their silent support. Enala's heart went out for their quiet bravery – that these people were willing to give their lives to cease the wars that had torn their world apart.

As the last of the volunteers stepped into the circle, Enala sensed the ebb of magic begin to grow. The priests' voices rose in a slow chant, their words curling through the crowd like a breath of smoke. The language was unrecognisable, but the power in each syllable was could not be mistaken. The hall rang with magic, its throb beating across Enala's mind like a drum.

A glow emerged then from the hands of each priest, stretching up to engulf the volunteers in a dome of pure magic. The blue, green and white of the elements twisted and turned, absent of darkness, shining with the purity of natural magic. The light bathed the volunteers, illuminating their fear, their hope, their sacrifice.

Then the chanting of the priests ceased, and the glow of magic faded away.

A hush fell over the hall, as those who had gathered held their breaths and waited. Enala waited with them, eyes fixed on the circle. Had the priests' magic failed? Each of the volunteers still stood, looking from one to another in confusion.

Whispers grew, spreading through the crowd like fire.

Then a man stepped forward from the volunteers, the others moving aside to let him pass. Silence fell instantly as every soul present turned to stare at the man.

Except he was no man. Enala would never mistake that face, those wild, electric blue eyes.

This was Jurrien, the Storm God of Lonia.

As one, the ring of priests fell to their knees. The crowd quickly followed, bowing in a wave beneath the eyes of the God. His gaze swept the room, the piercing blue eyes seeming to stare into the soul of every man and woman present.

"I am Jurrien, master of the Sky," he spoke at last. His tone was soft, yet his voice boomed across the hall.

The old man from the secret meeting rose, his blue robes rustling as he stood. "Greetings, Jurrien. Welcome to our world."

Jurrien gave a slow, sad smile, but said nothing. Instead, he turned to watch the other volunteers, and waited.

Enala swallowed, the breath catching in her throat. So this was how the Gods had been born, why they could not release Antonia or Jurrien from the *Soul Blades*. They had been freed from the spirit realm only by the courage of these volunteers – these brave souls who had sacrificed their bodies so that the Gods might be made flesh.

Stomach clenched, Enala turned to watch the remaining volunteers.

As she turned, a man stepped forth. His hair was long and grey, his eyes turning white as he walked – though it was clear he was not blind. Light shone from his skin, his eyes, his very being. His arms were thick with muscle, though he was clearly well into his fifties. His bare feet slapped on the smooth wooden floor as he joined Jurrien.

The hush embracing the room, if possible, gathered strength.

Enala stared at the man she did not recognise, though she knew his name long before he spoke.

"I am Darius, master of the Light," the God rumbled, his voice filled with power.

Enala stared at the man, at the God who had vanished long before her birth. She looked into the white glow of his eyes, searching there for some hint of the betrayal to come. She wanted desperately to scream, to demand the truth from him.

He will abandon you! She yelled to the silent crowd, but the words did not come out.

Smiling, Darius turned as well to the gathered volunteers, and waited.

Swallowing her anger, Enala turned from the God of Light and scanned the crowd of volunteers, seeking out the familiar face of Antonia. But she could see no children amongst them, no likeness to the young Goddess. The silence stretched out, the crowd waiting for the emergence of the third God.

"No, child, get back here!" a woman's sudden shout shattered the quiet.

Enala spun, staring as a young girl weaved through the crowd. Men and women turned to watch her, mouths open in astonishment. Her lime green dress fluttered as she ran, the silk slipping through her mother's fingers, the woman just a step behind her. Enala's heart went out to the woman as she recognised the desperation in her eyes.

As the girl reached the circle of priests she paused, turning back to her mother. "It's okay, Mum. Everything is going to be okay. She is with me, she will always be with me," she flashed a final smile, and then she was through the ring of priests, and her mother was screaming, fighting against the arms reaching out to stop her.

The girl strode two steps into the circle and froze. A ring of green light lit the air, drifting down to wrap around her fragile body. Sadness tightened in Enala's chest as she watched the transformation, watched as the girl's eyes changed, the innocent green giving way to the violet wisdom of the Goddess.

The mother's screams faded as the woman sank to her knees, face in her hands. Tears streamed from her eyes and she reached out one trembling arm for her daughter. But she was already gone.

As the light died away the girl turned back to the crowd. Her eyes glowed with violet power, the change unmistakable. Those eerie eyes surveyed the crowd, a bewildering contrast to the youthful body she had taken.

The youthful body she had stolen.

"I am Antonia, Goddess of the Earth."

The silence in the hall was palpable. The other volunteers retreated back into the crowd, leaving only the three Gods in the centre of the hall. Enala could only stare, breath held, sure there was more to come.

She did not have to wait long.

A creak came from the back of the hall as the outer doors opened. Two boys slipped inside, their eyes wide, desperately seeking out something or someone. They made their way closer, moving amidst the kneeling crowd, their eyes drawn inexorably towards the circle of priests.

As they reached the circle, the voice of one rang out in recognition.

"Father!" the boy pushed his way through the circle and ran to Darius. "Father, what have you *done?*"

The other boy joined him and the two of them stood alone amidst the priests, staring up at the man who had been their father. Yet whoever that man had been, it was not their father who looked back now.

Sadness swept across the face of Darius as he looked at the boys. "I am sorry, children. Your father... he loved you very much," he crouched then, staring into the eyes of each of them. "He has made a great sacrifice, but I swear to you, his sacrifice will not be in vain."

Tears appeared in the eyes of the boy who had not yet spoken. "Who are you? Where is Father?"

Darius reached out and gripped the child's arm. "He is still here, child. For a time at least. He wishes more than anything he could stay with you, but he says this was something he had to do. To make the world a better place for you."

The boy's head bowed and he started to sob. The sound rang loudly in the wooden hall, even as the crowd watched on in silence.

"*No!*" Enala turned as the other boy screamed. "*You are not him!*" he growled. "You will never be him!"

Darius tried to reach for the boy, but he flinched back out of reach. "You are no God," his words curled through the hall. "You are a demon, a darkness summoned here to destroy us!"

"No, child. I am the spirit of the Light. I am Darius," Darius offered his hand again, seeking peace.

"*No!*" before anyone could stop him, the child turned and fled the hall, his angry screams cut short as the doors slammed behind him.

Enala shuddered as the scene faded away, recognition screaming in her mind. She knew the boy, knew his voice, his face.

The boy was Archon.

ERIC SUCKED in a breath as he found himself back in the council room in Fort Fall. He stared around the room, his eyes wide, his heart still racing with the terrors of the vision.

He saw fear and shock in the eyes of Gabriel and his sister, and knew they had witnessed the same thing.

The Great War, the slaughter, the birth of the Gods.

And the boy.

Archon.

He turned to stare at the man. His presence cast a darkness across the room, but he recognised now the pain at its core, the pain of loss.

"It was you," he whispered.

Archon nodded. "Now you see why I hate them, why I have always hated them. They are nothing more than the demons you so despise."

"They saved us," Eric replied. "They pulled us from the wreckage our people had created, stopped the slaughter."

"And replaced it with *what?* With nations cowering beneath their thumb, ruled by puppet kings such as my brother to fool the people into thinking they still control their destiny?"

"What was the alternative?" Gabriel looked into Archon's dark eyes. "You? What have you ever done for the people?"

Archon stared back. "I have given *my* people hope, though they were rejected by your *wondrous* Gods," his arm swept out to the north. "They have united beneath me, for my promise of freedom from the wasteland. They gladly give their lives so that I might throw down the tyrannous Gods and kings who put them there."

Eric shook his head, straining to break free of Archon's bonds. "Do you not see your hypocrisy? That you let your people to die for your cause, but refuse to accept your father's own sacrifice?"

Archon looked down at him, disappointment in his eyes. "I had hoped you would see reason, my child," he waved a hand. "You cannot win, cannot hope to defeat me. Even should you somehow bring all three God powers against me, you do not have the knowledge to win. I have spent five hundred years mastering my craft – you are nothing to me."

He sighed then, shaking his head. "I will give you three days to consider. After that, I shall take my armies and my magic, and grind this fortress to the ground. One way or another, the time of the Three Nations is over. Farewell, kinsmen," with a final wave he swept from the room, vanishing into the shadow of the corridor.

Eric breathed out a long sigh as he felt the darkness release him. Reaching up he pulled the Sword of Light free of its sheath, drawing comfort from the surge of white fire that swept through him. Slowly his fear subsided and he looked around the room.

"What do we do now?"

CHAPTER 18

Eric reached for his mug of ale and took another long gulp of the bitter drink. He shuddered at the taste – he preferred the spiced wine Michael had served so long ago in Lon – but right now he needed the vigour. A shadow clung to his spirit, the knowledge of events five hundred years in the past weighing him down.

He was the ancestor of Archon, the ancient enemy of the Gods, the man whose darkness had hung over the Three Nations for more than a century. And the Gods, the very entities the Three Nations had worshiped for five hundred years, were usurpers, thieves who had taken the lives of innocents to come into this world.

And now Archon was offering them salvation, offering to spare the lives of every man and woman in Fort Fall, if only they joined him.

The weight of responsibility was more than he could bear.

"You are not alone, Eric," Inken's hand settled on his and he looked up, dragging himself back from his waking nightmare.

They sat alone in their room, in the chairs before the fire. The hour was late, but Eric knew he would not sleep tonight; not after Archon's appearance. Terror clung to his soul – that their enemy could walk so easily amongst them, could destroy them any time he wished. Even after all the time he had spent with the Sword, after the hours he had practiced each day with its power, Archon had overwhelmed him without effort.

They were mere puppets before the man's power.

Even more than the revelations, it was the screams of the dying which haunted him. How many men and women of the Three Nations had already fallen? Hundreds? Thousands? What was the point of it all now, knowing they could not win? That Archon's magic was beyond any defence they could muster?

Eric shuddered, unable to find a reply to Inken's words. He looked at her, trying to summon a spark of hope, of defiance. But he could not find it. For the first time since Alastair's death, he could not see any hope of victory.

"It is in the past, Eric," Inken whispered. "You are nothing like him; none of you are. Your ancestors were heroes, men and women who refused to give up, whatever the odds. You are no different – you will find a way to save us all, Eric. I believe in you."

Eric nodded, his eyes starting to water. "We cannot join him, we can't…" he trailed off. "And yet, I don't see how we can defeat him, Inken. He walked past all our armies, past our Magickers and dragons and guards, into the centre of the greatest fortress in the Three Nations. And there was nothing we could do to stop him," he took a deep breath. "What if it's all for nothing? How can I ask more to give away their lives for a lost cause?"

Inken stood and moved across, lowering herself onto his lap. She reached out, trailing a hand through his hair. "No one can make this decision for you, Eric. But I have faith in you, in all of you. So did Antonia, and Jurrien, and Michael and Alastair."

Eric stared into her hazel eyes. "I just wish I knew *why*," he replied. "Why did they believe in me, after all I have done?"

"Because you are *good*, Eric. Because you are strong. Because despite all that has happened, you have never hesitated to do the right thing. To stand against the darkness."

Eric released a long breath and looked down into the fire. Inken's words drifted through his conscious and the weight on his shoulders lightened, if only a little.

But even so, indecision still gripped him. "Are we even fighting for the right side?" he asked. "You did not see it, see the pain on the woman's face. She was only a *child*, Inken. Why would Antonia have chosen her?"

To his surprise he saw tears in Inken's eyes. "I don't know," she looked away, her hand drifting to her stomach. "I cannot..." her voice broke as she trailed off.

A twisting ache spread through Eric's chest as he watched her. Reaching out, he grasped her wrist. "Inken..."

Inken shook her head. "I cannot imagine her agony, to lose her child. I do not know what I would do if ours..." her eyes widened and she bit off her last words.

Eric gaped, staring into the depths of her hazel eyes. The twisting in his chest tightened as his heart started to race. He opened his mouth, then closed it again, struggling for the words.

Inken grasped his hand, clutching it tight to her throat. "I'm sorry," she murmured, her voice breaking. "I wanted to tell you, I don't know why I didn't. It never felt right, not with everything... not with death hanging over our heads."

"Inken..." Eric murmured. He stared at her, a warmth rising in his throat. "Inken..." he leaned in and kissed her.

She kissed him back, her tongue finding his as they came together. The warmth of her hands slid across his skin, slipping beneath his shirt and pulling him tight against her. Blood thumped hard in his ears as they entwined, her fingers twisting in his hair, reaching for him. And then they were falling, falling, falling.

And the fur rug before the fire rose up to greet them.

ENALA LAY on her bed and stared up at the blank stone ceiling. The chill air nipped at her skin despite the fire burning in the heath, and she yearned to crawl beneath the covers. But she could not bring herself to move, could not break free of her silent reverie.

Images flashed through her mind: the terrified faces of those ancient soldiers as they faced certain death, the terror and panic on the face of the woman as she chased after her daughter, the hatred on the face of the boy who had become Archon.

It was all too much.

And over everything loomed the dark Magicker's threat. His unstoppable armies and magic seemed to hover overhead, poised to strike their final blow to the fortress.

It was up to her and Eric to stop him.

How? Closing her eyes, Enala sent the question out into the void, praying for an answer.

But there was only silence. Opening her eyes, she rolled onto her side and stared at the *Soul Blade* where it lay propped against the wall. The very sight of it sent a shiver down to her stomach. She could almost taste the darkness lurking within the thing, waiting to strike. Her stomach churned, seeing again the fate of Sylvander, watching as the magic of the *Soul Blade* burned him to ash.

I can only wield it because of him, a creeping horror grew within her as she thought of Archon's blood running in her veins.

She heard the door squeak and looked up to see Gabriel enter. They now shared the room with two beds, though this was the first night since Gabriel had been freed.

Their eyes caught from across the room.

"I still cannot believe it," Gabriel whispered, moving to sit on his bed. "How many cousins of cousins of cousins do you think we are to each other?"

Enala laughed, the thought a welcome distraction. "Too many to count, probably. I guess Aria's secret adoption policy worked better than she could ever have imagined. My family is apparently not as endangered as we'd thought," she reached out and squeezed his hand, drawing comfort from his presence.

Gabriel shook his head, his smile slowly fading. "Do you think we have a chance?"

Enala swallowed. "I don't know. If I can summon the magic of the *Soul Blade*, we'll have the power of the Earth and Light behind us… With the power of the other war Magickers, we might just manage to match him."

Gabriel stared at her. "But we won't have Jurrien's power."

"No," Enala sighed. "Not his God magic at least. Eric's magic does come from the Sky though. And as I said, there are other Magickers to lend us their strength."

"You remember what happened when Eric used his magic against the demon in Sitton. It was not enough," he swallowed. "But maybe with the other Magickers…"

"We can beat him," Enala said again, her voice growing stronger.

"Okay," Gabriel breathed. "But what of his army?

Without the Magickers, what chance do the soldiers stand if the beasts come again?"

"If we can find a way to hold back Archon's magic, I have every confidence the men and women of the Three Nations will find a way to stop his beasts," she paused, staring at Gabriel. "They did before, the last time. They stood together and held the walls against man and beast alike. It was only Archon's magic that defeated them in the end. We won't let that happened again."

Gabriel smiled. "I believe you," he squeezed her hand and she found herself smiling back.

Without thinking she reached out and brushed a strand of hair from his face. As her fingers touched his cheek she almost gasped and her heart began to pound. She lingered, watching as Gabriel's face softened, his eyes drifting closed. Then, before thought or reason could stop her, she leaned across and pressed her lips to his.

His eyes widened and for half a second she thought he would pull away. But then he was kissing her back, his hands in her hair, his tongue hard against hers, and it was all she could do not to lose herself in the moment.

When they finally pulled apart, Enala found herself panting. She stared into Gabriel's eyes and saw the fear there had faded, replaced by desire. She knew that same desperate longing burned in her eyes, but as he leaned in again she placed a finger on his lips to stop him.

"What? Don't tell me you've finally found something to live for?" she teased.

Warmth spread through her stomach at the fire in Gabriel's eyes. "I have never met anyone like you, Enala."

Enala smiled, feeling suddenly hot in the cool room. But still she hesitated, doubt lingering in her mind.

Reaching up, she stroked his hair. "It was not so long ago, was it?" she breathed, remembering the tale Gabriel had told her back in Lon. "Not so long since you lost her. I'm sorry…"

She looked away, suddenly regretting the kiss. It had only been a few months since Gabriel had been engaged to another woman – a woman who had died in the wreckage of Oaksville. After all that had happened, had he ever been able to process that loss?

And hell, we're related! Enala swore at herself.

Enala looked up as Gabriel's hand brushed her chin. "Yes, I loved her," he murmured, and she saw his sadness. "I miss her, miss my family. But…" he paused, looking down. "But they are part of my past. Archon wiped that past from me, back in the desert. It no longer seems a part of me. I have changed too much, faced so many things since that time. I am not the same man who worked in my father's forge," he stared at her, and Enala could not look away.

This time when he made to kiss her, she did not stop him.

THE FIRE WAS long dead when Gabriel finally slid from the bed, though the freezing air almost drove him back beneath the thick covers and the warm body waiting there. The first light of the morning had just begun to shine through the window, but he had lain awake for hours, staring into the sleeping face of the woman beside him. Her peaceful presence brought joy to his soul, but deep within, he knew it could not last.

There was a darkness inside him, even without the lingering touch of Archon's magic. One born in the ruin of Oaksville, one that drove him to anger, to hate.

He shivered as he slipped out the door, the morning air outside even cooler than inside the room. Regret twisted in his stomach as he closed the door behind him, but there was no going back now. He could not stay. Despite what Enala had said, they did not stand a chance against Archon. Not unless he acted.

Jurrien had told him to pick up the *Soul Blade* when they ran out of other options. It seemed that time had come.

Slipping through the silent corridors of the fortress, he made his way toward the council room. They had left the *Soul Blade* there, locked and guarded by two soldiers who stood outside. No one wanted to go near the thing after what had happened to Sylvander, even if they wrapped it in cloth first.

Gabriel was not sure what he would do about the guards yet, but he knew what he had to do now. Archon's vision had shown him the truth behind Jurrien's words, the truth the God had done his best to hide. There was only one way to free the Storm God: to sacrifice himself, and allow Jurrien's spirit to possess him.

Just as his ancestor had done all that time ago.

It did not take long to pass through the empty hallways. He encountered only a handful of soldiers along the way, those few who preferred an early breakfast before taking up their stations for the coming day. Not that there had been any attacks in the last two days. Archon had given them three days, and so far, he had kept his word. An uneasy peace hung over the fortress, the men making the most of the rest. They all knew it would be over soon enough.

At last the door loomed, as nondescript as any other he had passed on the way. It stood unguarded and open, and Gabriel's stomach twisted as he realised May must have ordered the *Soul Blade* moved after all. Even so, he pushed the door wider and moved inside.

"Good morning, Gabriel," Gabriel jumped as Eric spoke from the corner.

He spun, searching out the young Magicker. "What are you doing here?" he hissed.

Eric shrugged. "I couldn't sleep," he stood, moving across the room to the table. "Apparently, I'm going to be a father. The thought has my mind spinning."

Gabriel joined him and together they looked down at the *Soul Blade*. It still lay beside the table where it had fallen, untouched. Its faint blue glow filled the little room. Gabriel shuddered, remembering the last time he had touched it. Would he have the strength this time to hold back the magic, at least long enough to free the Storm God?

"What happened to the guards?" Gabriel asked absently.

"I sent them away," Eric spoke softly. "I thought I would wait for you. I had a feeling you would come."

Gabriel looked across in surprise. "How?"

Eric shrugged. "Intuition? Reason? I'm not sure. But I've seen the look in your eyes, the fear there whenever Archon is mentioned over the last two days," Gabriel looked away from the knowledge in Eric's eyes. "You fear you are like him, don't you?"

"Why else would he have chosen *me* to haunt?"

"Because you don't have magic," Eric whispered. "It makes you vulnerable. But in truth..." he shuddered. "In truth he has come to me too, in my dreams. I did not remember them, not until he walked into this room. You are not the only one he has haunted. You are not the only one who has darkness within them."

Gabriel saw the ghost in Eric's eyes and reached across to grasp his shoulder. "I forgive you, Eric," he felt a tremble of relief as he spoke the words, as he felt the hate lift from his soul.

Eric's eyes watered as he stared back. A single tear spilt down his cheek. "Thank you, Gabriel," he choked.

They stood there in silence then, staring at the *Soul Blade*.

"Now is not the time," Eric said at last.

Gabriel looked across at him. "What do you mean?"

Eric met his gaze. "Now is not the time," he repeated. "If you truly wish to do this, you have to say goodbye, Gabriel. You owe the others that much. Enala, Caelin, Inken, they love you – they deserve better," he breathed out. "Besides, if Jurrien is freed, Archon will know. He will know we have rejected his offer, and we will lose our last day of peace. Better to wait, if that is what you mean to do."

"When?" Gabriel croaked, holding back tears of his own.

"You will know, Gabriel. You will know."

CHAPTER 19

Caelin stood atop the rampart of the second wall and looked out at the enemy. They had unblocked the gates of the outer wall, burning the rubble and wooden doors to clear a path for their army. Now they lined the ramparts and packed the grounds at the foot of the wall, waiting just beyond the range of the defenders' arrows. He knew more would be waiting outside the gates, eager to join the fray when the assault began.

He glanced across at May, reading the fear on her pursed lips as she stared out at the challenge facing them. This wall was higher, thicker, stronger, and the defenders had rested for three days. Even so, their morale was low, their courage crumbling beneath the memory of the beasts.

"We'll hold them, May," he growled.

The woman looked up and forced a smile. "I know, Caelin, I know. I just hope Eric and the others can do their job."

Laughing, Caelin shook his head. "Let's let them worry about their job, and us worry about ours, Commander."

"Easier said than done," May muttered and then shook

her head. "No, you're right. There's only so much one woman can do."

"I'm not sure about that," Caelin turned as Inken walked up. Her eyes were alight with fire and he was surprised by the hope there. "We can certainly do more than these blokes here," she waved at Caelin and Gabriel.

Caelin chuckled. "What's your tally again, Inken?" his chest tightened at the question. The competition between himself and Alan to slay the most enemy had been just one of their many bets. He bowed his head, sending up thanks again for the big man's bravery.

"I don't feel the need to count," Inken smiled and winked. "I know your numbers could never come close to mine."

"How much does a demon count for?" May grinned as she joined their banter.

"Oh, I don't know, I'd say at least a hundred," Inken offered.

It was Gabriel's turn to laugh then. "Good, that catches me up somewhat then."

Caelin grinned, glad to see the life in the young man's eyes. It was the first time he'd truly seemed himself since their imprisonment beneath the citadel of Ardath. A desire rose within him to reach out and draw Gabriel into a bear hug, but he resisted.

"So it's settled then," Caelin turned to look out at the enemy. "It's a draw between us men and you women."

"Pfff," Inken stepped up beside him. "In your dreams, little man," with her last words, Caelin knew she missed Alan's presence as much as he did.

He reached out and squeezed her shoulder. They stood together and waited then, the heat of the morning warming them. The crash of waves came from the distance and the tang of salt hung heavy on the air. Caelin breathed it in, relishing in the freedom of life.

His gaze drifted along the wall to the centre where Eric and Enala stood. There they would make their final stand, backed by the combined might of the Magickers of the Three Nations. He wished with all his heart he could stand beside them, but he would only be a liability in that fight. He and Gabriel and Inken alike, though he did not know how they had convinced the other two to stand aside. If it had been his love waiting to face Archon…

He shook his head as horns rang out from the enemy camp. Releasing a breath he had not realised he'd been holding, Caelin glanced at his companions. Inken nodded back, already stringing her bow. Steel rasped on leather as May and Gabriel drew their swords. Caelin reached down and did the same, his eyes drifting out to watch the enemy come.

May's cry rang out as the enemy came within range, carrying down the wall as her officers repeated the call. The twang of bowstrings followed as the first volley took to the air, then the screams of the dying as the enemy wilted beneath the deadly rain. A second volley followed, and a third, and then the enemy was at the wall and there was no more time to keep count.

Beside him, Inken tossed aside her bow and drew her blade. Caelin edged closer to her, determined to keep his friends safe. Gabriel stood on her other side, and May to his right, but he still felt the gap amongst them. Alan's presence had been enormous and they would miss his steely courage in the coming fight.

The thump of wood on stone heralded the arrival of the enemy. Staring at the ladders, Caelin gripped his sword tight and sucked in a breath.

"Ready?" Inken asked.

Caelin nodded. "Let them come."

ENALA LOOKED down at the enemy, watching as volley after volley decimated their ranks. Yet their numbers seemed without end and they came on, determined to wipe the defenders from the wall. As they closed in, the enemy archers began to fire back, and black shafted bolts flashed up towards them.

Ducking beneath the crenulations, Enala glanced at Eric. He stood resolute beside her, a host of Magickers at his back. They came from every nation and discipline: The Sky Magickers of Lonia, the Earth Magickers of Plorsea, and the Light Magickers of Trola. They stood together atop the walls of Fort Fall, ready to give their lives to keep the darkness from their hearths.

Eric glanced at her. "Ready?"

Enala swallowed, looking down at the *Soul Blade* sheathed at her side. Dread curled up in her stomach and she had to will herself not to vomit. Her knees shook as raw terror robbed away her strength, but she nodded. "As ready as I'll ever be."

Closing her eyes, she reached down and drew the *Soul Blade* from its scabbard.

As her hands closed around the leather hilt a flash of green light lit her mind, burning its way up from the cold steel. Energy surged through her as a harsh glow threaded its way along her veins, twisting ever deeper. She gasped as pain burned her wrist, tearing at her concentration. Her eyes watered as the pressure within her built, but she bit back a second cry.

From deep within a flame rose, her power responding to the threat of the foreign power. Its red light flickered, and then a tower of fire rose, beating back the twisting vines spreading from the *Soul Blade*. The two powers twisted in her mind, thrashing against one another for supremacy.

Somehow, Enala sensed it was a battle her magic could not win, not without direction. Swallowing her fear, she reached out and grasped the flickering red flames and drew them to her. The magic fought against her touch, the flames turning to fangs that bit and tore at her soul, but still she held on, determined.

At last the red flames calmed, and with a rush of elation she twisted her power into lines of red and sent it out to wrap about the God magic.

The green light flashed again, igniting the deepest corners of her mind, but she did not flinch now. She held on as the God magic fought against its bindings and tore at her, desperate for freedom.

You can do it, Enala, from somewhere came her brother's voice, and biting her tongue, Enala drew her magic tighter. With one final jerk, the column of green collapsed in on itself, succumbing to the binds of her power.

Enala breathed out and opened her eyes, finding Eric's concerned face not three inches from her own.

She smiled. "I have it."

Eric nodded back. "Well done. Then let's go to work," he turned to face the ranks of enemy below.

Soldiers stood ahead of them, fending off those attackers who had already reached the battlements, but they parted now as Eric and Enala walked to the fore. The Magickers followed, flashes of their magic sizzling outward as they cleared the enemy from the ramparts.

As Eric reached the edge of the wall he reached up and drew the Sword of Light. White light washed over the wall as flames leapt along the length of the blade. Enala glanced down at her *Soul Blade*, staring with hate at its brilliant green. It felt corrupted, *wrong*. Even so, they needed it.

But even with the two God powers and all the Magickers aligned behind them, Enala doubted it would be enough. They still lacked the Storm God's magic, and Eric and herself could not come close to mastering the God powers they possessed. The Earth magic of the Goddess might be pumping through her body, but she had yet to truly wield it. She would need to rely on instinct and guess work in the coming battle. The thought did not fill her with confidence.

But still, they had to try. She glanced at the other Magickers, seeing the fear on their grim faces, and knew she could not back down. The odds they faced in the coming fight were far worse than hers. They had only their mortal magic to protect them.

Enala drew in a long breath of salty air, struggling to calm her racing mind. Together they were about to draw the wrath of Archon down upon them. God powers or no, it would be a miracle if any of them survived.

Below the enemy flooded across the killing ground between the walls, an endless black tide, fearless, unstoppable. Except they were about to stop it, to burn them all where they stood. Their angry voices rose up to wash over the defenders like thunder, but that would soon change.

Moving to stand close to Eric, Enala reached deep within and unshackled the power of the Earth. Light spread from the *Soul Blade*, its green washing out to mingle with the white of the Sword. The glow slowly brightened, flashing out to cast the soldiers below in eerie shadows. For the first time that day, the enemy hesitated, their charge faltering as they paused to look up.

But they were not without protection either. As with the beasts before, they were clothed in Archon's magic. She could sense it now, a darkness rising from them like a foul scent, shielding them from fire and magic alike. It rose up above them, mingling with the power of the Sword and the *Soul Blade*.

Thunder rolled across the Gap as the two forces came together, though the sky above remained clear. Enala gritted her teeth as she felt the force of darkness pushing back, driving off their power.

It's too strong, but even as Enala formed the thought, she sensed the building of power behind her as the other Magickers stepped up to join the fray. Light spread from their hands, red and white and blue and green shooting up to join the fray. Less than the God powers, but joined they still created a formidable force.

Flame flashed across the sky, followed by the rumble of thunder as lightning crackled. Enala gritted her teeth, driving the magic of the *Soul Blade* outwards, straining to unleash its power on the enemy below. Bit by bit, the darkness started to give way to the elemental power streaming from the wall.

A sudden *snap* reverberated through the air, followed by a whoosh as the dark magic flickered and went out. The combined magic of the Three Nations poured through into the void, streaming down towards the enemy below.

The roar of Archon's forces turned suddenly to screams as their magic erupted into life and chaos spread through their ranks. The flames came first, the white fire burning down to strike the massed ranks on the killing grounds, followed by the flash and crackle of lightning. Together they scorched all they touched.

Green light flashed again from the *Soul Blade* as its power rushed from Enala to join the fray. Hate curled around her soul as she watched the slaughter. These men had come here to kill them, to destroy her people and murder her friends. They had allied themselves to darkness – this was what they deserved. Their souls were not worthy of pity, of mercy.

The massacre spread through the enemy ranks, sweeping

them back from the wall. As one they turned and fled, desperate to retreat back to the protection of their master.

Enala would not allow it.

Raising the *Soul Blade*, Enala drew on its magic, rejoicing in the surge of power flooding her weary body. Its green light flashed out over the enemy, chasing them across the killing field.

A smile twisted Enala's lips as her spirit soared with the magic. Reaching out, she gripped the ground beneath their feet, the green light of the Earth seeping deep into the soil. Then, with casual ease, she hauled it back.

As one the enemy crumpled like leaves as the ground shifted beneath them, driving them to their knees. Terrified faces looked up at the wall, desperate for mercy, but they would find none there. The earth groaned and tore apart, swallowing pockets of men before they could so much as scream.

Looking down at the enemy, Enala began to laugh, taking joy from their terror. Magickers turned to stare at her, but she waved aside their concern. She breathed out, releasing her grip on the earth. As the shaking slowed the enemy climbed to their feet and fled towards the far off gate, desperate to escape her deadly power.

With a shake of her head, Enala waved the *Soul Blade* again.

A groan rose up from below as the ground before the outer gates exploded, hurling chunks of dirt and stone across the killing field. Vines twisted their way up into view, a great thicket of impassable thorns taking form in the instant between blinks. The snakelike vines whipped upwards, tearing into the enemy who still stood atop the ramparts of the outer wall. On the killing field the enemy drew to a halt, staring at the impassable barrier now blocking their path.

Then the thicket moved again, turning from the now

empty wall to the enemy below. Snakelike threads of green flashed out, snatching men from their feet and dragging them screaming into the impenetrable depths of the copse. Hundreds fell, torn to shreds before the might of the Earth, before the power in Enala's hands.

Turning away, Enala nodded to the other Magickers. "They're all yours," she smirked.

She moved away down the ramparts, thrilling in the pull of the power within her. Before she could take three steps a hand grabbed her by the shoulder and spun her. Growling, Enala swung the *Soul Blade*, the razor sharp steel striking for Eric's head. The Sword of Light rose up to block the blow and sparks of green and white scattered across the bricks.

Eric stepped back, his eyes wide with shock, his mouth agape. "Enala, what the *hell* was that?"

Enala stared back, the *Soul Blade* slipping from her fingers. It clattered to the stones, the green glow dying to a whisper. As she released it, the hate curling its way around her soul fell away and she gasped. The blood fled her face and she swayed, feeling suddenly faint. She wavered, and would have fallen had Eric not caught her.

"What… What have I done?" she whispered.

Eric shook his head. "It was necessary," he shook her, forcing her to look at him. "We said before this started we could show them no mercy, that we had to break their spirit. I'd say we've done that," he paused. "Except it was not you, was it?"

Enala shuddered. "No… yes… I'm not *sure!*" she closed her eyes. "I… I don't think I've ever felt hate like that, so intense, so powerful."

Eric's eyes flashed and he drew her into his arms. "You did well, Enala. It was the *Soul Blade*; it was whatever black magic Archon left embedded in it."

She nodded, feeling tears in her eyes and burying her

head in Eric's shoulder to hide them. "I don't know how much longer I can do this, Eric," she gasped, her words half-muffled. "How long I can keep fighting. It's too hard, too awful."

His arms squeezed her tight. "I know. Even the Sword has its own darkness. Each time I use it, it feels as though I lose a bit more of myself, like a bit more of me is burnt away. But we have to keep going, just a little bit longer."

Enala bit her tongue to keep herself from crying. Before she could find a reply, a scream from behind interrupted her thoughts. They spun together and saw the group of Magickers staggering backwards, their faces pale. One stumbled a step too far and tripped through the gap in the crenulations. He disappeared without so much as a scream.

"Pick up the *Soul Blade*," Eric hissed, moving past her, the Sword of Light crackling in his hands.

Enala swallowed. Steeling herself, she reached down and lifted the *Soul Blade*. Its power swept through her once more and the bitter bite of hatred returned. She struggled to push it down, holding the love for her brother and her friends close to her heart.

Taking a breath, she followed after Eric.

Below, the killing ground lay piled with the enemy dead, with the thousands who had fallen to their magic. Now the few survivors no longer fled, but were turning back to face them, their faces twisted with a wicked joy. Enala squinted her eyes, straining to see what was happening.

A dark light seeped through the thicket by the gate, spreading out to cover the last of the enemy force. Where it touched her vines they withered and died, whilst the ranks of enemy straightened, their burns and injuries fading to nothing.

The darkness spread across the plain and through it came Archon, his stride calm and measured, as though he did not walk through a field of his dead. The feathered cloak fluttered out around him, caught on the ocean winds, but he did not slow. His face registered no emotion, no hint of compassion for his fallen soldiers. His eyes stared straight ahead, fixed on the ramparts where Eric and Enala stood.

"What now?" Enala whispered.

"Now it ends," Eric growled, the veins of his wrist straining as he gripped the Sword of Light tighter.

Wind whipped around them and then Enala felt the familiar lifting sensation beneath her feet. She flashed Eric a grim smile and nodded. Together they lifted off the wall and dropped to the killing field below. Behind them the Magickers hesitated, looking from one to the other. But after a moment they followed, the Sky Magickers amongst them lifting the others and carrying them down.

Enala caught the eyes of the leaders and nodded, then returned her attention to Archon. A wave of relief swept through her; at least they would not be alone in this fight. The other Magickers had already helped to break Archon's magic once today. Perhaps they might stand a chance after all.

They came together in the centre of the field: Archon standing alone amidst the legion of his dead, Eric and Enala with all the might of the Three Nations behind them.

Archon wore a grim smile as his cold blue eyes surveyed them. "So, Enala," he rasped. "You have finally tasted the magic of the *Soul Blade*. How does it feel, to wield such power, to cast such destruction upon your enemies? Does it call to you?"

Enala swallowed and scowled back. She gripped the *Soul Blade* tighter, the truth of Archon's words clear on her face. "It doesn't matter – we have made our decision. We will never serve you."

Archon laughed. "If only life were so simple, my child.

My offer was only meant to lessen your suffering, to spare you the pain of what is to come," he spread his arms and Enala sensed the dark power crackling around them. "But make no mistake; you *will* serve me. Your refusal will not stop that," he took a step towards them and Enala could not help but shrink back.

But Eric stood strong. "You are wrong, Archon."

"Ah, young Eric, ever the optimist. But you do not see," Archon waved a hand and the very air around them darkened. "You never stood a chance in this fight, my child. You have only ever been able to delay the inevitable. But the end was never in question," his cold eyes locked them in his gaze. "I will break those feeble bodies of yours, shatter your souls. And then I will unleash the untamed God powers on each of you."

A chill swept through Enala's heart as Archon's words seeped in. Could that truly be his plan – to crush their resistance and then allow the God magic to take them? She shivered, remembering the helpless terror as the God power had taken control of her body. To suffer that fate for eternity…

Archon laughed. He waved at the dead around him. "In truth, I am impressed by your strength, your ruthlessness. You have made me proud," he smiled. "But no more. This ends today. I will see this fortress torn down, stone by stone, and the last resistance of your Three Nations ground to dust," with that Archon raised his fist.

Shadows swirled around his clenched hand, spreading outwards in a ball of all-consuming darkness.

Enala swallowed and gripped the *Soul Blade* hard in her fist. She glanced at Eric and nodded.

Eric nodded back. "Now or never?"

CHAPTER 20

Eric swallowed his fear and roared. The white-hot flames of the Sword of Light bathed his face as he pointed the blade. Light flashed and a rush of energy swept through him, leaving his every muscle quivering and his magic flickering with renewed strength.

Archon still stood in place with his arm raised, concentration etched across his ageless features. Eric stared at the gathering darkness, the very sight sending a shiver of fear right to his soul. They had to stop him, before he could unleash that power. A rush of magic came from beside him as Enala drew on the power of her *Soul Blade,* then from behind as the other Magickers gathered their strength.

Now or never, Eric repeated the words, and pointed the Sword.

White fire rushed from the blade and raced towards the dark Magicker. Enala's cry echoed his own, followed by the rush of Earth magic, and then there was only Archon, and the battle for survival.

Archon threw down his fist as the inferno reached him. With a *whoosh* the flames vanished into the gathered darkness. A second later the earth beneath him tore open, revealing a crevice leading down to the depths of hell itself.

Archon only smiled as he hung in the air, his head rolling on his shoulders as though to remove a crick in his neck. He drifted over the gap and dropped back to the earth.

Fear gripped Eric, but there was no time to retreat now. He reached again for the magic of the Sword, drawing on the power of the world around him, and hurled it at Archon. The lines connecting the world bent inwards before the white energy of the Sword and then its invisible force struck the dark Magicker, hurling him out over the gaping canyon.

For a second Archon's eyes widened, but he still did not fall. Instead he twisted in the air, a dark grin on his face, and threw out his hand. Eric's heart fell into his stomach as a wave of darkness swept towards him. Backing away, Eric summoned the white magic within and hurled it outwards. Pure energy crackled around him as the power of the Light rose up to meet the darkness.

A boom came as the two forces met, but within seconds the light was overwhelmed. The dark surged forwards and Eric barely managed to throw himself clear. He rolled across the hard ground, coming to a rest alongside a fallen body. Looking away from the burnt ruin of a man, Eric pulled himself to his feet, the Sword still clenched tight in his hand.

Archon stood calmly ten feet away, arms folded and a thin smile on his lips. Gritting his teeth, Eric fed his anger to the magic of the Sword, and charged. Flames crackled along the blade as he swung it at the dark Magicker, its white light casting them all in shadow.

With an almost sadistic slowness, Archon reached up and caught the Sword of Light with his empty hand. Eric cursed as the blade shuddered in his fist and his arm went numb, but he refused to drop his only weapon against the darkness. Straining his arms, he released the power of the Sword from his grasp, allowing it free reign. The magic crackled and roared, the heat of its white fire sweeping out to bathe them both.

Archon cursed and thrust the Sword aside. His fist swept out and caught Eric in the face. As it connected a dark energy coursed through him and suddenly he was airborne, hurtling backwards toward the group of Magickers. Raising his arms, he braced himself for impact and prayed the Sword would not injure him.

Before he could hit the hard ground a gust of wind rushed up to catch him. He gasped in a breath of cold air as the winds lowered him gently to the ground, and nodded his thanks to a woman in blue robes. The other Magickers gathered around him then, and together they turned towards the dark Magicker.

Enala beat them to it. The green flash of her *Soul Blade* swept out across the field, followed by a rumble from deep within the earth. Dirt flew through the air as vines erupted from the ground, the thick tendrils thrashing out to trap Archon in their iron grasp.

Archon smiled and raised a hand. A dark glow seeped from his skin, and as the thorny vines reached him they suddenly stiffened and turned black. Then they were turning back on themselves, leaving the dark Magicker untouched and rushing for Eric's sister.

Eric raised the Sword of Light and swung it, unleashing its white inferno on the thicket. The flames swept through the black and green, turning all they touched to ash. Smoke spread across the open ground, hiding Archon from view as Enala stumbled back to join them.

Straining his eyes, Eric searched the smoke for sign of Archon. He could sense his dark magic building again. The power made his head throb, more powerful than anything he'd ever felt before.

Then suddenly Archon was there, arms raised, and a wave of darkness swept towards them. Eric flinched back, the Sword raised before his face, its magic rising to meet the oncoming force. But this time the black magic did not so much as slow. It came on, death incarnate, ready to claim them all.

A brilliant flash of light lit the air, and then a rush of energy swept past him. Fire and lightning crackled in its midst, the very earth itself spitting open at its passage. He staggered as the combined magic of their allies warped the world around them. With a boom it struck Archon's dark magic and shattered it. Gathering force, it swept on.

Archon roared as the magic found him and ignited. The air shook and the ground splintered, cracks racing out as a shock wave knocked them from their feet. Flames soared into the sky and crashed down towards them, but before Eric could reach for the Sword's magic, Enala was there. She raised her empty fist and hurled the fire back on itself, protecting them all from its wrath.

Eric spared her a nod as he climbed back to his feet. Behind them, he could feel the energy gathering as the Magickers prepared another attack. Taking a firmer grip of the Sword, he added its strength to theirs. Power warped the air between them, the skies overhead darkening as lightning rippled across the underbellies of the clouds.

A low growl echoed across the barren field. Eric turned back to the pillar of smoke rising from where Archon had stood. A boom shook the air and a gust of wind rushed outwards, tearing the smoke from the ground and snuffing out the last of the flames.

Archon stood amidst the scorched earth, his face twisted now with rage, his shoulders hunched as he summoned his power. Darkness collected in his fists, swirling out like storm clouds – though Eric could sense nothing of the Sky in that magic. Only evil, only death.

Throwing out his fist, Archon unleashed the chaos gathered there.

Fear swept across the faces of the Magickers as Archon's power surged towards them, but they did not waver. They stood as one, arms raised, and unleashed their gathered magic. The forces surged towards each other, meeting again with a boom and a roar. This time though it was the black magic that won, swallowing up the swirling colours of their attack. Ripples of energy raced outwards as the magic scattered, forcing Eric and Enala to retreat.

The other Magickers were not so lucky. They staggered as their magic shattered, some crumpling to the ground with the shock of their magic's loss. Blood gushed from the eyes and noses of others as they stumbled blindly amidst their comrades.

Either way, it did not matter. The wave of shadow magic came on, unrelenting.

And together, the Magickers of the Three Nations fell screaming before the power of Archon.

GABRIEL STARED as the Magickers aiding Eric and Enala disappeared beneath the wave of dark magic. A dread silence fell across the wall, the defenders on the battlements reduced now to silent spectators in their own war. They stood helpless before the powers aligned beneath them, their fates in the hands of those below.

And they were losing.

Swallowing, Gabriel turned away. The time had come. He felt a pang of regret as he looked down at Enala one last time. Despite Eric's words, he had said nothing of his decision to the girl. And now it was too late.

Tears burned in his eyes but he wiped them away, pushing down his fear. This was a sacrifice he had to make. There was no other choice; they would not survive without aid, and there was only one being powerful enough to shift the balance.

"Gabriel, where are you going?" Inken's voice stopped him at the top of the stairs.

He turned back, the lies catching in his throat as her eyes caught his. He bowed his head. "I am going to free Jurrien. It's the only way we stand a chance."

Inken stared, mouth open. Emotion swept across her face and for a moment Gabriel thought she would try to stop him. She shook her head, glanced at Caelin, and closed her eyes. A tear ran down her cheek, then she was stepping up to him, pulling him into her embrace. He hugged her back, drawing strength from her presence.

He felt a strong hand on his shoulder and looked up at Caelin. "Good luck, Gabriel," the sergeant's voice was soft, almost breaking. "You're a brave soul."

Gabriel nodded back as he disengaged himself from Inken. She wore a small smile on her face now, but she did not look away. "Thank you, Gabriel. Good luck."

Gabriel sucked in a shaky breath and turned away before they saw his tears. He forced himself not to look back, knowing that if he did, he would lose his nerve. The pull of life was strong now, the call of the shadows a dim reflection of what the world could offer him.

Friends, love, life.

But he had to leave that behind, say goodbye to the promise of a new future.

If only so the others could have what he longed for.

The race to the citadel seemed to pass in an instant, his

feet treading the familiar path by intuition alone. His mind was far away, joying in the three days he had spent with Enala. They had passed far too quickly.

At last he found himself back in the council room, staring down at the blue glow of the *Soul Blade*. The guards on duty only nodded as Gabriel swept past – he was expected. Eric and May had made sure of that.

Gabriel blew out a long sigh, his chest constricting not with exertion but fear.

I can do this! He whispered in the silence of his mind.

You can, a voice answered back, and whether it was his own, or some last vestige of the dark magic, or Jurrien, or someone else, he could not have guessed.

Either way, it was enough.

Reaching down, Gabriel wrapped his hand around the hilt of the *Soul Blade*.

ENALA SWORE as she flung herself backwards, a dark shadow tearing through her jacket. The metallic scent of blood bit the air, sending her back another step. Pain stabbed at her arm. She spared it a glance and then looked away. Blood soaked her sleeve, but already the Earth magic was rising from the *Soul Blade*, driven by instinct, restoring the strength in her arm.

She had already repeated the feat several times for both herself and Eric. She moved by instinct alone now, at one with the green glow of the earth magic, sending it out to heal the cuts and bruises before they could slow them.

Yet despite their best efforts, Archon remained untouched, with barely a mark on his clothes or skin. With the other Magickers dead, they were hopelessly outmatched. But then, even with their aid it had never been a fair fight.

Still they would not surrender. A chill ran through Enala's blood at the thought of the fate Archon planned for them. She would rather die than allow the God magic to make a puppet of her again, than to watch on, helpless, as it destroyed her friends. To suffer beneath the yoke of her magic as a thousand years passed, unable to have even the final relief of death.

Fear fed Enala's anger and she brought about the *Soul Blade*, drawing on its power to attack again. The earth shook beneath her feet, a crack tearing open and racing towards their foe. Archon watched it come, an amused smile on his lips.

Drawing on her own magic, Enala shot her brother a glance. Eric nodded back, and as the gulf opened up beneath Archon, they unleashed their attack. Lightning leapt from Eric's hands as Enala hurled her flames.

Their combined energies lashed out, striking Archon squarely in the chest. The dark Magicker only raised his arms and laughed, but they were not done. Pointing the Sword of Light, Eric unleashed its magic. White fire joined the conflagration, and then an invisible force gripped Archon and drove him down into the crevice.

A boom came from below as lightning and fire burst up from the crack, but Enala did not hesitate. Elation stirred in her chest as she screamed, the green light of the *Soul Blade* flashing in the morning sun, and the earth snapped closed.

Cheers erupted from the wall behind them and Enala's heart pounded hard in her chest. She glanced at Eric, seeing her own disbelief reflected on his face.

"Did we do it?" she whispered.

A dark, booming laughter cut off his reply. Silence fell across the wall as the sound echoed across the killing field. Eric and Enala edged closer to one another, eyes scanning the empty ground, waiting.

With a long, grating groan the earth broke back open. Archon rose up from the fissure, his feathered cloak torn and shredded, but a smile on his lips. He drifted across and alighted on solid ground. Reaching up, he unclipped his cloak and tossed it away. It struck with a heavy thud, loud in the silence.

"Are you done?" Archon gave a dark chuckle.

Enala shuddered, despair rising up within her.

You cannot defeat me, Enala staggered as Archon's words rang in her mind. She spun to stare at Eric and saw his terror, and knew he had heard the words too. *You cannot even keep me from your minds, you poor, frail mortals.*

Archon stepped closer, his grin widening, his teeth glinting in the light of their swords. Magic swept out from him, stretching up like great wings of darkness. Tendrils of black magic wove through the air, reaching for them, calling to them.

Enala shrank away, a voice answering deep inside her, stirring the shadows of her soul. Beside her, the colour fled Eric's face as the magic caught them both. In her chest, Enala felt her hate stirring, her rage and desire rising up to claim her.

Gasping, Enala doubled over, desperate to fight the forces wrapping about her soul. The flames of her magic rose to defend her. It burned at the darkness, tearing at its edges, but the black was like a flood, overwhelming. Bit by bit the spirit of her magic died away, snuffed out, suffocated.

A groan rose in Enala's throat as she sank to her knees. She stared down at the *Soul Blade*, willing herself to hurl it away. But her hand refused to move. It remained fixed around the sword's pommel, and with creeping dread she sensed the first prods of the God power as it seeped into the void left by her magic.

"No," Enala sobbed, her body frozen now, helpless before the power of the *Soul Blade*. "No, please, not again."

Fear rose within her, stronger than belief. Never before had she experienced such terror as on Witchcliffe Island, when the God magic swept her away. Her will and soul had been nothing to it, mere play-things to torment and torture. She had never wanted to touch the damn thing again. It had only been for her friends that she had taken up the *Soul Blade*, to defend them against Archon's power.

And now... now they would die by her own hand.

Enala sucked in a breath as the first surge of power tore through her body. The God magic had discovered her weakness, that her magic was lost beneath the darkness of Archon's power. Enala fled into the depths of her subconscious, searching desperately for a hint of the flame, for some small ember with which to fight. But she found only darkness.

And the burning touch of God magic.

Throwing back her head, a scream rose from her throat.

Then, all at once, the dark magic surged back from her, fleeing her mind as though sucked out through a vortex. The red of her magic flickered back into existence and with a rush of joy she caught it and hurled it at the God magic. The green flames gave way before its heat, retreating back into the *Soul Blade*.

Enala opened her eyes to the boom of thunder, the crackling of lightning. The air rippled with power, the taste of it like ice on the wind. A column of lightning as thick as the towers of Fort Fall fell from the sky, enveloping Archon in its electric blue. The crack as it struck deafened her.

A blast of wind rushed across the killing field, sending Enala rolling backwards over the barren ground. She clutched desperately at the *Soul Blade* as she rolled, suddenly desperate to keep its magic.

In her heart, she knew who had arrived, what had happened.

Grief twisted in her soul as a figure fell from the sky. He landed with a thud on the ground between them and Archon, a sly smile on his familiar lips, power shining from his eyes. It was Gabriel, Gabriel as she had never seen him before.

But it was not the man she had grown to love. She could see it in his eyes, in the ancient wisdom there, in the once brown irises now changed to crystal blue.

It was Jurrien who stood before her now, not Gabriel.

Jurrien, wearing the body of the man she loved.

"Jurrien," Archon's voice boomed across the field. Darkness flashed and the lightning vanished, the wind dying away.

Archon strode from the cloud of smoke where the lightning had fallen, his chest heaving, darkness curling all around him. The earth crunched beneath his feet, scorched black and crystallised by the heat of the lightning.

And his face… Enala had never seen such rage on a human's face.

"In the flesh," Jurrien smiled back. "Did you miss me?"

"Oh, I will enjoy this," Archon growled. "I will enjoy sending your spirit screaming back to the void. The time of the Gods is *over!*"

Archon's last word came out as a scream. Darkness grew from every inch of the man now, curling about him like a living thing. He faded into the magic as it spread from him, as though he were a part of it, as though he were more shadow than real man.

Ice seeped into Enala's veins as she watched the shadows grow. She could sense the power thumping through the air. The sickly twist of dark magic was so thick she could taste it. There was no denying it now; the man within the magic was no longer mortal, no longer even human. No human could withstand the transformation now twisting the dark Magicker's body.

The magic swept out, swirling and changing. Great wings of fire took shape first, stretching up to the sky as black embers scattered on the wind. Feathers of darkness formed, fire lighting from their tips. A hooked beak reached out for them, burning teeth lining the twisted keratin. Within seconds nothing remained of the man who had been Archon.

In his place stood a Phoenix, its burning wings casting them in shadow, the heat of its flames driving them backwards. It towered over the three of them, its bulk filling the killing field, far larger than any dragon, taller even than the walls behind them.

Enala staggered backwards. Slipping in the mud, she fell to the ground, unable to look away from the colossus towering over them.

The great beak opened and a scream tore the air. If she hadn't already been on the ground, the sound would have sent Enala to her knees. As it was, she clapped her hands over her ears and waited for the world to end.

When the scream finally ceased, she heard Archon's whisper in her mind.

Time for this game to end.

A fiery wind buffeted them as the flaming wings beat down, lifting the beast into the sky. Turning in the air, it swept towards the fortress.

CHAPTER 21

Eric staggered to his feet as the Phoenix lifted off, its burning wings carrying it skyward. In his mind he heard Archon's words, but they were dim compared to the memory screaming in his ears.

"Then Archon took his place on the battlefield. He flew overhead, morphed beyond all recognition, darkening the heavens with his magic," Antonia's words from so long ago rang in his head, her warning now clear with the beast before them.

Archon had surrendered his humanity long ago, had become one with his own power. Dark magic was the antithesis of everything natural and good, flaunting the laws of magic and the physical world.

With it, nothing was beyond his power.

Eric watched as clouds gathered around Archon. Flames leapt from the Phoenix's wings to spread across the sky, and he remembered how Antonia's tale had ended. Archon had unleashed his power and an inferno had fallen from the sky, burning the ranks of their army to ash.

They could not let that happen now, not again.

A roar sounded from overhead and Eric spun, his heart

surging as the gold dragons dropped from the sky. The sun glittered off their scales, turning the sky into a gold-speckled tapestry. As one they alighted around them, growls rumbling up from their chests.

It is time, Enduran's voice echoed in his mind. *We must stop him here, or all will fall.*

The dragon stepped forward as the others ringed them and offered his leg. Eric nodded, but turned back to Gabriel – or Jurrien, he guessed now.

"Do you have a plan?" he shouted over the howling wind.

Jurrien laughed. "The plan is yours, Eric. Gabriel seemed to think you had one. All I know is, alone, we cannot match his power. Last time I tried, he snuffed my magic out like a candle."

Eric sheathed the Sword of Light as he climbed up onto Enduran's back. He nodded as Enala slid past him and took her seat in front of him. She flashed him a weary grin.

"Mind if I steer?" she laughed.

"You're the dragon rider," he turned back to Jurrien. "Well, we have all three God powers now," he pointed to the sky. "So we stop him, whatever the cost."

Jurrien nodded, the hint of a smile on his lips. "Lead on then, young Eric."

Eric felt the muscles of the dragon bunch beneath him, and quickly wrapped his hands around Enala's waist. Then Enduran leapt for the sky and Eric's stomach fell into his boots. The dragon's wings swept down as his roar echoed off the walls around them and then they were surging upwards, driving ahead to where the dark Phoenix waited.

The gathered roar of the other dragons came from behind as Enduran's tribe joined them, followed by a boom as Jurrien took to the sky. Glancing across, he saw lightning flickering in the God's fists as he flew past them.

Swallowing, Eric reached up and redrew the Sword of Light. Its energy surged through him but he kept its flames extinguished, ensuring they would not do any harm to Enala. She still held the *Soul Blade* clenched in her fist, its green glow glittering on the scales of Enduran's back. He held her tight as they raced upwards, closing fast on the beast Archon had become.

Enala glanced back as they flew and he saw a wild joy on her face, a sharpness to her eyes that had been missing before. She swung the *Soul Blade* and pointed it skyward, her wild scream carrying to him over the thump of wings.

Eric smiled as he remembered the first time he had laid eyes on this girl, his sister. He had been dying on the black sands of Malevolent Cove, but even so the image remained crystal clear: Enala astride the dragon Nerissa, her golden hair billowing in the wind, her brow creased with righteous anger.

He saw that girl again now and the sight warmed his heart. They would need her courage in the battle to come.

Hoisting the Sword of Light, he drew on its energy. His mind tingled with its power, but he was still searching for a plan, for a way to halt the inferno Archon was about to unleash.

"We have to stop his attack," Eric shouted over the wind. "Jurrien, you and I will fight fire with fire. Hopefully we have enough to match what he throws at us. Enala, do what you can to protect the fortress from whatever gets through!"

Enala nodded but she did not look back. Instead she hoisted the *Soul Blade* and stood, a wicked grin on her face as she balanced on Enduran's back. Then she turned and slid back down so that she faced the ground, the *Soul Blade* already flashing as she worked its magic.

Thunder crackled in the storm clouds above them, but Eric could sense no rain or wind within them. These were no natural clouds, but dark things, born of Archon's black magic. They held only one thing – death.

Then a roar shook the air and the sky opened up.

And the flames began to fall.

∼

FEAR CLUTCHED Inken's chest as the dragons took flight, chasing after the black beast that had risen from the mud.

Archon.

The name sent a shiver down to her soul. The man's shadow had hung over their lives for so long now, leaving a dark taint on even the most joyous of memories. Always there, waiting in the distant future, waiting to destroy them.

But now that future had finally arrived. Archon had come, his legend made flesh. They had watched together from the wall as he slaughtered their most powerful Magickers, as he brought Enala and Eric to their knees. Only Caelin's strong arms had stopped Inken from racing to their aid then, and a wave of relief had swept through the defenders as Jurrien arrived.

But now they stood helpless, unable to aid their friends in the desperate fight in the skies above the fortress. There atop the battlements of Fort Fall they waited, tame sheep for the slaughter.

A rumble carried down from overhead and Inken sucked in a breath of fear.

The clouds gathering around the Phoenix had vanished, washed away by a firestorm now falling towards them from high above. Flames licked across the sky and Inken flinched as she felt the first kiss of their heat on her face. Around her the men and women of the Three Nations started to scream and run, but she could only stand and stare, knowing there was nothing they could do to escape the doom rushing towards them.

Above, the dragons still flew towards the firestorm. A surge of hope flickered in Inken's chest as light leapt from the leading dragon. The blue flash of lightning joined it and she knew Eric and Jurrien were fighting back. She just prayed they had the strength to halt the inferno.

Lightning collected around the dark figure of Jurrien, spreading out to coat the sky. White fire joined it, rushing from the Sword of Light to swirl around the dragons, its strength building with each second.

Inken's ears popped as a sudden energy surged in the air, and then the forces of the Light and Sky were rushing up to meet the oncoming inferno.

A deafening crash fell across the wall as the two forces met. Light flashed, blinding the defenders, and it seemed the forces would tear the sky itself asunder. Tears streaming from her eyes, Inken forced herself to look away as white spots swept across her vision.

Please, please, please, she chanted the silent prayer in her mind.

A gust of air struck her then, knocking her from her feet. She tumbled across the cold stone and only the crenulations stopped her from toppling from the wall. Groaning, she blinked her eyes to clear them and looked up, desperate to see her fate.

Overhead the sky had cleared, the waves of black fire all but destroyed.

Not quite, she realised with a trickle of despair. Spots of flame still marked the sky, tumbling down towards them, too close to stop now. Closing her eyes, Inken waited for the end to come.

Then she gasped as the wall beneath her shook and the earth rumbled. Struggling to stand, Inken stared across at

Caelin, mouth wide, unable to speak. The rumbling grew around them, turning to a roar, and then the ground behind the wall split open and a cliff-face of rock rose into the air. Groaning and crackling, the rock grew upwards, surpassing the wall and the pale faced defenders, and spread out overhead to form a shield against the flames.

Inken shivered as dull booms came from above, the flames crashing onto the rock with impotent fury. She hugged herself, tears stinging her eyes, and sent her silent thanks to Enala.

Slowly their rocky shelter receded back into the ground, disappearing into the field behind them until it seemed it had never been. Breathing out a long sigh, Inken searched the sky for sign of the dragons.

Before she could find them, the horns of the defenders began to sound.

Climbing to her feet, Inken stumbled to the edge of the ramparts and looked out across the killing field.

Through the smoke below came the black cloaks of the enemy, emerging like the ghosts of the past. Beasts ran amidst them, Raptors and felines and lizards alike, the whole host of Archon's army come to claim their revenge.

Atop the wall, the defenders watched them come. Not a single man or woman wavered. Pride for her people swelled in Inken's chest. Each of them had witnessed the battle below, the bravery of their Magickers as they went to their death. They had watched as Eric and Enala refused to give an inch to Archon, as they refused to surrender.

Now they faced the tooth and claw and steel of the enemy, and they would live by that example.

Smiling, Inken reached down and drew her blade. It was almost a relief now to see the enemy return, to feel her helplessness swept aside. This was a threat she could face, an enemy she could defeat.

Caelin stepped up beside her, a smile on his face. "Let's go to war."

ENALA LET out a long breath as Archon's firestorm died on the rocky shield she had torn from the earth. Then she turned her attention back to the sky, and the black creature Archon had become. Reaching into the *Soul Blade*, she sent a pulse of magic into Eric and Enduran, and allowed its healing warmth to flow through her own body.

Thank you, child, the dragon rumbled in her mind.

"Thanks, Enala," Eric echoed the dragon's words, his voice raised over the crack of the wind.

"Do you have a plan?" she shouted back.

Eric laughed, nodding to the smoke drifting around them. "That was about the extent of it."

Enala's heart pounded hard in her chest, but she grinned back. Joy swept through her soul at being a-dragon-back again, to soar through the sky with nothing but the strength of the dragon holding her aloft. It was freedom to her, a final connection to her parents and the gifts they'd given her. If she was to die today, she was glad to have had this last ride.

You are welcome, little one, she heard Enduran's voice and smiled.

It is good to be with you, Enduran. But let us hope this is not our last ride, she thought back.

A tremor shook the dragon and she smiled at Enduran's laughter. Ahead the phoenix loomed, its black wings beating the sky. Flames curled out around it, tainted by its dark magic, but there were no clouds now.

"Enduran!" Eric shouted over the howling wind. "Send the others back. There is no point in them risking their lives in this fight."

No, the roar of the other dragons tore the air. *This is the final battle. We shall not flee.*

Enala smiled, warmed by their presence. Beneath her Enduran roared his own response, and then the world erupted in flames, and there was no going back for any of them.

Archon folded his wings and dropped towards them. Around them the jaws of the dragons opened and they unleashed their fire. The dark flames of the Phoenix threaded down to meet them, mingling with the red of the dragon fire and then exploding outwards. Heat washed across them, forcing Enala to draw on her own magic to protect herself from its burning touch.

Behind her she heard Eric shout and then sensed the surge of the Sword's power. White flames leapt past her as Eric pointed the blade, racing up to join the conflagration overhead. Then a boom rocked her in her seat and she looked across to see lightning rushing from the hands of the Storm God.

She stared up, watching the blue and black, the red and white flickering across the sky, and knew she could not hold back. Raising the *Soul Blade,* she threw herself into the green of its magic, seeking out some way to attack the Phoenix up here in the sky, so far from the powers of the Earth.

But this was God magic she held, and with a thrill she remembered what that meant. While normal magic could manipulate the world around it, God magic could *create*, could pull power from the air itself.

Gritting her teeth, Enala released herself to the draw of the God magic, willing it to aid her. In her mind's eye, she imagined the sky filling with stone.

Enala's ears popped and a shudder went through her as energy poured from the *Soul Blade*. She looked around to see great boulders appearing in the air around them, and with a scream she turned back to Eric. *"Catch them!"*

Eric smiled and spared her a nod. White flashed from the Sword of Light and then the boulders were racing upwards, slicing through the inferno overhead without resistance. A scream came from beyond the flames, echoing across the sky, and Enala threw back her head and laughed.

Around them the wind shrieked, rushing past to gather in Jurrien's hands. Enala glanced across at the Storm God, her eyes widening as she saw the forces swirling around Gabriel's body. Wind roared in from every direction, tearing through the flames licking the sky. Lightning thundered, flickering amidst the winds as a tornado of electricity swept around Jurrien.

With a scream of rage, Jurrien threw out his hands, directing the hurricane upwards. Wind howled and then the tempest of wind and lightning was racing into the depths of the firestorm overhead, hurling it back at the Phoenix.

The black scream came again, more beast than human, and then the Phoenix was falling, twisting in the air to sweep past the host of dragons. For a second a rush of elation swept through Enala, but terror still clung to her soul and she knew they had not won yet.

Her fears were confirmed as the wings of the Phoenix swept out, halting its fall. Spinning, the black wings swung towards them and a wave of flame raced out to catch the nearest dragon.

The gold dragon's neck arched backwards as it screamed, the dark flames eating through flesh and scale and wing. With a final roar, its wings crumpled and it began to fall.

Panic gripped Enala as she threw out her arm. A ray of green streamed from the *Soul Blade*, racing down to catch the injured dragon in its warmth. Within the span of seconds, she watched its flesh knit back together and golden scales reform like feathers from its skin. The dragon yelped, the reversal catching it by surprise. Then the wind caught in its restored wings and it surged back up towards them.

Lightning crackled and Enala looked across to see the clouds regathering around Jurrien.

The Phoenix drew to a halt in mid-air, its head twisting, almost in curiosity.

Have we not fought this battle before, Storm God? Archon's words hissed through Enala's mind.

"Yes," Jurrien roared. "But this time we have the Light. Eric, now!"

Enala twisted around to look at Eric, expecting fire or raw energy to rush from the Sword. But her brother's eyes were closed, the light of the Sword washing over his face.

"Eric, what are you doing!" she shrieked.

Then the Phoenix screamed, convulsing in the air as chunks of darkness tore from its wings. The sound stabbed at Enala's ears and sent a tremor through Enduran. Closing her eyes, Enala strove to force the noise from her mind, to focus against its darkness.

She heard Jurrien shout his hatred and sensed the rushing throb as the Storm God unleashed another attack. Forcing open her eyes, she watched through tears as the reformed twister rushed down to engulf the Phoenix.

The beast screeched again, flames tearing from its body as it shook, wings beating hard to escape. But the winds had already caught it, trapping the creature within the power of the twister.

Thunder shook the sky as the first bolt of blue fire struck, tearing fresh chunks of darkness from the cruel body. The wind roared, catching in the Phoenix's wings and whirling it around. Another crash and another screech followed as the lightning crackled, burning at the foul creature.

Enduran's great head shook and his wing beats faltered,

the awful sound tearing at his strength. Enala struggled to cover her ears, unable to release the *Soul Blade* for fear of losing its power. At any moment she might need it.

Glancing back again at Eric, she saw blood trickling from his ears. A sudden shudder swept through him and he started to convulse. His hand slipped from the dragon's back, and he would have fallen if she had not reached out to steady him. Still the white flashed from the Sword of Light, and with a rush of realisation, Enala knew what he was doing.

Eric had delved into the arsenal within the Sword, and finally unleashed its greatest power. He was using the magic of the Light to fight Archon's magic, to render him defenceless against their attacks. And watching the Phoenix writhing within the twister, the winds and lightning tearing it to pieces, she knew it was working.

But how long could he last?

Enala shuddered as she twisted on the dragon's back to face her brother. Blood ran from his eyes and nose, streaming down his throat, and she knew he was giving everything he had to hold back Archon's magic.

Gripping tight to the *Soul Blade*, Enala reached for its magic and sent it pouring into her brother.

A cough came from Eric and she breathed out in relief as the flow of blood slowed. Smiling, she held him close, offering her silent comfort. The darkness within the *Soul Blade* seemed less now, a small thing beside the love she felt for her brother and those below. She held that feeling tight, and gathered her strength.

Then Eric gave an awful groan and coughed. Blood splattered her shirt as his head lolled and his eyes rolled into the back of his head. His hand remained clamped around the Sword of Light, an iron grip that would not release until death, but the rest of his body went limp.

Enala pulled him close as the howling wind ceased with a

sudden tearing sound. The lightning flashed blue one final time and went out. The air cleared, the storm clouds sucked away in a rush of noiseless movement.

The dragons hovered in place, their wings beating hard as they turned to face where Archon had been. As the last of the clouds faded away, a single word hissed through their minds.

Die!

Enala raised the *Soul Blade* as the Phoenix reappeared, coalescing from a ball of darkness back to the flaming bird of before. But before she could reach for the *Soul Blade's* power, darkness exploded from its flaming wings and rushed outwards in all directions.

The dragons roared, their wings beating hard in desperate retreat as they tried to escape the flames. But there was nowhere to go, no place to hide in the empty sky. Enala screamed, an icy hand clutching her heart as she stared at the unstoppable tide closing on them.

Around her the dragons roared again as the flames found them, a terrible, gut-wrenching noise, their agony made sound. Gripping Eric tight, Enala squeezed her eyes shut and waited for the end to come.

She did not have to wait long. Tongues of flames licked at her flesh, igniting waves of pain that rippled through her body. Agony filled her, robbing her of the breath to even scream. Her voice caught in her throat, her mind exploding, her sanity washed away on a river of pain.

The magic of the *Soul Blade* poured into her, into Eric and Enduran, but it could not hold back the burning agony, could not stop the torturous fire. It was not enough to save them.

Enala's stomach rose into her chest as they began to fall, Enduran still beneath them, but his strength gone. Wind whipped at Enala's hair, her clothes, its icy touch agony on her blackened flesh. She screamed then, finally finding her voice. But now she could not stop, could not cut it off.

Opening her eyes, Enala watched the earth race up to meet them.

And then everything went black.

CHAPTER 22

Inken ducked beneath a wild swing and plunged her blade into the chest of the man facing her. Stepping back, she felt the breath of an axe sweep past her face. Then Caelin was there, his short sword smashing into the head of the hulking giant who had just made the wall.

As the man toppled backwards, Inken heard a growl from behind and spun. A Raptor stalked across the ramparts, a hungry longing in its sickly yellow eyes. She screamed a warning to Caelin as it leapt, throwing herself to the side as it swept past. Its claws tore through the fabric of her sleeve and a burning sting lanced from her arm as they found flesh.

Then she was up, already spinning to drive her blade into its side. She had lost her sabre what seemed like hours ago and she now wielded a short sword. Its razor sharp blade bit deep into the beast's stomach and lodged between its ribs. She released the hilt as it swung to bite her and threw herself backwards.

Caelin raced in from its other side and drove his own short sword into the Raptor's neck. The beast screeched, staggering on the slippery stones, turning from one to another.

But the blades had made their presence felt, and as it tried to charge them the strength went from its limbs. It toppled to the ground and lay still.

Recovering his blade, Caelin stabbed it through the creature's eye to ensure it was dead. Inken stepped up and retrieved her blade before anything else came at them.

They stood together for a moment in a pocket of calm, back to back as they surveyed the battle. Along the wall the enemy streamed up their ladders to throw themselves at the defenders. The roar of the beasts chilled her, the clack of their claws on the stone wall mixing with the clanging of steel.

But despite the odds, the defenders were holding their ground. They fought with grim faces, stretched with exhaustion, their clothes and armour torn and broken, but they *stood*. Comrades in arms, they refused to give an inch to the dark creatures and men fighting beneath Archon's flag. Hundreds of them had fallen, but for every man that fell another defender would step up to take his place in the line.

Inken unleashed a wild laugh, adrenaline surging through her veins as another black-garbed man rushed at her. He fell within seconds, another victim to add to her countless tally. Pride filled her as she watched the defenders fight around her. Nearby she glimpsed May, moving through the men and beasts like a dancer, a sword in one hand and a dagger in the other. Even the dark creatures of the wasteland gave her dance of death a wide berth, and behind her the defenders mustered.

All along the wall, the brave souls of the Three Nations held strong, fighting back to back in places, determined to make the enemy pay dearly for their lives. Defenders streamed up the staircases, reinforcements rushing from the third wall to join them. It seemed an unspoken command had gone out – that this was the final battle, that they would hold them at the second wall or fall in a glorious final stand.

Then a boom rang out from overhead, crashing over the wall like the tolling of a bell. Inken stole a glance up as the enemy closed again, and choked back a cry of despair.

The dragons were falling, tumbling from the sky as black fire licked at their golden scales. The flames were eating them alive, burning away the flesh and bone of all but one of the wondrous beasts. Inken stared as that last golden body plummeted towards the earth. A green glow covered the dragon, shaking off the last of the black flames, and she knew it was Enduran, and that Eric and Enala still clung to his back.

The falling dragon disappeared behind the spires of the citadel, followed the distant echo of a thud. A groan rippled through the defenders as their eyes went to the sky, watching for the Phoenix, waiting for the firestorm to fall.

Inken watched as Archon streaked through the sky, but for now he seemed to have forgotten the fortress. The Phoenix chased after the fallen dragon, a trail of flame licking out behind it, and vanished behind the walls of Fort Fall.

Tears stung Inken's eyes and she bit back a groan.

"Eric!" she roared as the enemy came at them again.

Every fibre of Inken's being screamed for her to go to him, but instead she threw herself at the enemy. She blinked through her tears, swinging her sword with a wild rage she could not control. She refused to give in, refused to accept defeat now, not after they had all sacrificed so much. The enemy flinched back before her fury and fell beneath her blade. Caelin joined her, his own blade a blur, a rage burning in his eyes that almost matched her own.

Yet their ferocity was not matched by their fellow defenders. The sight of the dragons falling had stolen something from them – their courage, their hope. She could sense it in the air, in the hesitation of the men around her. Despair hung across the wall like a cloud, stealing away their strength.

They all knew the truth. With the last of their Magickers gone, it would not be long before Archon came now. And when he did, there was no one left to protect them from his wrath. They would be helpless before his magic.

In contrast, the enemy had drawn strength from the sight, and attacked now with renewed fury.

Bit by bit, the defenders gave ground before the enemy. Inken struggled against the pull, surging forward again and again, drawing the boldest of the defenders with her. But one by one they fell around her, and others no longer stepped up to replace them.

The enemy numbers swelled, the weight of their bodies forcing her back. Her sword flashed like a living thing, an extension of her own body that lanced out to slay the black tide before her. But now she hardly had space to move, and one step at a time she retreated with Caelin towards the stairs.

She glanced at her friend and caught the desperation in his eyes. A blade lanced for his throat and she threw up her sword to deflect it. Caelin shook himself and took another step back, nodding his thanks.

Then they were at the stairs and there was no choice left but to turn and flee. Her sword heavy in her hand, Inken grabbed Caelin's hand and spun, leaping for the first step. The bigger man came after her, and together they raced after their retreating comrades.

Ahead of them defenders streamed across the field between the walls, churning the ground to mud beneath their boots. Inken gasped as beasts jumped down from the ramparts overhead, landing without trouble despite the height. Raptors raced after the defenders, leaping high to land on the backs of fleeing men. Their weight drove them to the ground as the razor sharp teeth flashed out to tear chunks from their helpless victims.

Inken's heart lurched with fear as they reached the ground and joined the fray.

"It's a rout!" Caelin's voice carried over the screams of the dying.

All around them their people were being slaughtered as they ran, falling to the claws of the beasts and arrows from the enemy atop the wall they had just lost. And every second more of the enemy reached the ramparts above, adding their weight to the slaughter. A crash came from nearby as a battering ram slammed into the gates.

Inken could hardly find the will to run. Her eyes scanned the scene, staring at the slaughter as though she were apart from it, as if this were happening to someone else. Another crack came from the gates as the wooden beam holding them shattered. Then a fresh wave of enemies poured into the fight, rushing through the gateway to join the slaughter.

She looked at the third wall and the scant defenders atop its ramparts – those few who had obeyed their orders and remained at their posts. The gates stood open, just a hundred yards away.

So close, but so far.

Even so, they had to try. Steeling herself, Inken charged into the fray, dragging Caelin with her. Her sword licked out, catching the enemy fighters as they stood and hacked at the fallen defenders. Guilt clawed at her soul as they ran past their injured comrades, their desperate screams chasing after them. But there was no time to save them – it was everyone for themselves now.

Staring ahead, Inken fixed her eyes on the open gates and prayed they could reach them in time. But even as the thought came the wooden doors began to close, swinging in towards them. A cry of despair came from the men around her as others picked up speed, desperate to reach the relative safety of the third wall.

The strength fled Inken's legs as she staggered to a stop. The gap between the gates quickly closed, shrinking to a thin sliver through which a few stragglers managed to slip. She stared at the wall, her gaze catching on the eyes of the men above. Caelin drew to a stop beside her, his shoulders slumped, despair carving deep shadows beneath his eyes.

Side by side, they turned to face the oncoming enemy, swords raised in defiance. The other defenders gathered around them, forming a thin wall in the middle of the field. Shoulder to shoulder, they watched the black tide sweep towards them. Claws shone and fangs flashed in the mouths of the massive felines as the enemy charged.

Then a boom came from the wall behind them and Inken spun. The gates were opening again and those nearest the gates were throwing themselves to the side. From beyond came the rhythmic thump of hooves on the hard ground.

Inken's breath caught in her throat as the first of the horsemen appeared. They rushed through the gateway like a river from a narrow gorge, the red horses of the Plorsean cavalry. At their head rode King Fraser and Elton, a wicked joy on their faces as they charged at the enemy. Lances pointed, they raced past the survivors of the second wall and plunged into the unsuspecting enemy. Caught in the open, beast and man alike fell to their steel-tipped lances.

A cheer rose up from the men atop the third wall as the Plorsean cavalry turned and charged again, crushing the enemy as they tried to reform beneath the shelter of the second wall. Pressed in on themselves with the stone to their back, they died by the hundreds.

Beside her Caelin gave a whoop of joy, raising a fist in triumph. "They made it!" he turned and lifted Inken off her feet. Swinging her around, he shouted again. "They made it!"

Inken joined his laughter, but reason quickly returned as he lowered her back to the ground. They had lost the second wall, and the Plorsean cavalry could not change that. Their turn of fortunes would not last long. Already the enemy was forming up again, gathering atop the wall. Arrows rose up from the ramparts to fall on the Plorseans and several horses crumpled in the deadly rain.

"Come on," she shouted back. "Let's go."

Together they stumbled towards the open gates.

ARCHON STRODE across the burning ground, the flames dying at his touch. The body of the dragon lay nearby, its last pitiful gasps echoing from the walls of the fortress behind him. He ignored it; its death was of little concern. He had eyes only for his ancestors now. Jurrien had vanished, but he would deal with the wily God soon enough. For now, he was preoccupied with his magic, with the dark threads of power he had wrapped around the two Magickers, binding their souls to their broken bodies.

They lay beside each other on the icy ground, their arms outstretched, almost touching. Their legs and arms lay at awful angles, their bones shattered by the impact. In normal circumstances their hearts would have already given out, but Archon refused to give them the satisfaction of death. His magic washed over them, holding them to life.

The Sword of Light lay nearby. Smiling, he reached down and lifted it from the ground. Light flashed from the blade and then died away. Shaking his head, he moved to Eric's side.

"Such a curse," he whispered, staring at the blade. "If only I had known."

Leaning down, he placed it in the boy's hand. The light flashed again and a groan rattled up from Eric's broken chest.

Archon smiled, sensing the flow of God magic streaming

from the Sword into Eric's undefended body. It would not take long to take hold, to crush the feeble resistance of his soul and gain dominion over his body.

Moving away again, he recovered the *Soul Blade* Enala had wielded.

"My sweet daughter, please, accept my gift," his voice was hard as he reached down and placed the blade in Enala's hand.

"*No,*" the groan came from the girl's torn lips, but his magic kept her unconscious.

Her back arched as green light flooded from the *Soul Blade*. He grinned, watching as it took hold, burning through her veins to cast off the feeble remains of her magic.

Turning away, he walked to the dragon and sat on its broken head.

Smiling, he waited for his Gods to be born.

CHAPTER 23

Enala groaned as sensation came rushing back. To her surprise she felt no pain, but even so the sudden return to reality was overwhelming, her whole body throbbing with the shock of her return. Biting her lips, she forced herself to open her eyes.

"*What?*" she whispered, unable to comprehend the sight that greeted her.

There was nothing. No burning sky or broken dragons, no Fort Fall, no Archon. Only empty white, stretching out to eternity without so much as a shadow to break the nothingness. She lay amidst that emptiness, alone in oblivion.

Standing, Enala looked around, mouth wide as she struggled to come to terms with her surroundings. She shuddered, knowing she could only be dead, that her soul had been sent to the otherworld. Her breath caught in her throat as she thought of spending eternity in this place, alone but for the memories of the world she'd left behind. She would surely go mad.

"Where am I?" she breathed, tears burning in her eyes. This could not be happening, could not be the end.

Her words echoed out across the void and returned to mock her. She groaned, reaching up to cover her ears, her eyes, anything to deny the reality around her.

"You are in the spirit realm," Enala jumped as a girl's voice spoke.

Heart pounding hard in her chest, Enala spun, the hackles on her neck rising in warning. She gasped as her eyes found the girl behind her, and if anything, her heart beat faster.

Antonia stood before her, her violet eyes pinched with sadness. She wore the same lime green dress as in the vision Archon had shown, and her auburn hair hung limp about her shoulders. A pale glow seeped out around her, staining the whiteness of the void an emerald green. Enala stared into the ancient wisdom hiding in the depths of her eyes, unable to find the words to speak.

"Hello, Enala," Antonia gave a sad smile. "It's nice to finally meet you."

"I... I... How are you here?"

Antonia reached out, drawing Enala into her arms. "You put up a brave fight, Enala."

Enala shuddered and sank to her knees, the comfort of the Goddess doing little to warm her despair. "We lost," she whispered.

"You did better than any of us could have ever imagined," she squeezed Enala tight and drew back. "I'm sorry..."

Enala looked away. "I thought we had him there, at the end."

"You almost did. I wish I could have given you the strength to finish him, but Eric's soul was not strong enough to cope with the God magic pouring into his body. It burned him, body and mind, until he could hold on no longer. Our magic was never meant to be used by mortals."

"What will happen now?" Enala could not keep the

despair from her voice. "To the others, to Inken and Caelin and May, all those soldiers in Fort Fall?"

"You will kill them all," Antonia murmured.

A shiver ran down Enala's spine. "*What?*"

"Archon has done as he promised. He is holding your body to life and has put the *Soul Blade* in your hands. That is why I am able to come to you. But even as we speak, my power is flooding your body, taking it for its own. This time you will not have the strength to take it back, Enala."

"No, no, no," Enala wrapped her arms around her chest. "I have to wake up."

Reaching up, she twined her fingers through her hair and pulled. The fragile strands tore from her scalp, sending pain shooting through her head, but it did nothing to change the void around them.

"There is no fighting it, Enala," tears watered in Antonia's eyes. "Your body is broken. Were you to wake, even for a second, the pain would drive you insane and the God magic would take you anyway."

"Then what?" Enala leapt to her feet. "Do we just sit here and watch? Watch as I slaughter every man and woman in that fortress? Watch as the light fades from the eyes of my friends?"

Enala stalked across to the tiny Goddess, rage burning away her despair. She wanted to kick and scream and *fight*, anything but sit here as helpless witness. She could not bear it, could not sit back as the God power destroyed everything she had fought for. There had to be *something* they could do.

Antonia bowed her head, refusing to look her in the eye. "There is something," she murmured.

"*What?*" Desperation made Enala bold. Reaching out, she grabbed the Goddess by her dress, dragging her close, forcing Antonia to meet her gaze. "*What can we do?*"

Tears spilt from Antonia's eyes. "I promised I would

never ask again," she tore herself loose of Enala's grasp and turned to stare out into the empty whiteness. "Not after last time. I cannot do it."

Enala hesitated, shocked by Antonia's grief. She approached slowly, placing a hand on her shoulder. "What is it, Antonia?"

Antonia turned, misery in her violet eyes. "To ask someone to make the ultimate sacrifice. To ask you to give me your body and allow me to be reborn."

Enala staggered back as the dreadful truth of Antonia's words rang in her ears.

"No," she breathed, staring at the Goddess. "You can't ask that; you can't make me."

Antonia shook her head. "I would never. It is your choice, Enala, yours alone."

Groaning, Enala spun, searching the void for some escape. But there was only the emptiness, the relentless nothing of the spirit plain. Despair clung to her soul, and she wrapped her arms around herself again, desperate for comfort. She longed for one last moment in reality, to breathe in the scents of the forest, to ride on a dragon's back one final time, to find comfort in the arms of the man she loved.

Gabriel.

Enala closed her eyes, feeling again the pain as she realised his sacrifice. Now Antonia had asked her to make the same choice, to give away her life so the rest of the Three Nations might survive.

"What will it be like?" she asked at last, her voice no more than a whisper.

"You will feel no pain," Antonia's words were laced with grief. "For a time… your soul would remain, bound with mine. But eventually…" her voice broke, "eventually it would succumb. Your being would be enveloped by me, become a part of me, and you would be no more."

Enala took a deep, shuddering breath, summoning the last dredges of her courage. Looking up, she found the violet glow of the Goddess' eyes.

"Do it."

～

LIGHT. Brilliant, shining light, everywhere Eric looked. He spun, searching for a break, a single flaw or contrast to offer some hint of reality. But there was nothing – only the never-ending nothingness.

Finally, he abandoned the search. Releasing his breath, he sank to the ground, still struggling to come to terms with the reality around him.

"What is this place?" he breathed.

What had happened, there at the end? They had been so close, so close to destroying Archon's darkness. If only he could have held on a few moments more, if only he'd had the strength. But the white fire had swept through his body, flooding every crevice of his mind. It burned at his soul, tearing at his every thought, his every memory. Even now he struggled to put the pieces of the battle together.

Jurrien's voice had been whispering in his mind, images flashing through his thoughts, leading him into the depths of the Sword of Light's power. He had seen then what he had to do, how to use the magic of the Light to bind Archon's power.

And it had almost worked. Deprived of his dark magic, the Phoenix had lost its form and been trapped within the tempest of Jurrien's magic.

But the power of the Sword had been too much, and Eric's soul had finally given way before its all-consuming flame. He'd found himself falling, his magic crumbling to dust as the Light overwhelmed him.

Perhaps that was why he found himself here in this empty domain.

Eric looked up as a distant thud echoed through the void, the sound like a rock dropped on a tiled floor.

Or the thud of heavy boots.

Another thud followed, and another, coming close. A tingle spread down his spine as he spun to search the void anew. Heart pounding in his chest, Eric pulled himself back to his feet. He stared into the white, searching for the first hint of danger, half-expecting Archon to appear from some hidden crevice.

Instead he was met by the image of an old man. Lines of age streaked his face and his skin hung from his cheeks in paled bags. Thin white hair grew down to his knees, its wiry lengths fading into the emptiness around them. He wore grey robes of rough fabric, but came unarmed, his empty hands trembling as he walked. A faint glow came from the man and his white eyes were filled with sadness.

"Eric," the man rasped, his voice as soft as falling snow. "It is nice to finally meet the man beyond the veil."

A tingle of recognition ran through Eric and for a second he thought of his mentor, Alastair. Sadness filled him, but he knew this was not his tutor. This man was far older, his age beyond counting.

"Who are you?" he asked, a creeping suspicion rising in his throat.

The old man sighed, sadness sweeping across his face. "I am Darius."

The name tolled in Eric's mind, ringing like a bell through his memories as he looked on the face of the God of Light. He recognised him now, though the man seemed to have aged far faster than his siblings.

A sickness curled through Eric, a violent anger at the spirit standing before him now. The God of Light had abandoned the Three Nations centuries ago, and in his absence the power of Archon had grown to fill the vacuum.

"Where have you been?" Eric hissed, unable to control his rage. "What are you doing here, now, after a thousand lives have been lost, when the war is all but done? *Why?*" he all but shouted the last word.

Darius closed his eyes, the wrinkles on his forehead knotting with pain. "You do not understand," his eyes opened again, catching Eric in their ancient depths. "I have been *here*, Eric. I have been here all along."

Eric found himself frozen in the God's gaze. "What do you mean?" he growled. "Where are we?"

"We are in the spirit realm, in a portion of it twisted by Archon and trapped within his *Soul Blade*," Darius paused. "His very first *Soul Blade*. I believe you call it the Sword of Light."

"*No,*" Eric staggered back, his heart freezing in his chest, unable to believe the words. He shook his head. "No…"

Ice spread through his veins as he stared at the wasted figure of the God of Light, at the ancient spirit standing amidst the nothingness of the void.

No, it can't be.

But Eric could not deny the truth standing before him. He felt his world turning on end, the story of Darius and his absence cracking the very fabric of his reality.

The God of Light had not abandoned them. He had been trapped, locked away for eternity.

"All this time?" Eric breathed, a sharp pain burning in his chest. "*How?*"

Darius moved past him, his movements slow, weighed down by his centuries of imprisonment.

"We never expected him to return," emotion laced his

voice, sad and filled with regret. "Five hundred years ago there was a boy who hated us, who hated me because I took his father from him," he shook his head. "It has been our everlasting shame, that three mortals gave up their lives for us to be born. But we did not expect the hate it would nurture in the boy, the path it would send him down."

"His name was Archon, son to Nickolas, brother to Artemis – your ancestor. While his brother ultimately accepted his father's sacrifice, the boy Archon could not do the same. Both wielded powerful magic, but my birth sent them down separate paths. Artemis welcomed the new world, joining us in our efforts to rebuild his nation and bring peace to the Three Nations. But Archon, he spurned us and the future his father had sacrificed himself to build. Instead he turned to the darkness, embracing the power offered by black magic, and used it to slay the priests who had brought us into the world."

"But you did not kill him," Eric whispered.

"No," Darius met his eyes. "We have never used our power to kill. When we caught him, he was banished to the wasteland in the north. And that was the end of it."

"Except it wasn't, was it?" Eric's anger bubbled up again but he pressed it down now. Who was he to judge the mistakes of the Gods?

"We thought we had done the right thing, showing mercy, even to one so steeped in dark magic. We did not expect his hatred to fester, for him to surrender so completely to that darkness. He spent decades in that wasteland, brooding, preparing his revenge. And we forgot," he paused. "But when he stabbed me in the back, somehow, I knew it was him."

"How did it happen?"

Darius shook his head, the pain on his face evident. "I took another criminal north, leaving him where he could do no more harm to our people. I did not expect an ambush, certainly not by such a powerful magic. Somehow Archon had discovered where I usually appeared to release the banished, and there he waited for me, concealed by his dark magic. Before I sensed his presence, he drove his foul blade through my back."

"Then how did we get the Sword?" Eric frowned.

Darius gave a wry smile. "I am the God of Light. Even with my magic pouring into the *Soul Blade* and the life fleeing my mortal body, I was not going to allow my magic to fall into his hands. I broke free of his dark magic, and we fought – the Light against the darkness. But Archon had grown more powerful than I could possibly have imagined, and I quickly realised it was a battle I could not win."

"Archon knew it too. He hammered at me with his magic, determined to see me fall. But when I felt his final attack building, I reached back and tore his *Soul Blade* from my flesh. I held it high, feeling its pull tugging at my spirit. But I had enough strength left for one final effort, and with the last of my power I hurled it into the void, back to Trola and the host of Magickers waiting in the Temple of Light."

"And they thought you had abandoned them," Eric croaked.

Darius waved a hand. "I have spent a century listening to the thoughts of the Trolan royalty. I know what they thought, Eric. But I never had the strength to reach them," his words were filled with sorrow. "So many died, thinking I did not care."

Eric stared at the God of Light, imagining his desolation as centuries of Sword wielders passed by while he lay trapped within the blade. He could not begin to envision the pain, the despair of such a fate. It would have driven Eric mad. Yet here Darius stood, withered by his entrapment, but *alive.*

One question still remained though: was it too late to turn the tide of the battle?

"We need your help, Darius. Archon, he's winning."

Darius shook his head. "No, Eric. He has *won*. Even now the Sword's magic is burning through your body, giving it life, taking control. Soon you and your sister will become the very demons you fought to stop. The Three Nations will fall before your power."

"I won't let that happen," Eric stepped towards the God and grabbed his wrist. Before Darius could free himself, Eric pulled him close. "I know what I have to do. Gabriel has already done the same, sacrificed himself to allow Jurrien to be reborn. I can do the same for you."

Darius tore his arm free. "You do not know what you ask," he looked around the void, the white nothingness. "I cannot return to the world now, not after all this time. Here… it is peaceful. I can feel the pain, the sorrow coming from beyond the veil. I cannot face that world again."

"You must!" Eric grabbed the old man by the shoulders and shook him. "The Three Nations need you, they need the God of Light to return to our world. Whether you meant to or not, without your power the world outside has withered, and evil has crept into the void left by the Light. Dark magic has wiped entire lands clean of life, and not even Antonia can restore them. If Archon wins, there will be no more light, no more life. Only darkness."

Anger flashed in Darius' eyes. "That is not my fault. I fought this fight, gave my magic to your world. I tried to help you foolish creatures. *And how did you repay me?*"

Eric refused to retreat before the God's fury. "And do you not want revenge for that? Don't you want to show Archon your true power? To cast him down as he did to you?"

"Do not try to bait me, boy. I do not need revenge,"

Darius growled. He turned away, then back again. "You won't stop, will you? You won't give up?"

"Never."

Darius sighed, a weary resignation crossing his face. "I guess one way or another, my peace has come to an end then," he drew in a deep breath and stared down at Eric. "You are sure?"

Eric swallowed, thinking of all he was about to give up. Inken's face drifted through his thoughts and pain twisted in his chest. She would be alone now, their child left without a father. But he could see no other way to save them, to save them all.

Closing his eyes, he summoned his courage and nodded. "Do it."

CHAPTER 24

Inken stood atop the ramparts of the last wall and stared down at the endless ranks of the enemy. It had not taken them long to reform on the killing ground below. They looked up at the defenders now without fear, knowing the end was within sight, that victory would soon be theirs. They filled the space below, knowing the defenders had nothing left to hurl at them. The dragons were dead, their Magickers destroyed – even their stocks of arrows had run dry.

Her stomach clenched with regret. *If only we had run, Eric, all that time ago in Lon. We could have been free.*

But it was too late now for regrets, for second thoughts. The time had come for the Three Nations to make their last stand, to take their final breaths of freedom. With the arrival of the Plorsean army, the combined might of the Three Nations now stood atop the wall, ready to defy the forces below one final time. The weight of responsibility weighed on all their shoulders. Behind them the land stood open, their friends and families defenceless.

Caelin and May stood to her left while Elton and King Fraser waited on her right. The king had driven his army hard, leaving the stragglers behind in his desperation to reach the fortress. His forced marches had caught them up with Elton's vanguard, and the bulk of the Plorsean army had arrived together.

Their reunion had been quick, stolen hugs and tears turning quickly to the matter at hand. Inken's heart soared to see the king again. They had conquered the darkness together, the three of them, and had emerged stronger for it. Now they had one final battle to face together and she was proud to stand alongside them.

Behind them there had been no sign of the Phoenix or dragons or Eric and Enala. Inken drew strength from that, from the thought there might still be hope. It flickered in her chest, its tiny flame keeping her alive.

If Archon had not returned, it could only mean their friends continued to fight.

"Here they come," Fraser spoke. His voice rose to a boom. "Here they come, boys and girls. Let's show them what we're made of!" he drew his sword, the steel flashing in the afternoon sun.

Inken smiled, reaching down to unsheathe her own blade. If she had to die, she was glad to do so with the company around her.

Below the enemy surged forward, their hateful voices rising up to wash across the battlements.

Together the men and women of the Three Nations watched them come.

∾

THE SENSATION BEGAN as a tingle in Eric's arms, a warmth

AARON HODGES

that quickly spread through the rest of him. But the feeling felt strangely detached from him, as though he were perceiving someone else's body. Then his arms moved, shifting as though by a will of their own, reaching down to push him from the mud. Pain shot through his elbow as something went *crack* and he made to scream, but his mouth did not respond.

A groan rattled up from his chest, but he felt curiously disconnected from the movement, as though it had been someone else's groan.

Relax, Eric. This is no longer your fight. Sit back and watch, Darius' voice whispered through his mind.

Eric's eyelids fluttered and opened, revealing a world torn by chaos. Dark clouds raced across the sky, the sun streaming through gaps to light the world below. The earth beneath him was blacked and broken, while a few yards away the body of a dragon lay dead.

Sadness clenched his chest as his eyes lingered on Enduran, then drifted up to the man sitting atop the dragon's head.

Archon looked back, his eyes shining with hate.

A hand settled on his shoulder. He looked up and warmth blossomed in his chest, a love far stronger than any mortal emotion.

"Antonia," the word slipped from his mouth.

The face of Enala stared back, but changed, her eyes now a brilliant violet and filled with the ancient wisdom of the Goddess. A tear spilt from her eyes as she reached out to touch his cheek.

"Darius, brother, how is this possible?"

"A long story, my dear sister," Darius sighed as heat spread from her fingers.

He nodded his thanks as the warmth spread and the

broken parts within him knitted themselves back together. Within seconds he found himself whole, and stood. Together they turned to face Archon. A boom of thunder shook the sky, followed by the crackling of lightning. Then Jurrien stood on his other side, his face dark with anger.

"Brother," he nodded at Darius. "Glad to see you again. I'm about ready to be done with this pitiful excuse of a mortal."

Archon laughed as he climbed to his feet, but Darius saw the hesitation on his face. He could not have expected this. The man had no empathy; he had never been able to understand how his father could have given his life to create a better world for his children. For Gabriel, Enala and Eric all to have made the same decision was beyond Archon's comprehension.

"I am hardly mortal," Archon hissed, his breath misting on the cold air. He dropped from the dragon, landing lightly on the blackened ground.

Darius closed his eyes, joying in the breath of wind running across his skin, in the scent of mud and the feel of the earth beneath his feet. Memory of such sensations had long since faded in the void of his imprisonment, and he experienced them now with renewed wonder. Truly, Eric had given him a gift beyond measure.

"You were born of my Earth, Archon. Now we shall return you to it," his sister's voice was laced with anger.

Reaching across, Darius grasped her hand. "Careful, little sis," she scowled at him for using his nickname for her. "Even with the three of us, he is still dangerous."

Pain flashed across Antonia's face. "Believe me, Darius, we know that all too well."

Darius nodded, regret at his absence eating into him.

"Let's end this," Jurrien growled.

CAELIN SCREAMED as a blade swept past his guard and slashed across his ribs. He staggered backwards, an awkward swing of his sword knocking aside a second attack. Inken stepped past him, her blade flashing out to crush the helmet of his attacker. Then Elton was at his side, steadying him, and he nodded his thanks.

Swallowing his pain, Caelin hurled himself back into the fray. Blood ran from his arm but it did not slow him. An axeman charged him and the wicked blade came around in a wild swing. Ducking back, he charged in as the axe swept past. The man's eyes widened as he buried his sword in his chest.

Stepping sideways, Caelin spun as footsteps crunched behind him. Elton shouted and flung himself backwards, and Caelin managed to pull back the blow before it landed.

Elton nodded at him and raised an eyebrow. "A little jumpy there, Caelin. Try not to do the enemy any favours would you?"

Caelin laughed, the blood surging in his veins. Grinning, he shoved Elton aside as another man charged them, parrying a blow and then slamming his elbow into the man's face. As he prepared to finish him, Elton swept past and stabbed the man in the chest.

Panting, Caelin shook his head. "Thief."

Elton only laughed, already moving on to his next opponent.

A low growl came from behind and Caelin spun to see Inken engaging with a feline. Elton stepped up beside him and together they charged to their friend's aid.

"Nasty looking one," Elton commented as Inken retreated from the beast.

Inken laughed. "How can you tell?"

Caelin stared at the approaching beast, its long fur bristling as it crouched low. The golden eyes studied them with a frightening intelligence. Though fewer in number, the felines had proved just as deadly as the Raptors, and he had no wish to underestimate this one.

As it slunk towards them they spread out, splitting the cat's attention as much as they could on the narrow ramparts. Blood ran from the beast's jaws, matting in the fur beneath its chin. Its claws were extended, scraping on the stones beneath it.

"Now!" Caelin screamed as the thick muscles of the cat's back bunched.

The beast sprang towards them, its paws raised to smash them from their feet. Inken threw herself sideways, her sword sweeping up to deflect its blow. Caelin leapt forwards, the jagged claws coming within an inch of his face, and lashed out with his sword. A judder ran up his arm as the blow struck bone and was turned aside.

Then the momentum of the beast's charge carried it past. They turned and watched it come again, waiting for an opportunity to strike. The cat moved with unbelievable speed, giving them only a second to react before it charged.

This time Caelin was not fast enough. The air exploded from his lungs as the massive paws smashed into his chest, sending him bouncing back to the stone. He heard a scream from somewhere overhead and a cry, then he rolled. The scrape of claw on stone grated in his ears as the beast's paws smashed the ground where he had fallen.

Wheezing hard, Caelin climbed to his knees, watching as Elton and Inken drew the feline's attention. It stalked towards them, the sergeant forgotten behind it, and he smiled. Lifting his sword, he finally caught his winded breath and stood.

Before he could strike, the beast charged the others, its

wild roar echoing across the wall. Inken stumbled back, slipping on the slick stone, and the feline leapt. Caelin cried out as it smashed Inken from her feet and sent her crashing to the stone. Its jaws opened, revealing the massive fangs.

Caelin acted without thought, hurling himself forward to land on the back of the feline. Driving his sword deep into the beast's back, he held on for dear life. Beneath him, the cat threw back its head and screeched. It twisted and leapt, desperate to throw him off.

With a final shake, Caelin's fingers slipped from its fur and he bounced across the stone, his blade still embedded in the beast's back. Before he could move, it bounded forward and sank its jaws into the flesh of his leg.

A scream slipped from Caelin's throat as its fangs tore into his flesh. He scrambled backwards but found himself trapped, the iron jaws refusing to release him. He looked into the yellow eyes of the creature, almost imagining it smiling. With a shake of its massive head, it hurled him across the ramparts.

Then Inken was there, charging at the beast with a short sword in each hand. Before it could turn to face her, she drove the twin blades deep into the feline's chest.

Inken danced back out of range as its claws swiped at her. But this time the blades had found their mark. The strength went from it in a rush and the beast collapsed to the ground.

Caelin groaned, pulling himself to a sitting position and leaning his head back against the ramparts. Pain washed through his body and without looking he knew he was done. His last stand was over. Blood gushed from his leg, spreading across the stone with frightening speed.

Inken strode across and crouched beside him, tearing the jerkin from her shoulders. Caelin sucked in a breath, biting back a scream as Inken wrapped the jacket around his wound. Tying it off, she looked around, and he saw the desperate fear in her eyes.

"It's okay, Inken," he coughed. "Leave me."

Inken shook her head. "Why did you do that, Caelin?"

Caelin shrugged, fighting back the pain. "Couldn't let the future mother go off and get herself killed."

"Fraser told you?" Inken swore. "That man needs to learn how to keep his mouth shut."

Smiling, Caelin shook his head. "Eric, actually. He asked me to look out for you. I didn't want to let him down."

"In that case, I'll be giving him a piece of my mind when he gets back."

"I'm sure that will terrify him," Caelin gave a weak laugh. He stared at the blood now soaking Inken's jerkin. "There's too much, Inken. I don't think I'm going to survive this one."

Inken swore again and shook her head. "I'll be damned if you're going to die on me, Caelin. Elton!" the young commander stood over them, his back turned and his sword raised to fend off any enemy that came near.

He glanced back at them, concern written across his face. "How is he?"

Inken shook her head. "Not good, we need to get him to the healers."

Elton nodded and, with a final glance to ensure there was no one close, crouched down and took Caelin under his shoulder. Caelin groaned as the young commander took his weight, his leg pulsing with the beat of his heart.

"Quit your complaining," Inken whispered in his ear. "It's your own fault you got half your leg bitten off."

Caelin gritted his teeth, unable to respond through the pain.

Together, Inken and Elton carried him towards the stairs and the citadel below. Men streamed past them in the opposite direction, rushing to reinforce the defenders on the wall.

They joined the steady stream of injured stumbling down towards the distant infirmary.

Not that Caelin had much hope of making it that far.

As they reached the ground men and women rushed towards them, but his friends shook them off. Despite his protests they would not leave him in the hands of strangers.

They would not let him die alone.

Even so, a man joined them, leaning down to inspect Caelin's leg as they continued in the direction of the citadel. The purple diamond on his chest marked him as a doctor from the Earth temple. A rush of sadness swept through Caelin as he remembered Michael, and the diamond his friend had worn proudly to the end.

"What happened?" the man asked.

"Feline," Inken grunted.

"Got the bugger," Caelin managed to croak.

Inken smiled. "Pretty sure I had to finish him off for you," he didn't miss the wink she flashed at the young doctor.

Before any of them could continue, a boom shook the ground beneath them. Caelin groaned as his friends staggered and almost fell. He looked up to see the earth rippling like a wave, throwing men and women from their feet as it rushed across the open field.

A second before it struck Inken and Elton dropped to the ground, pulling him down with them.

Then the world erupted in chaos.

A DEEP EXHAUSTION wrapped around Enala as she stared across at Archon, a desperate weariness that stretched down to her very soul. Magic coursed through her veins, its touch soft yet all-consuming. Her legs moved, her eyes sweeping out to meet those of Gabriel and Eric, but the movements were beyond her comprehension now.

Brothers, the Goddess' thoughts whispered in her mind.

Are you ready? Darius replied.

Hatred unlike anything Enala had experienced swept through her, followed by the surge of God magic. It swirled in her chest, but the power no longer seemed alien or threatening. It was a part of her, its green tendrils embedded with her very being. The *Soul Blade* was no more; it had crumbled to dust as she stood, its remnants catching in the wind and scattering across the ocean.

There was only *her* now.

Antonia smiled. "Let's put an end to this, brothers."

The dark laughter of the false God shook the air, but Antonia was not afraid. For the first time in centuries, the three of them stood together once more, their mastery of the elemental world complete. No force on earth could stand against them.

"Come now, my old nemeses, you cannot think that shrivelled excuse for a God can help you?" Archon grinned. "There is nothing left of his spirit. *I can see it!*"

At his final words Archon threw out his arms. The air crackled as darkness gathered in his palms and surged towards Darius. Her brother stumbled backwards, a thin, pale light rising to meet the attack. But the darkness smashed through it and caught Darius in its awful power.

And the God of Light crumpled like leaves before an autumn breeze.

"*Darius!*" Antonia screamed, reaching out for the soul of her brother.

Fear not, sweet sister, Darius' words echoed in her mind, even as Archon's laughter gathered force.

"So much for the God of Light," Antonia shivered in disgust as the dark Magicker's words hissed in her ear.

Antonia spun, but she was not fast enough. Pale fingers whipped out and grasped her by the throat. She choked as the icy fingers began to squeeze and a dark shadow clawed its way inside her. She kicked feebly in Archon's grasp as he lifted her into the air.

"So much for your sacrifice, children. You could have ruled the world, could have conquered these puny people. But instead you chose death," Archon growled, holding her high.

Fighting against the darkness burning at her spirit, Antonia reached out and hurled her magic at their foe. The ground erupted beneath them and a fist of earth smashed Archon from his feet. Antonia spun through the air as his iron grasp released her, twisting to land gracefully on a rocky column that reached up to catch her.

She smiled as Archon regained his feet, glad at least for her new body's agility. Then the joy faded, sadness rising to replace it. She could feel Enala's soul within her, already shrivelling, overcome by Antonia's being.

I will not let your sacrifice be in vain, she whispered in her thoughts.

"They did not choose death," Jurrien dropped from the sky to land beside her.

"They chose life for everyone they loved," Darius appeared from thin air on her other side.

Archon growled, brushing dust from his clothes. "I see you are still a master in the fine art of running away, Darius."

Darius grinned. "You have grown used to battling the limited powers of mortals, Archon. Yes, we are masters. Together, there is nothing we cannot do."

"*You know nothing of my power!*" Archon roared.

Archon raised his arms and darkness congealed around him, swelling outwards to engulf his body. A tingle of warning came from deep within Antonia and the image of a Phoenix rose from Enala's memories.

But she could sense Darius' magic rising in response, the Light bubbling in his raised fist. He gave a wild howl, the sound filled with the pain of centuries, and threw out his arm. Light erupted across the plain, casting the world in a brilliant white. A beam of power shot towards Archon, smashing through his darkness, pressing it down, driving it back to whence it came.

Archon's face twisted with rage as the darkness retreated. For a moment his magic faltered and his features warped, revealing the horror beneath. Time had ravaged his mortal body, boiling his skin into waxy lines, eating away his teeth and turning his ice blue eyes to white. His hair had died away, leaving only a few tangled wafts that fluttered on the breeze.

With a scream, Archon threw out his hand and the image vanished, replaced again by the ageless face of the dark Magicker. He pointed a finger and a spear of darkness tore through Darius' light, shearing its way towards her. Antonia shook her head, her magic racing out to defend her, and a shield of stone erupted from the ground to block the darkness.

Lightning crackled from Jurrien as the Storm God joined the fray. The electricity dancing along his body raised the hairs on Antonia's arms, but she was too preoccupied to notice. Magic swelled in her chest as she tore her shield aside, allowing her brothers to attack. Blue and white fire rippled through the gap as they unleashed their power.

Antonia drew more power from within, determined to add her strength to the fray. It would take all of them to end this, and though she drew no pleasure from the destructive might of the Earth, she would make an exception for Archon.

Vines split the ground beneath the dark Magicker, whipping up to bind him tight. Black flames rippled from his body, burning the shoots to ash, but they were everywhere now, the thicket re-growing in the instants between blinks. Drawing a breath, Antonia pulled at the vines, trapping Archon tighter as they tore at his mortal body.

Archon thrashed amidst the green of her creation, but she sensed his power weakening now, and knew Darius was working his own magic. The Light throbbed around them, driving back the darkness. She smiled, relief pouring through her. Before Archon had overwhelmed her magic without effort, but now he was suffocating, his power cut off at its very source.

Another pulse of darkness swept from Archon, eating at her power, but Antonia gritted her teeth and poured more of herself into the fray. Beside her, Jurrien took to the sky, raising his fists to summon the storm. Wind swirled around him, hail and lightning rushing in to join his hurricane. Darius throbbed with power, light flashing from the body he wore, so bright even Antonia had to look away.

The darkness around Archon shrank further, the black fire dying with each boom of light. With a final flicker, the shadows around Archon went out, disappearing to nothing. Beneath the glow of Darius' power, the ancient face of Archon reappeared amidst the thicket of vines.

"*No!*" Archon screeched. The word rang with his mortal fear, his sudden terror, and Antonia knew Darius had trapped his power.

Without it, Archon was helpless.

"It's time," Darius' voice was quiet, filled with sorrow.

Antonia nodded, feeling the same emotion sweep through her. In all their time in the mortal realm, they had never killed, never used their powers to take a human life. Yet Archon left them no choice now, no other alternative.

He could not be allowed to live.

"*Please*," Archon had ceased to struggle now. He hung limp amidst her vines, his body shrunken with age, the fear in his eye a pitiful sight.

But Antonia would not be fooled. Given one second, a single opening, and Archon would turn them all to ash.

Releasing a long breath, Antonia summoned her power and dove deep into the earth. A rumble came from far below as the ground shook. Then with a shriek of shattered rock a fissure opened beneath their feet, tearing apart the fabric of the earth itself. A soft red light came from far below, the fires of the earth themselves, their unquenchable heat awaiting their sacrifice.

Above Jurrien nodded, and as one the three Gods drew on their magic.

Lightning boomed as Jurrien unleashed the storm. The dark clouds rushed down into the bramble of vines, tearing the last remnants of darkness from Archon. He screamed, limbs thrashing amidst her entrapments as lightning burned and the vines pulled him down beneath the crust of the earth.

Darius rose into the air, drifting across until he hovered over the crevice. Below Jurrien's storm still raged, the flicker of lightning catching amidst the red glow of the earth's core. Flames roared as white fire took form around the God of Light, burning with the heat of the sun. Closing his eyes, Darius pointed at the conflagration far below.

White fire rushed down into the crevice. A roar carried up to them as the inferno joined the hurricane.

Pain tore at Antonia's spirit as she sensed the life fleeing the body below, but she knew the job was not done yet. Regret clawed at her soul, but she did not hesitate. The air popped as she sent a last wave of magic down into the earth.

A column of light burst from the fissure: white, blue and

red mingling in the sky overhead. A final shriek came from far below, desperate and filled with fear. But there was no stopping her magic now, no mercy left to save Archon. The red glow of molten rock crept up to meet the storm, its power inexorable.

With a final roar, the insatiable fires of the earth claimed their ancient enemy.

WHEN THE SHAKING FINALLY CEASED, not a soul moved. The enemy stood silent amongst the soldiers of the Three Nations, staring at the sky in silent expectation. A note of finality hung in the air, a sense that the battle was over, the outcome decided. They had only to wait and see whose side had emerged victorious.

Inken held her breath, her eyes with those of her comrades, praying for a glimpse of her friends in the skies above Fort Fall. Caelin sat beside her, his face twisted with pain but his eyes still on the sky, Elton on his other side. Together they waited.

Eric and Enala came first, soaring over the fortress as the clouds cleared before them. Gabriel followed behind them, his arms folded as the wind tossed his auburn hair. Inken felt a twist of pain as she looked at him, knowing he was no longer the man she knew. It was Jurrien, wearing the body of her friend.

Even so, Inken could not keep the elation from her spirit. They had survived, had won the final battle and cast down the dark powers of Archon. Tears ran down her face as she watched them come, her hands covering her mouth as she struggled to contain her joy.

Cheers rang out across the fortress as men and women threw up their hands in victory. Blades clattered to the ground as the enemy dropped their weapons, the despair of defeat sucking away their strength. Without Archon they knew they could not stand against the magic of the Gods. Their cause was lost; there was no point in throwing away their lives as well.

As one the beasts turned and fled, tails flashing as they raced from the battlefield, eager to put as much distance as they could between themselves and the power that had defeated their master.

Inken watched the three drift down, coming to rest in the field on which they stood. Swallowing, she glanced at Caelin.

"Go," he waved a hand, obviously fighting back pain but still managing a smile.

Inken surprised herself with a yelp of delight. She sprang to her feet, leaving Caelin behind with Elton, and raced across the barren field, her boots slipping in the torn up mud.

Ahead Eric turned to watch her come, but as their eyes met he did not move. Instead, sadness swept across his face and his shoulders slumped. Inken slowed as she stared into the eyes of the man she loved, her heart thudding hard in her chest.

Something was different. Something was wrong.

Step by step, she drew closer, the terror rising in her stomach.

At last she stood before the three of them.

And she knew.

Eric's gaze enveloped her, filled with love and sadness, but the difference now was unmistakable. She could see it in his eyes. They were no longer the blue of lightning, but a pale white, filled with an infinite depth. An ageless knowledge stared back from those eyes, soft and caring.

But Eric was not there.

Inken turned to Enala, opening her mouth to scream, to ask why, to demand an answer, but the words caught in her throat. Enala's eyes had turned to violet and glowed with power, but there was no sign of her friend there.

Sinking to her knees, Inken felt her hope crumble to dust.

CHAPTER 25

I nken sucked in a breath as she stood staring at the door to the council room. Reaching up one last time, she wiped the tears from her eyes. A shudder ran through her, but she swallowed hard and pushed down her grief. Grasping the handle of the door, she shoved it open and strode inside.

Eyes turned towards her as she marched past the guard and took an empty seat. She glimpsed pity in the faces of her comrades and tried to ignore it. But her sadness only deepened as she looked at those seated around her. May and King Fraser sat at the head of the table, Elton and Caelin joining them on either side.

There was no one else.

Biting back fresh tears, Inken slumped in her chair, the memories of her fallen friends flashing through her mind. The kindly, wrinkled face of Alastair, the warmth of Michael's generous spirit, the iron strength of the old warrior, Alan.

She remembered the wild strength of Enala's smile, her unquenchable determination in the face of evil. And

Gabriel's quiet presence, even when gripped with madness, solid, reliable.

And Eric…

So many lives, gone before their time.

Looking around the table, she attempted a smile in the face of the sorrow reflected in the eyes of her friends. It came out as a grimace, but the others said nothing. Each wore fresh clothing and looked better for a full night's sleep. That, and the healing magic of the Goddess.

Inken closed her eyes, seeing again the warm green glow emerging from Enala. *Antonia*, she reminded herself with an angry growl. The light had spread out across the fortress, falling on the defenders and enemy alike. Wherever it touched, broken bones and torn flesh had knitted itself back together within seconds. Those on the edge of death had suddenly sat up and looked around. One by one the fallen had regained their feet and turned to stare at the three Gods standing in their midst.

Inken fought back a sob as she recalled the words Eric had spoken, their tone so different from that of the man she loved.

"People of the Three Nations," his voice carried to the furthest corners of Fort Fall. "I am Darius, and I have returned. The Magicker, Eric, has given his life to return me to your world. The brave souls of Enala and Gabriel have done the same for my siblings, restoring us to life," he waved to the Gods to either side of him. His head bowed then, and Inken saw the shame in his eyes. "I am sorry I abandoned you, though it was Archon who trapped me. But he is gone now, destroyed. His shadow will never touch our lands again."

A chorus of cheers rang out across the fortress, enveloping the brave men and women who had put their lives on the line to protect their homes, their families.

Amongst them the enemy still stood, their eyes wide with fear. They stared at the Gods, their faces filled with dread.

Somehow, the eyes of Darius found each of them. "As for you who have fought against us…" his eyes hardened. "You may return to your homes in the north. When we are done healing the damage you have caused to the Three Nations, we will come to you. Those of you who have committed no crime will have the chance to return. *Now go!*"

Darius' final words shook the air itself, and as one the enemy turned and fled.

After that, the three Gods had bid their farewell, fading away until there was nothing left of them but empty air.

And Inken sitting alone in the mud, staring at the space where Eric had stood.

Back in the council room, the dagger in Inken's chest twisted again at the memory, driving deeper. The pain was too much and she could not hold back her groan.

Caelin's eyes found hers from across the table. "Are you okay, Inken?"

Inken blinked back tears. "How could this happen?"

"Our hearts go out to you, Inken," she hated the kindness in Fraser's eyes. "The Three Nations will never forget their sacrifice."

"Ay," May bowed her head. "They were brave souls, each of them. They saved us."

Within, Inken railed against the unfairness, the cruelty of this awful world. A rage burned in her, and no matter how she tried, she could not put it out.

"I don't care!" the words tore from her. The others jumped as she slammed her fist into the table and stood. "I don't care," she grated again. "They took him from me. Took them from us all!"

"They had no choice, Inken," Caelin murmured. "You know that. It was the only way to stop him."

"Who? Archon?" she snapped back. "They *created* him, planted the seed of hatred in a boy too young to know better. It was never our fight, it was *their's*. So why do they still live, while everyone and everything I have ever loved is dead?" the last words came out as a sob, her voice breaking before her sorrow.

Caelin stood and moved to her side. She shuddered as his arms pulled her to him. His fingers stroked her hair as he offered his meagre comfort, but she could not stand it. She struggled in his grasp, her breath coming in sobs, her vision blurred by tears.

Memories of Eric flashed through her mind: the day they had met in the desert of Chole, how he had fed her and comforted her. The time in the forests of Dragon Country, their night in the thermal stream, their desperate fight against the red dragon. The quiet escape of the temple in Sitton, and the tears as she had forced Eric to leave her.

And their reunion here in Fort Fall, and Eric's joy as she told him of their child.

She tore herself loose from Caelin as the last thought taunted her. Her hand drifted to her stomach as she whispered. "How could they have done this?"

Caelin squeezed her shoulder. "It was their choice, Inken. Gabriel's and Enala's and Eric's. You know that," he released a long breath. "He did it for you, for all of us. To give us all our freedom, to give your child a future."

"*Our* child," Inken hissed, pulling away again. She hugged herself, looking around the room in search of an ally. "It's our child," her voice broke. "How can I do this without him? *Alone.*"

A tremor went through her, the familiar despair rising up to steal away her strength. Her knees trembled as she sank into the chair and buried her head in her arms.

"You will never be alone, Inken," May's voice was firm.

"So long as we live, we will be here for you. You only have to ask."

Inken shook her head. "I just want him back," she breathed. "I want them *all back*."

"We all do," Fraser replied. "But we can't. They're gone, Inken, and there is nothing we can do to bring them back. We can only respect the sacrifice they made for us by living our lives. Together we can rebuild the Three Nations. Without Archon's shadow hovering over our lands, we can finally prosper again."

May nodded. "There are three Gods again," Inken could not miss the wonder in the commander's voice and she hated it, hated her for it. "Together they will rid our lands of the last of Archon's beasts. They can restore the Badlands around Chole. Our nations will prosper once more, and we will have peace."

"But at what cost?" Inken demanded. "We will build our dreams on the souls of the innocent."

"What else would you have us do, Inken?" there was sadness in Fraser's voice. "We cannot bring them back."

"I would have you *fight*," Inken snapped, not really believing the words but knowing she hated them, hated the Gods for everything they had done. For saving her, for forcing her to live in a world without hope. "I will hate them until the day I die," she said into the long silence that followed her outburst.

Standing, Inken turned and walked away. The silence followed her, suffocating, but she could not stand the pity in their eyes any longer. She strode out into the long corridors of the fortress and took the first doorway outside. She found herself in an open courtyard, the sun streaming down from the bright blue sky.

For a moment the world seemed a brighter place, free of the darkness of just a day before. The yellow rays of the sun warmed her skin, digging their way deep inside, until even the hate gave way before it, if only a little.

Her legs carried her to a stone bench. She sat and closed her eyes, feeling the heat of the sun mixing with the cold breath of winter, and knew it was all a lie. Winter was approaching, and with it the last of her hope would curdle and die.

Staring up into the empty sky, Inken wept for the future that might have been.

EPILOGUE

"This doesn't sit right with me," Antonia sat on a rock, staring across at her brothers.

Two months had passed now since the events at Fort Fall, and peace had finally settled over the Three Nations. Together they had worked with the new leaders of Plorsea, Lonia and Trola to put the pieces back together. Each nation had suffered horrible losses and without her help many would have starved in the harsh winter snows.

But spring was now approaching and the Three Nations were safe. They had hunted down the last of the dark creatures Archon had unleashed on the Three Nations and a fragile peace had finally settled, breathing life back into the land.

Archon was finally gone, his army defeated, his magic finished.

Antonia could hardly believe it.

Days ago the Three Nations had begun to send their emissaries into the wastelands of the north, to talk with the people there and offer the hand of peace. It would take time, but King Fraser and the councils of Lonia and Trola were eager to welcome the innocent back into their lands. In truth, they needed them now, after all they had lost.

"I agree," Darius interrupted her musings. "There is peace, but in my heart I feel a wrongness. Our rebirth has sown the same seeds of hate that led to our fall the last time," he closed his eyes. "And I'm tired."

"But they need us," Jurrien answered, his blue eyes looking from Antonia to Darius. "Look what happened in your absence, Darius. The world was torn apart again, and a darkness far worse than we could ever have imagined almost took our place. Now they finally have peace."

"Ay," Darius met their brother's gaze. "But for how long? How long before another rises up to strike at us, to stab us in the back when we least expect it? How long before the hatred we have sowed bears fruit?"

"And how many will die without us?" Jurrien argued. "How long before the wars begin again?"

"That is up to them," Antonia whispered. She closed her eyes, feeling the soul dying within her. "It has been five hundred years since the priests called on us to save their lands. The people have changed, grown. They *want* peace, they *want* freedom. Two of the Three Nations are now ruled by councils. What is our place now? To rule over those elected by their own people?"

"We will become tyrants to them, Jurrien," Darius added.

Jurrien scowled. "At least we'd be benevolent ones."

Antonia laughed, enjoying the warmth of her brother's humour. It was good to see the weight lifted from his shoulders. In Darius' absence, Jurrien had shouldered the burden of his brother's responsibilities. They had not sat well with him, and he had grown unbearably grim.

She took a breath, sensing the soul stirring in her chest.

"I cannot bear the guilt again," she looked at her feet. "To feel another's soul die within me."

Jurrien sighed. "You're right, of course, little sis."

Antonia scowled and flicked a hand. Jurrien yelped as the rock beneath him shifted, sending him tumbling backwards. He came back up with his hands raised in surrender.

"All right, all right," he grinned. "You win."

Antonia sighed. "So it is time?"

Darius nodded. "They don't have long, I think. If we don't act now, there would be little point."

"You truly think they can be trusted?" Jurrien asked. "If we return ourselves to the spirit realm, there will be no one to save them should the darkness come again."

"You're wrong," Antonia smiled. "They will stand together; they will find a way to win, whatever the odds. It's what they do."

Letting out a long breath, Darius nodded. "It's decided then?"

One by one, each of them nodded.

Antonia smiled, reaching out to grasp the hands of her brothers. Their skin felt soft beneath her fingers, and she took joy in the touch. Soon they would feel no more, see no more, hear no more. They would be spirits once more, watching over the land, but never able to touch it.

In a way, it was a relief.

Looking from Darius to Jurrien, Antonia smiled.

"See you on the other side, brothers."

ERIC BLINKED as sunlight pierced the canopy of trees stretching out overhead. Rubbing his eyes, he looked up at the leafless limbs, glimpsing hints of blue between the branches. The trees swayed to a gentle breeze, but beneath the canopy the air was still, at peace. He yawned then, struggling to find the strength to sit up. A dull ache throbbed in his chest, stretching down to his very soul.

A surge of elation took him as realisation finally struck.

He was alive, free, his body his own again.

Looking around, he found his own amazement reflected on the faces of Gabriel and Enala. They blinked back at him, their eyes wide, their mouths open with astonishment. The rustling of nearby animals carried to their ears, but the peace in Eric's soul did not relent. In his heart he knew they were safe, that it was only the gentle creatures of the forest. The chirp of birds and buzz of insects rose around them, mingling together to form the sweetest song he had ever heard.

Farewell, children, the words whispered on the air itself, and Eric had to fight back tears.

Thank you, Eric thought back, wonder at his sudden freedom replacing the grief of the God's departure.

Eric stood with a groan and stumbled across to his sister. Offering his hand, he drew Enala to her feet and embraced her. Gabriel joined them, the tears streaming down his face matching their own. They stood together, overwhelmed by the raw emotion of the world, of life.

Finally they drew apart and looked at the wilderness surrounding them.

"What now?" Enala asked, a smile on her face.

"Now, we live."

～

ENJOYED THIS BOOK?

Then follow Aaron for a free short story:
www.aaronhodges.co.nz/newsletter-signup/

AFTERWORD

Wow, what a journey. It still amazes me that the concept for this story came to me in a first year English class for high school. It took another ten years for those first stumbling words of Eric's journey to be introduced to the big wide world. But anyway, thank you to everyone who has joined me on this journey. I hope you enjoyed the Sword of Light Trilogy! And fear not, I will be returning to the Three Nations in the future.

As always, reader feedback is a huge part of its continued success, and all reviews on your vender of choice would be appreciated.

FOLLOW AARON HODGES:
And receive a free short story…

Newsletter:
http://www.aaronhodges.co.nz/newsletter-signup/

Facebook:
www.facebook.com/Aaron-Hodges-669480156486208/

Bookbub:
www.bookbub.com/authors/aaron-hodges

Printed in Great Britain
by Amazon